Praise for *Melmoth*

"Masterful. . . . Scary and smart, working as a horror story but also a philosophical inquiry into the nature of will and love. Perry did as much in her richly praised novel *The Essex Serpent*, but this is a deeper, more complex novel and more rewarding."
—*Washington Post*

"Ms. Perry, whose last book, *The Essex Serpent*, was a breakout hit, again proves herself a master of atmosphere."
—*Wall Street Journal*

"The past few years have brought a glut of fashionably affectless and amoral fiction, to which Sarah Perry's fierce, full-hearted books about love and ethics feel like the perfect antidote."
—*NPR, "Our Guide to 2018's Great Reads"*

"A gothic masterwork."
—*Entertainment Weekly*

"Perry's new novel *Melmoth* is another Gothic stunner. . . . A scary novel that chills to the bone even as it points the way to a warmer, more humane, place. . . . By the end of *Melmoth*, you are left with a feeling that you have experienced something wholly entertaining, and that you have found humanity and compassion in the process."
—*The New York Times Book Review*

"Reels you in, using the same trick of all the best ghost stories, from *The Turn of the Screw* on: Is there really a ghost before you? Or do you see the projection of your own secret sins and desires? What is more frightening than the human?"
—*New York Times*

"A novel that manages that vanishingly rare feat—being at once hugely readable and profoundly important. . . . Perry's masterly piece of postmodern gothic is one of the great literary achievements of our young century."
—*The Guardian* (UK)

"The author of *The Essex Serpent* casts another haunting spell in this exquisitely written gothic novel." —*People* magazine

"Filled with thought-provoking ideas on historical guilt and personal responsibility, as well as a depth of learning. . . . The message at its heart is an uplifting one; even if redemption for wrongdoing cannot always be achieved, there is power in bearing witness." —*Financial Times*

"An unforgettable achievement. . . . Though rich in gothic tropes and sinister atmosphere, the novel transcends pastiche. Perry's heartbreaking, horrifying monster confronts the characters not just with the uncanny but also with the human: with humanity's complicity in history's darkest moments, its capacity for guilt, its power of witness, and its longing for both companionship and redemption." —*Publishers Weekly* (starred review)

"This fever dream of a novel will prove as compelling and all-consuming as *The Essex Serpent*." —*Library Journal* (starred review)

"[A] stylized, postmodern work by a masterly writer. . . . A sobering, disturbing, yet powerful and moving book that cannot fail to impress. The stories-within-stories and the Jewish themes recall Dara Horn's *The World to Come* and Donna Tartt's *The Goldfinch*, although *Melmoth* presents different kinds of nightmares." —*Booklist* (starred review)

"A gorgeously wrought tale that feels as timeless as its title character and as real as the monster you're sure is sitting at the foot of your bed. Perry doesn't waste a word of this lean, taut novel. . . . By the end you're happily trapped in its eerie embrace."

—*BookPage*

"A single-handed revival of the Gothic tradition."

—*New York* magazine

"Ingenious. . . . Haunting, disquieting and memorable, and showcase[s] Perry's dazzling creative powers."

—*Star Tribune* (Minneapolis)

"[A] spine-tingling, gloriously creepy tale. . . . This is horror done masterfully."

—*The Globe and Mail*

"Imaginative, intellectually engaging, and genuinely creepy in places, *Melmoth* is a worthy entry to the Gothic canon."

—*Toronto Star*

"A richly layered novel that will likely blossom even further with repeated readings. . . . Atmospheric, emotive, and hauntingly beautiful, there's so much to explore and so much to savor that it will undoubtedly follow you long after you finish."

—*AU Review*

"In a passage about the sensation of knowing Melmoth is there watching, Perry offers the perfect description for the way it feels to read her book: 'a kind of frightened longing, like a man who sees a lover he has hopelessly longed for, and in his lover's hands a noose.' It's a heartbreaking novel, one filled with fear and regret and horror, one that forces readers to confront some of mankind's greatest atrocities, past and present. And yet, its gorgeous lyricism and stunning prose make it difficult not to fall deeply for *Melmoth*, just as its fascinating characters and nested storytelling make it impossible not to get pulled into its darkness." —Bustle

"The best word to describe *Melmoth*, the latest novel from *Essex Serpent* author Sarah Perry, is *lush*. This is a novel where every sentence has been wrapped in layer upon layer of velvet." —Vox

"Arguably the most eagerly awaited novel of the year. . . . A playful, bona fide page-turner."

—*Daily Mail* (UK)

"A brilliant, spooky meditation on the sins of history. . . . If *The Essex Serpent* mined Victorian history for a legend and worked it up into a romance with broader social themes, then *Melmoth* repeats that trick in multiple dimensions." —*New Republic*

"In rich, lyrical prose, Perry weaves history and myth, human frailty and compassion, into an affecting gothic morality tale for 2018. Like David Mitchell and Sarah Waters, Perry is changing what a modern-day ghost story can look like, challenging her readers to confront the realities of worldwide suffering from which fiction is so often an escape. A chilling novel about confronting our complicity in past atrocities—and retaining the strength and moral courage to strive for the future." —*Kirkus Reviews* (starred review)

Praise for *The Essex Serpent*

"A novel of almost insolent ambition—lush and fantastical, a wild Eden behind a garden gate. . . . It's part ghost story and part natural history lesson, part romance and part feminist parable. I found it so transporting that 48 hours after completing it, I was still resentful to be back home." —*The New York Times Book Review*

"Richly enjoyable. . . . Ms. Perry writes beautifully and sometimes agreeably sharply. . . . *The Essex Serpent* is a wonderfully satisfying novel. Ford Madox Ford thought the glory of the novel was its ability to make the reader think and feel at the same time. This one does just that." —*Wall Street Journal*

"Gloriously alive." —*NPR*

"A fabulous summer read. . . . If *Middlemarch* heroine Dorothea Brooke had heard of dinosaurs, she might have gone tromping through the salt marshes with Cora Seaborne."

—*Christian Science Monitor*

"The sumptuous twists and turns of Perry's prose invite close reading, as deep and strange and full of narrative magic as the Blackwater itself. Fans of Sarah Waters, A.S. Byatt, and Elizabeth Gilbert's *The Signature of All Things* should prepare to fall under Perry's spell and into her very capable hands. Stuffed with smarts and storytelling sorcery, this is a work of astonishing breadth and brilliance."

—*Kirkus Reviews* (starred review)

"The vivid, often frightening imagery . . . and the lush descriptions . . . create a magical background for the sensual love story between Sarah and Will. Book-discussion groups will have a field day with the imagery, the well-developed characters, and the concepts of innocence, evil, and guilt."

—*Booklist* (starred review)

"In Perry's excellent second novel . . . a fatal illness, a knife-wielding maniac, and a fated union with the Essex Serpent will dictate the ultimate happiness of [the] characters. Like John Fowles's *The French Lieutenant's Woman*, whose Lyme Regis setting gets a shout-out here, this is another period literary pastiche with a contemporary overlay."

—*Publishers Weekly*

"Compulsive. . . . Narrative and voice coil together until it is very difficult to stop reading."

—*The Guardian* (UK)

"Irresistible."

—*People*

"Astonishing. . . . Perry's prose is rich, textured, and intricate. . . . A thoughtful and elegant book about the human need for knowledge and love, and about the fears and desires we bury."

—*Vox*

"Triumphs on every level, whether in its rich, evocative prose or its authentic Victorian detail, its credible, multifaceted characters or its high-stakes drama. . . . Perry likened writing her novel to a 'possession.' Reading it, we find ourselves under a similar mesmerizing spell."
　　　　　　　　　　　　　　　—*Star Tribune* (Minneapolis)

"*The Essex Serpent* is Sarah Perry's first book to come across the pond to us from Great Britain, and it is a corker. . . . Even the most minor characters are filled with a particular life, light and love. . . . One of the best, most memorable novels I have read in long years."
　　　　　　　　　　　　　　　—*Daily Herald*

"As engrossing as its reputation would suggest. . . . Perry's command of language as a tool to evoke time and place proves remarkable."
　　　　　　　　　　　　　　　—*Paste* magazine

"The most delightful heroine since Elizabeth Bennet in *Pride and Prejudice*. . . . Perry creates that delicate illusion of the best historical fiction: an authentic sense of the past—its manners, ideals and speech—that feels simultaneously distant and relevant to us. . . . By the end, *The Essex Serpent* identifies a mystery far greater than some creature 'from the illuminated margins of a manuscript': friendship."
　　　　　　　　　　　　　　　—*Washington Post*

"A work of great intelligence and charm, by a hugely talented author."
　　　　　　　　　　—Sarah Waters, author of *Fingersmith*

"Dickensian in scope, depth, and exquisite use of language. . . . At once love story and mystery, deeply penetrating layered characters with wit and grace, *The Essex Serpent* reveals the mundane beast that spawned wild rumors, and the stranger, less easily unmasked beasts within us."
　　　　　　　　　　　　　　　—*Historical Novels Review*

"Perry's second novel is a dazzling and intellectually nimble work of Gothic fiction."
　　　　　　　　　　　　　　　—SFGate.com

"Had Charles Dickens and Bram Stoker come together to write the great Victorian novel, I wonder if it would have surpassed *The Essex Serpent*? No way of knowing, but with only her second outing, Sarah Perry establishes herself as one of the finest fiction writers working in Britain today. *The Essex Serpent* is nothing less than an all-out triumph."   —John Burnside

"A suspenseful love story. . . . *The Essex Serpent* recalls variously the earthiness of Emily Brontë, the arch, high-tensile tone of Conan Doyle, the evocation of time and place achieved by Hilary Mantel and Sarah Waters and the antiquarian edgelands horror of M. R. James."   *—New Statesman*

"Perry's achieved the near impossible. . . . A thing of beauty inside and out. . . . A stunning achievement."
                                              —The Independent (UK)

"Irresistible. . . . You can feel the influences of Mary Shelley, Bram Stoker, Wilkie Collins, Charles Dickens and Hilary Mantel channeled by Perry in some sort of Victorian séance. This is the best new novel I've read in years."   *—Daily Telegraph* (UK)

"An exquisitely absorbing, old-fashioned page-turner. . . . *The Essex Serpent* is shot through with such a vivid, lively sense of the period that it reads like Charles Dickens at his most accessible and fans of *Jonathan Strange & Mr. Norrell* will also find much to love."   *—Daily Express* (UK)

"Perry fully inhabits many of the concerns and stylistic elements of the 19th century novel—but its interests are still contemporary ones: desire, fulfillment and questioning the world. . . . Her language is exquisite, her characterization finely tuned. Based on *The Essex Serpent* and its predecessor, it's clear that Perry is a gifted writer of immense ability."   *—Irish Times*

"A Victorian-era gothic with a Dickensian focus on societal ills, Perry's second novel surprises in its wonderful freshness. . . . Perry's singular characters are drawn with a fondness that is both palpable and contagious, and the beautifully observed changing seasons permitted space to breathe, all making for pure pleasure."

—*The Observer*

"Sarah Perry's novel of 19th century England tackles big ideas. . . . Reversals and sharp darts of psychological insight combined with a sense of the substance and feeling of late 19th-century ideas in bloom make this a fine novel, both historical and otherwise."

—*Newsday*

MELMOTH

MELMOTH

A Novel

Sarah Perry

ch.
CUSTOM
HOUSE

P.S.™ is a trademark of HarperCollins Publishers.

MELMOTH. Copyright © 2018 by Aldwinter Ltd. Excerpt from AFTER ME COMES THE FLOOD © 2020 by Aldwinter Ltd. All rights reserved. Printed in the United States of America. No part of this book may be used or reproduced in any manner whatsoever without written permission except in the case of brief quotations embodied in critical articles and reviews. For information, address HarperCollins Publishers, 195 Broadway, New York, NY 10007.

HarperCollins books may be purchased for educational, business, or sales promotional use. For information, please email the Special Markets Department at SPsales@harper collins.com.

Originally published in the United Kingdom in 2018 by Serpent's Tail, an imprint of Profile Books Ltd.

A hardcover edition of this book was published in 2018 by Custom House, an imprint of William Morrow.

FIRST CUSTOM HOUSE PAPERBACK EDITION PUBLISHED 2019.

Designed by Crow Books

The Library of Congress has catalogued a previous edition as follows:

Names: Perry, Sarah, 1979– author.
Title: Melmoth : a novel / Sarah Perry.
Description: First U.S. edition. | New York, NY : Custom House, 2018.
Identifiers: LCCN 2018029870 (print) | LCCN 2018032295 (ebook) |
    ISBN 9780062856418 (ebook) | ISBN 9780062856395 (hardcover) |
    ISBN 9780062856401 (paperback) | ISBN 9780062856425
    (international edition) | ISBN 9780062859686 (large print)
Subjects: | BISAC: FICTION / Romance / Gothic. | FICTION / Literary. |
    FICTION / Occult & Supernatural. | GSAFD: Gothic fiction.
Classification: LCC PR6116.E776 (ebook) | LCC PR6116.E776 M45 2018 (print) |
    DDC 823/.92—dc23
LC record available at https://lccn.loc.gov/2018029870

ISBN 970-0-06-285640-1 (pbk.)

19 20 21 22 23 LSC 10 9 8 7 6 5 4 3 2 1

In Memoriam
Charles Robert Maturin

Keep your mind in hell,
and despair not

Silouan the Athonite quoted in *Love's Work* by Gillian Rose

J. A. Hoffman
c/o The National Library of the Czech Republic

December 2016

My dear Dr. Pražan—

How deeply I regret that I must put this document in your
hands, and so make you the witness to what I have done!

Many times you said to me: "Josef, what are you writing? What
have you been doing all this time?" My friend, I would not tell
you, because I have been the watchman at the door. But now
my pen is dry, the door is open, and something's waiting there
that will turn what small regard you have for me to ruins. I can
bear that well enough, since I never deserved your regard—but
I am afraid for you, because beyond the threshold only one light
shines, and it's far more dreadful than the dark . . .

Ten days have passed and all the while I have been thinking only
of my fault, my fault, my most grievous fault! I do not sleep. I
feel her eyes on me and with hope and dread I turn, but find I'm
all alone! I walk through the city in the dark and think I hear
her footsteps and I find that I'm holding out my hand—but she
offered me her hand once, and I doubt she'll offer it again.

I leave this document in the custody of the library with
instructions that it should be delivered to you when next you are
at your desk.

Forgive me! She is coming!

J. A. Hoffman

Part 1

Look! It is winter in Prague: night is rising in the mother of cities and over her thousand spires. Look down at the darkness around your feet, in all the lanes and alleys, as if it were a soft black dust swept there by a broom; look at the stone apostles on the old Charles Bridge, and at all the blue-eyed jackdaws on the shoulders of St. John of Nepomuk. Look! She is coming over the bridge, head bent down to the whitening cobblestones: Helen Franklin, forty-two, neither short nor tall, her hair neither dark nor fair; on her feet, boots which serve from November to March, and her mother's steel watch on her wrist. A table-salt glitter of hard snow falling on her sleeve, her shoulder; her neat coat belted, as colorless as she is, nine years worn. Across her breast a narrow satchel strap; in the satchel, her afternoon's work (instructions for the operation of a washing machine, translated from German into English) and a green uneaten apple.

What might commend so drab a creature to your sight, when overhead the low clouds split, and the upturned bowl of a silver moon pours milk out on the river? Nothing at all—nothing, that is, but this: these hours, these long minutes of this short day, must be the last when she knows nothing of Melmoth—when thunder is just thunder, and a shadow only darkness on the wall. If you could tell her now (Step forward! Take her wrist, and whisper!) perhaps she'd pause, turn pale, and in confusion fix her eyes on yours; perhaps look at the lamp-lit castle high above the Vltava and down at white swans sleeping on the riverbank, then turn on her half-inch heel and beat back through the coming crowd. But—oh, it's no use: she'd only smile, impassive, half-amused (this is her way), shake you off, and go on walking home.

Helen Franklin pauses where the bridge meets the embankment. Trams rattle on up to the National Theatre, where down in the pit the oboists suck their reeds, and the first violin taps her bow three times against the music stand. It's two weeks past Christmas, but the mechanical tree in the Old Town Square turns and turns and plays one final pleasing strain of Strauss, and women from Hove and Hartlepool clasp paper cups of steaming wine. Down Karlovy Lane comes the scent of ham and woodsmoke, of sugar-studded dough burnt over coals; an owl on a gloved wrist may be addressed with the deference due to its feathers, then gingerly held for a handful of coins. It is all a stage set, contrived by ropes and pulleys: it is pleasant enough for an evening's self-deceit, but no more. Helen is not deceived, nor has she ever been—the pleasures of Bohemia are not for her. She has never stood and watched the chiming of the astronomical clock, whose maker was blinded by pins before he could shame the city by building a better device elsewhere; has never exchanged her money for a set of nesting dolls in the scarlet strip of an English football team; does not sit idly overlooking the Vltava at dusk. Guilty of a crime for which she fears no proper recompense can ever be made, she is in exile, and willingly serves her full life term, having been her own jury and judge.

The lights change—the crowd surges on—Helen is taken on the noisy tide and pitches up against an iron railing, withdrawing her gloves from her pocket. It is then she hears—above the noise of wealthy Koreans bound for the brass-clad riverboats moored down in the dock—her own name lifted on the wind coming off the river. "Helen—Helen Franklin!"—called frantically, as if perhaps she's dropped her purse. She looks up, gloved hand to mouth, and sees—standing still beneath a street light, coatless and shivering—a tall man, blue-shirted, clutching a large dark object to his chest. Eye meets eye; an arm is raised. "Yes?"—imperious, impatient—"Yes! Come here, would you? Come here now, please." The man plucks at the fabric of his shirt as though that half-transparent silk irritates his skin: within, his body is violently shaking.

"Karel," says Helen, who does not yet move. It is Karel Pražan, who constitutes precisely half her complement of friends and acquaintances, their friendship struck up in the café of the National Library of the Czech Republic, there having been no free tables available that morning. He is tall, and carefully thin; his dark hair always gleams against his scalp; his shirts are silk, his shoes suede or calfskin, according to the season; he is not handsome, but gives the illusion of it, and seems always to have only just shaved. But even at this distance, jostled by passing children in bright padded coats, it is possible to make out the grayish pallor, the sunken eyes, of a man who does not sleep. The cold has touched his lips with bluish dust; the arm that clasps the object to his shaking chest is locked in place as if all the joints are fused. "Karel," she says, and moves unhurriedly towards him. Ten paces on she sees he holds a document file, its leather black and coarse; it is worn pale at the edges from much use; it is bound three times with a leather cord. The street light gleams on a mark in the corner, but she can't make it out. "Karel?" she says. "Put on my scarf. What's happened—where is your coat—are you hurt?" A likelier thought occurs. "Is it Thea?" She pictures Thea, his partner and certainly his better half, lifeless in her wheel-chair on the ground floor, eyes fixed at some point beyond the plaster ceiling, taken—as they'd always feared—by another clot of blood to the brain in the night. "Thea?" Karel is impatient.

"What? She's fine—no, I don't want it"—he pushes fretfully at the offered scarf, then surveys her as if he cannot think why she has troubled him.

"You will get ill."

"Take it back! I won't. I don't care. Look: I suppose we should sit down." He looks about, as if he might simply sit cross-legged on the pavement; then he lifts the leather file, and shakes it at her. She sees it is heavy, stuffed with documents and stained with water; he moves his thumb, and reveals in the corner a rubbed gilt monogram reading *J.A.H.* She notes with unease how he holds it with both avarice and distaste, as if it were an object he had coveted all his life, only to find that having paid the asking price it had a foul smell. "It's no good. I shall have to tell someone, and you of all people will bear it. I mean"—he breaks off, and laughs without merriment—"I believe she could walk up and look you dead in the eye and still you'd not believe it! Not a word!"

"She? Who is 'she'—have you taken this file, Karel—does it belong to some friend of yours? You ought not to play your tricks."

"Oh . . ." He grows vague. "You'll see." He begins then to walk on; calls over his shoulder that she must keep up, as though she were a child, and a tiresome one at that. She follows him down a cobbled alley beneath a stone arch which is hardly ten yards from the tourists' thoroughfare, but which you would certainly not find, were you ever minded to try. He pushes open a painted door, slips between heavy curtains drawn against the chill, and sits—beckoning—in a dim corner. The place is familiar—the wet fug on the windows, the green ashtrays, the 40-watt bulbs in their green glass shades—and Helen's anxiety diminishes. She sits beside her friend (he shivers, still), removes her gloves, smooths the sleeves of her cardigan over her wrists, and turns to him.

"You must eat. You were already too thin; you are thinner now."

"I don't want to eat."

"All the same—" Helen gestures to a girl in a white shirt, orders beer for Karel, and for herself, only water from the tap.

"You think me ridiculous," says Karel. He neatens his hair, serving only to demonstrate that he has aged five years in the short course of a week—lean face gone over to gauntness, stubble glinting white. "Well, perhaps I am. Look at me! I do not sleep, as you see. I sit up at night, reading, and re-reading . . . I didn't want to bother Thea, so I read under the covers. With a torch, you know. Like a boy."

"And what have you been reading?" The beer is brought; the water, with its single cube of ice.

"What was I reading, she says! Not a wasted word. How like you. Already I feel better—how could I not? In your presence it all seems—fantastic, bizarre. You are so ordinary your very existence makes the extraordinary seem impossible. I mean it as a compliment."

"I'm sure. Tell me, then"—Helen places her glass more precisely in the centre of its paper mat—"Tell me at least what you've been reading—is it this, here, in this file?"

"Yes." He shakes out a Petra cigarette, and lights it on the third attempt. "Take it. Go on. Open it up." The look he gives her then is one almost of malice: it puts her in mind of a child concealing spiders in a bag of sweets. She reaches for the file—it is very cold, having taken up more than its fair share of the night air; she unwinds the cord, which is bound tightly, and gives her trouble with its knots and turns; at last it gives unexpectedly— the file opens, and there spills out across the table a sheaf of yellowing paper. "There," says Karel. "There!" He stabs it with a forefinger then retreats against the wall.

"May I look?"

"If you want—oh wait, wait"—the door is wrenched open, the velvet curtains billow—"Is it her—has she come? *Do you see her?*"

Helen turns. Two boys come in—eighteen, no more, swollen with pride in earning a day's wages and spending it well. They stamp snow from their workman's boots, bawdily summon the waitress, and turn their attention to their phones. "It is only men," says Helen. "Two men, quite ordinary."

Karel laughs, shrugs, rises once more in his seat. "Don't mind me," he says. "Lack of sleep, you know—it's only—I thought I saw someone I knew."

Helen surveys him a while. Anxiety and embarrassment move across his face, and she feels curiosity sharpen in her like a hunger. But kindness wins out—he will speak, she thinks, when he can—and she turns to the manuscript. It is written in German, in a tilted copperplate as difficult to read as it must have been to master; there are crossings-out, and numbered footnotes: the effect is of a palimpsest pulled from museum archives, but the title page is dated 2016. Separately, fastened with a paperclip, one typed sheet of Czech is dated the preceding week, and is addressed to Karel.

"It's not intended for me," says Helen, turning the page face down. Unease causes her to say more sharply than she intends: "Ah, I wish you'd just tell me what's the matter—you're behaving like a child having nightmares. Wake up, won't you!"

"I wish I could! I wish I could! All right." He draws breath, places both hands flat upon the document, and remains very still for a moment. Then he says—casually, easily, as if it has nothing at all to do with the matter at hand—"Tell me: do you know the name Melmoth?"

"Melmoth? No. I'd remember it, I think. Melmoth—not

Czech, is it? Not quite English, either . . ." She says the name a third time, and a fourth; as if it were some new thing placed upon her tongue which might well taste bitter. This has a curious effect on her companion; it seems to animate him, to cause an avid shining in the bruised sockets of his eyes.

"No, why would you: it meant nothing to me, a week ago—a week! Is that all!" There is again that unhappy laugh. "Melmoth—she . . ." his hands dabble on the sheets of paper with a curious action that puts Helen in mind of a man fretfully soothing a bad-tempered cat. "D'you ever feel," he says, "the back of your neck prick—all the hairs lifting there—as if a cold wind had come into the room and hunted you out, and only you? It's nothing, you say to yourself—what's the English phrase—the goose walks over your grave?—but if you knew!" He shakes his head; lights another cigarette, draws deeply, stubs it out. "It's no use. You wouldn't believe me, and would be foolish if you did—here: take this, take the letter." He slips the typed sheet free from its paperclip. "I'll get another drink (God knows I'll need it) and leave you to read—take it, go on, aren't you all curious, you women, always putting your ear to the door?"

Helen is poised between a dark sea and a certain shore. Karel has never, in the years she's known him, shown fear of any kind, nor any inclination towards superstition, or to giving credence to legend. The change that has come over him is nothing less than the change from mortality to immortality: it all at once occurs to her, as it never has before, that he'll die; that death already has its imprint on him, on the days he's not yet lived, like a watermark on empty sheets of paper. He is at the bar, leaning with a stoop to his shoulders that is all the more troubling for being unfamiliar. She thinks how tall he had seemed, how upright his bearing, when he first approached her in the library café, there having been no other tables free. "May I?" he'd said in Czech, and not waited for her response, but having sat down turned his attention to some incomprehensibly complex diagram (intersecting circles; lines converging on a point), and to an apple pastry. Her own cup of black coffee, bitter and cold, was set beside a pamphlet which she was translating from German into English at the fee of nine pence a word. They had looked, Helen felt, like a peacock and a sparrow; Dr. Karel Pražan in a violet cashmere sweater, Helen Franklin in a cheap and colorless shirt. Certainly nothing more would have come of the encounter had Thea not arrived. Helen, looking up, had seen a woman of middle height and late middle years, standing with her hands in the pockets of woolen trousers with a deep hem, stooping to kiss Karel on the crown. Her hair was short and red; she smelt of cologne. She gave Helen a merry appraising look. "Have you made a friend?" she said to Karel in English; and Helen had blushed, because the inflexion, if not precisely unkind, had been disbelieving. Karel looked up from his notebook and surveyed Helen with vague surprise, as if in the intervening minutes he'd forgotten she was there; then said swiftly in Czech that he was sorry to disturb her, and that they would leave her in peace.

Conscious of a desire to wrong-foot this elegant pair, Helen had said in English, "Please don't go on my account: I'm leaving, anyway," and begun to return her work to her satchel.

Thea then had brightened, with the sudden blaze of delight which Helen later learned was characteristic of her ability to take pleasure at any time, from any source. "Oh, but that accent— you have brought me home in my time of exile! London? Essex, perhaps? Stay, won't you—sit, let me bring more coffee—Karel, insist she stays—she is leaving, and I won't have it!" There had been then a look of understanding that passed between Karel and Helen—*there is no use at all resisting, I'm afraid; it's all right, I quite understand*—which was a surer footing for friendship than any Helen had felt for years.

And indeed there had been no use resisting. That weekend, Helen Franklin—who resisted pleasure and companionship as assiduously as a Trappist avoids conversation—was welcomed into an apartment where Thea stirred a copper pan on the stove, and Karel sat at a scrubbed table measuring the depth of a curve on a convex glass disk. He was, she discovered, attached to a university department, his subject that of the history of the manufacture of glass, and all its uses both domestic and industrial. "It's a telescopic mirror," he had said, greeting his visitor with very little interest, and no sign of abandoning his task, "so the curve must be the depth of a parabola, and not a sphere."

Helen took off her coat and gloves, and handed Thea a bottle of wine (which she herself would not drink). Then obeying a gesture from her host she sat at the table, and folded her hands in her lap. "Tell me about it," she said.

"I am making a reflecting telescope," he had said, "grinding the mirror by hand, as Newton would have done, back in 1668." He set down the glass and showed her his hands. They were rough, and looked sore; remnants of some white paste adhered beside the nails.

Thea put bread and butter on the table. She wore on a long silver chain a curious green pendant, rather like a flower cast in glass. The copper pan spat on the stove. "He will never finish it."

"The focal length," said Karel, "is half the radius of curvature." He looked at Helen, who could not suppress her old pleasure in being taught, and listened with unfeigned interest as he explained his intention to create a mirrored surface by evaporating a layer of aluminium.

All that evening she watched her hosts. Thea, who had ten years on her partner, mothered and petted him—cuffed him, sometimes, if she felt he overstepped the mark ("Don't be nosy, Karel—let her keep her secrets!"). To Helen she was attentive and warm, though always with faint amusement, as if she found her guest odd, but not unpleasantly so. Karel, meanwhile, had an air of cultivated irony, of indifference, which slipped most when he was watching Thea, which he did with a kind of loving gratitude; or when treating Helen as if she were a pupil. Later Helen understood that his partner and his subject were really all that ever occupied his thoughts—that he was like a man who dines so well on the dishes he likes best that he has no appetite for anything else.

Helen—refusing wine; accepting only a very small portion of meat—said to Thea, "Do you teach at the university too?"

"I am retired," said Thea, with a smile anticipating Helen's protests that surely not—surely she was nowhere near retirement age.

"She was a barrister, back in England," said Karel. He gestured to shelves that bowed beneath the weight of legal textbooks. "She still keeps her horsehair wig, over there in a black tin box." Then he said, with as much pride as if it had all been his own doing, "She chaired a government inquiry, you know. Could have taken a title, if she'd wanted it." He took her hand, and kissed it. "My learned friend," he said.

Thea offered Helen buttered potatoes in a porcelain dish. Seeing her guest decline—seeing the half-eaten food on her plate, and the few sips taken from her glass of water—she said nothing. "It had been all work, and no pleasure," she said. "So I took a holiday in Prague, and that became a sabbatical, and that became a retirement. And then, of course, there was Karel."

Karel accepted a kiss, then looked with disfavor at Helen's

plate. It seemed he lacked his partner's tact: "You're not hungry?" he said; and then, "You're very quiet, I must say."

Helen said, "So they tell me."

"Well, then." Thea put down her fork. "How long have you lived in Prague?"

"Twenty years."

"And what do you do?"

"I work as a translator, though my German is better than my Czech."

"How wonderful! What are you working on at the moment—Schiller? Peter Stamm? A new edition of Sebald?"

"An instruction manual for operating Bosch power tools." (Helen smiled then; and she smiles now, remembering.)

"I can't pretend I'm not disappointed! And tell me: was I right—are you from London, or from Essex?"

"Essex, I'm afraid."

"Ah. Well, that can't be helped. And you came to Prague because—?"

Helen flushed. How could she explain her exile, her self-punishment, to these smiling strangers? Thea saw it: "Forgive me! I never quite lost the habit of cross-examination."

"If our guest were in the dock," said Karel, "I wonder what the indictment could be?" He peered at Helen over a glass of wine, then drank it. There was a flash of dislike in Helen then—for the pair of them, with their good clothes, their warm apartment, their ease; for their unlooked-for hospitality, their charm, their way of wheedling out confidences. But it was swiftly extinguished, because Thea said, with a repressing pat on Karel's hand, and a mollifying smile, "Did either of you see that old man in the library the day we met, crying over a manuscript? What do you think he was writing—love letters, perhaps, to some man or woman long dead?" And later, helping Helen into her coat, "I have so loved having you here—won't you come back, and we can talk about England, and all the things we hate about it, and how much we would like to go home?"

All this Helen recalls with a kind of disbelieving fondness, because they are gone now, those easy evenings; have seemed, in the few months since Thea's stroke, to have actually been erased. And now she is at this small table, with this glass of water—with this new Karel: stooping, uneasy, a little frantic. If whatever was concealed in that file, wrapped three times in leather cords, has had such malignant power, might it also disrupt her peace of mind? But—no!—it is impossible. That peace of mind, so hard won, is buttressed with stone. She draws the sheet of paper towards her, and reads: *My dear Dr. Pražan—How deeply I regret that I must put this document in your hands, and so make you the witness to what I have done . . .*

Helen Franklin, having read the letter, feels no chill—no lifting of the fine fair hairs at the nape of her neck. She greets it with interest, no more. An old man, confessing some long-forgotten sin (*my fault*, she murmurs: *my fault, my most grievous fault*), which doubtless could not, these days, tweak the eyebrow of the most ascetic priest. Nonetheless (she draws the paper towards her; reads: *my pen is dry, the door is open*), there is something curious in its fear and longing that is something very like the half-shamed anxious glances of her friend (*she is coming!*).

Karel returns with food: slabs of beef, thick gravy seeping into porous dumplings. "Well?" he says, with a not quite pleasant grin. Helen takes the offered plate; eats deliberately, in small bites, and without pleasure.

"Poor chap," she says. "Old, I suppose? Only a very old man or a very affected one would use a typewriter."

"Ninety-four. He looked as if he'd been pickled in vinegar, put in a jar. 'You will outlive me,' I said. 'Bring vodka to my funeral.' He laughed at that."

Helen notes the tense. "He has died, then? No beer for me, thank you." She sets down her fork, and gives him a quick kind look. "You know, it would be simpler if you just told me about it. If you told me all about it—the old man, and the woman you think you see. I don't like mysteries or surprises. How many times have I told you? I don't like them at all."

He laughs then—shrugs—clears his plate. The boys in their workman's boots have gone; in the corner a student sits smoking over her books. Karel returns the sheaf of papers to its file, and the tremor has gone from his hands. "All right," he says. "I'll tell you everything. That is: everything I have seen myself. The rest, we leave to Josef." He glances at the file. "And yes, he is dead." There is a long, silent moment: each bows their head, a little foolishly, out of mere good manners. Then Karel lights a cigarette from the candle on the table, leans back against the painted wall beside the velvet curtain, and says: "I met him first where I met you: in the library, in the morning, very early, six months ago at least . . ."

Morning, very early, at least six months ago: the National Library of the Czech Republic at the Klementinum, and a kind light shining on the pale bell tower of the Jesuit college it once had been. Karel, on compassionate leave from Charles University, Thea having suffered her stroke, went daily to his library desk to escape his guilt and shame. The woman in the chair for which ugly ramps had been fitted in his home was not—he could not pretend otherwise—the woman with whom he'd passed a decade. Thea, who could hardly cross the road without acquiring a dinner companion, or someone with whom to attend the Black Light shows for which she had a child's love; Thea, with her look of someone you could not trust with a secret, but to whom you'd tell it anyway—this Thea had, he feared, been effaced. On the steel footplates of her wheelchair her well-shod feet turned weakly in; her capable hands lay listless in her lap, or fumbled at the pages of a book. Karel found himself unsuited to the task of carer, which had been always Thea's role: who was there now to pet Karel in his childish moods, when he must clean, and carry, and press analgesics and distalgesics and antiplatelets from their foil packets, and carry them to Thea on a saucer? He wept onto burnt toast, and wished the tears were more sorrowful than angry. Thea said, "Oh get out, be off with you: do you think I need you under my wheels all day? Off to the library with you, and bring me something good to eat." Released from his duties—relieved, and guilty at his relief—Karel went to the Klementinum from Monday to Saturday, sat himself at desk 220 as he always had, photographing, mumbling, taking notes; in the afternoons (these being her allotted hours for work) meeting Helen in the café for cakes filled with poppy-seed paste.

On perhaps the second week—spring indecently in bloom—his gaze was drawn by an elderly man seated across the cork-tiled aisle at desk 209. He could not later say what it was that had made him look—a sudden movement, perhaps? The sound of a pencil's frantic scratching?—only that for several minutes he could not look away. The man wore a heavy coat, despite fine weather, and sat very still save for the motion of his right hand, which crossed and crossed a sheet of paper in a fine copperplate. All around him students typed rapidly before their glowing screens, or sat with eyes turned upward listening secretly to music; but this man had brought a pot of ink into which he dipped his pen with mechanical regularity. Beside that pot, Karel saw, was one of the small square stones that pave the streets of Prague, and which often erupt at the footfall of too many passersby, or at the upward press of a tree root; this he occasionally touched, without looking up from the page. Altogether the effect was of a breach in time through which Karel peered into some morning decades past: "I'll hear horses' hooves on the streets outside!" he thought. The document on which the man worked looked very like an academic treatise, with lengthy footnotes appended here and there; sometimes he would read over what he'd written, and shaking his head with a sound of disgust tear the paper into strips, earning censorious looks from nearby scholars. The desk beside him was empty, but the lamp was lit; the old man seemed to have drawn the chair towards him, and if someone approached—hopefully clutching their books to their chest: "May I?"—he raised his head, sternly shook it, and drew the chair a little nearer.

The following morning, coming early to the café for coffee and a pastry, Karel found the old man seated at an empty table. Curiosity put her palm between his shoulder blades and pushed him over; he set his own plate down, and said: "May I join you?"

Startled, the old man had cast his eyes about the room; then putting his palm on the chair beside him as if to indicate that he was shortly to be joined by another, said vaguely: "Oh—ah: well, that chair, I think, is free." His Czech was careful and decorous; his German accent that of a man for whom Prague's river would always, really, be the Moldau.

"You work hard," said Karel, gesturing to a leather file on the table. "You put us all to shame. What an ethic!" Then he said, "Karel Pražan, of Charles University; though not very often, if I can help it." He put out his hand.

"Josef Hoffman," said the man. "A pleasure." They shook, and the touch of palm on palm actually rustled, as though Hoffman were made of paper.

Not a great deal was exchanged that day—statutory pleasantries regarding the fine weather, and the difficulty of locating anything at all on the shelves these days, what with the staff being so young, and always putting some new system in place. But in the days that followed, if one saw the other a silent greeting passed between them, as if they were colleagues pursuing some common purpose. It was a pleasure to encounter Hoffman in the café, eating potato salad with a spoon; it was a pleasure to note that, yes, again, he carried that leather file, sometimes rubbing with his thumb the gilded monogram *J.A.H.*; that he kept the little paving stone in his pocket at all times. Karel never discovered what his occupation had been, but was delighted to find him knowledgeable in all kinds of subjects, and that he had never lived long in one country. He possessed a formidable memory for fact and figure, and took so great a pleasure in treating his new friend like a pupil that Karel concluded he must once have been the master of some country school: did he know, for example, that Saddam Hussein was once given the keys to the city of Detroit? That even the dead can get gooseflesh? The two often spoke in German, Hoffman moved to quiet laughter by Karel's inelegant phrasing, his impoverished vocabulary. In return for help with grammar and usage, Karel showed Hoffman how to operate a computer, which the old man treated with intelligent awe. All technology interested him, and he often spoke—with some sentiment—of an old radio he'd once used when he was young. He was in all things intelligent, courteous, quiet, and rather shy; if asked what it was that he was writing he would say, "Only an old man's recollections that will never be read," and without rancor change the subject. He was given to sudden fits of melancholy, and on those mornings did nothing but incline his head towards his friend, barely raising his eyes from the manuscript which seemed to be the sole preoccupation of his life. At these times Karel would see him cross out page after page, the nib of his pen scoring the paper; weeping in the arid way of the old, who have already wept themselves dry; then he would fretfully move the empty chair beside him this way and that; or lean first towards it, and then away . . .

So they'd gone on, the old man and the ageing one. If Thea's stroke and its consequences had knocked Karel off course, and presented him with daily evidence of his own selfishness, Josef Hoffman was a fixed point—and one which, what's more, required a redemptive degree of kindness. When Karel came to the library that last morning—a full year turned, the winter air clean and bright as polished glass, the courtyard rimed with frost—and found himself first to arrive (the custodians of the library cloakroom still drinking from their Thermos flasks; no security guards at their post) he laughed to think he'd at last beaten Hoffman to the door. Hoffman, who'd chide him so often for arriving at his desk an hour later than any good student should! It occurred to Karel to play a little trick: perhaps he might even transgress so far as to sit at desk 209, or in that always empty chair, and risk the old man's wrath. He slipped past the cloakroom unnoticed, a light coat thrown over his arm—laughing quietly at such an innocent deceit, the library empty, and his heels rapping out against the floor; the corridors, the oak drawers with their obsolete hoard of library catalogue cards, the view of the courtyard, all in their emptiness seeming entirely strange, as if he had never been there before. Then the great ironclad door, with its noisy latch; he lifted it, and slipped through. No librarians yet at their post, the ranks of desks miserably empty, like sockets from which teeth had been pulled; from the vaulted plaster ceiling plaster babies descended, screaming, as if behind the vault their soft fat feet were being scorched with branding irons. All this Karel saw, uneasy; what had been a place of comfort and industry now repelled him, so that he turned on the threshold to go back. How dark it was, with no lamps shining at their desks!—but, no: a single light was switched on, there, far at the back—left on overnight, perhaps, by some janitor heedless of the cost. It shone down and illuminated a sleeping scholar. Karel, coming slowly down the aisle between the desks, saw the outstretched arms that made an aching pillow for the stooping head; the curved back, the spill of white hair over the dark sleeve. "Josef!" said Karel to himself; hardly surprising, really, that the old man had taken a nap. "Josef?" he said, tiptoeing nearer, and speaking tenderly, as if to a sleeping child. Later he thought: why did it not occur to him, then, that Hoffman was taking his last long sleep? Ninety-four, and weary, and the library so comfortable and quiet—he reached the desk, and lightly put his hand on Hoffman's shoulder. "Josef!" he said, "Shouldn't you be at your work by now?" But Hoffman didn't wake, only fell aside, slumped against the green surface of the desk. The old head lolled against the shoulder—the hair was long and rough; it was the hair of a man who no longer cared what others might make of him, and Karel thought: was he always this man, with his shoes broken down and those great raw wrist bones erupting from the fraying cuffs of his greasy sleeves? "Josef," he said again, and this time shook the shoulder beneath his hand—again the head lolled, rotating on the thin corded neck, so that it turned a blind face up to its tormentor. The eyes were open—they were green—they gazed at Karel, imploring, in an expression of fear and dread; the mouth (Karel shudders, remembering) wide open, the lower jaw fixed awry, as if some unkind hand had tugged it aside as he lay screaming. The hands outstretched upon the desk were not at rest, but rigid, palms down, the fingers hooked, the nails scoring at the surface; there were pale marks visible, as if Hoffman had scrabbled frantically at the leather for minutes at a stretch; and scattered across the desk, in pieces as if crushed by a great weight, were fragments of stone. Beside him another chair had been prepared: it was tilted, as if he'd been deep in conversation with a companion who'd long since left; beneath the chair something unmoving, ill-defined, a scrap of dark fine fabric perhaps; oh, very dark, very fine, like the hem of a woman's dress; as Karel watched, it slipped, as fabric sometimes does—moved, again, as if a breeze passed over it. Karel, in a daze, put out his hand; then a window slipped its latch and blew back against the wall. He cried out, and turned: a jackdaw lighted on the sill, blinked its blue eye once, and left. That look, he later thought, was what recalled him to his senses: nothing on the floor after all but Hoffman's feet, twisted back against the joints of his ankles, and the deep unmoving shadows of the desk and chair. He ran out then, indecently fast (as if the old man might rear up! As if those hands might reach blindly out!), and encountering the security guards at last at their posts said, "An old man—a heart attack, I think?—you'd better call an ambulance." Then there'd been all the banalities: students turned away at the door half complaining, half relieved; bitter coffee shared from a flask, curious questioning from the staff; and if he shuddered to think of Hoffman's face, and the horrid gaping of his open mouth, it was only death, the old debt paid on all those years spent living. As he waited by the entrance, uncertain of death's etiquette (should he remain with his old friend—would there be suspicions, perhaps?) a solemn woman approached. "Dr. Pražan, yes? I found this," she said, "while cleaning." She paused, and narrowed her eyes. "There was a note saying we should give it to you. Not how we usually do things: most irregular. Not part of my job. Still," she said, "under the circumstances. It's his, isn't it? The dead one. Didn't think I knew him, but as soon as I saw this I could picture him clear as you standing there now. Those initials, there—always wondered what they stood for. Well, I know now, don't I? German, I suppose." Here, a very faint note of distaste. "Still, it's a shame." Reluctantly she handed it over; Karel took it, and left it unopened on his lap.

As Hoffman departed—mouth coaxed shut, and decently zipped up inside a nylon shroud—a police officer arrived, her manner that of a teacher disappointed in her pupils. When had the old man arrived? They couldn't say: doors were not always locked when they ought to be. What time was the file left at the cloakroom desk? Nobody knew: it had been tucked a little out of sight, and gone unnoticed an hour or so. Why, of all people, should it be left to—Dr. Pražan, did he say? He had no idea, and the authorities were welcome to it, so far as he was concerned. Had no one seen that one lamp shining? Had no one heard the lifting of the latch? No one had seen; no one had heard. Still (the police officer shrugged, and put on her overcoat): short of discovering a blade in the kidney, that was very likely to be that. The notice of refusal was taken down from the door: the students returned, and it was clear from their festive air that word had got round, and would brighten up the ordinary working day.

Karel pauses: lights another cigarette. The file is on the table between them. Outside, a group of girls in white ten-gallon hats go arm-in-arm along the cobbled alley. Snow has begun again to fall, sifting down against the kerb. The last girl—lagging behind, her feet sore in new shoes perhaps, or slowed by heaviness of heart— looks up at the window as she passes, and sees there a man and a woman, silent, grave, gazing down at something out of sight. They're entirely unalike, these two, but something in the cast of their faces—say, a kind of melancholy exhilaration—makes them seem cut from the same stone. The girl shrugs—moves on (a lovers' tiff, perhaps?)—and never thinks of them again.

"Still," says Helen. "Is it so bad, after all? Sorry, of course, for your loss; and the dead, they—" There is a pause so slight it passes Karel by. "It's an affront. The sight of it. It is *unbelievable*. But he was old, and likely knew nothing about it. Blew out like a light bulb that should have been changed, that's all."

"That he is dead doesn't trouble me. I miss him, that's all. It's what came later—" He stands, seeming suddenly impatient, or perhaps angry: Helen is conscious of having failed a task for which she never volunteered, and moreover is entirely unsuited. "Look, I must get back. Thea will wonder where I've gone— yes, all right, I'll take your scarf. And you take this—then you'll see." He unwinds the leather cord again, and withdraws a sheaf of paper. It is only half the contents. This he gives to her, without flourish or warning: he seems, she thinks, to have lost all interest in it. "Take it," he says. "Read it or not, I don't care. Come and see us next week—Thea sends love—then you can have the rest of it, if you like." Again, and for the final time, there's that look which sits so poorly on the face of a friend: a little private, a little malicious. It is this, above all, which gives Helen pause; then she takes the paper she's offered, and puts it into her satchel. "Well—take care," she says, meaning it more now than she ever has, but he's gone, on a dismissive gesture, out through the curtains, out through the door; swiftly, as if hunted.

Helen Franklin lives east of the river on the fifth floor of an apartment block. It is by no means inconvenient for the Metro, though certainly it could be closer; it is not the city's worst district, nor does it have much to commend it. There is a lift, which she doesn't use: she only ever takes the stairs, enduring patiently the aching limbs, the palms scored by the handles of heavy plastic bags. At the threshold she pauses, the door ajar, awaiting the inevitable call—a woman's voice, grainy, querulous: "Helen? Is that you?"

"Of course," she says. "Of course it's me," and goes in. Follow her in, and what you will see is this: the small dark flat, densely packed with furniture, which jostles, like condemned cattle in a crate; the white walls entirely obscured by prints, by photographs of family long past remembering, by certificates of forgotten achievements which were never any use, and blotted watercolors of ships in the dock. On each surface useless ugly objects of some kind: dried flowers colonized by spiders, matryoshka dolls, a porcelain elephant lacking his trunk. Lying beneath these, prostrate in defeat, are embroidered mats, doilies of cheap machine lace in polyester thread, and scraps of Indian fabric; there is above it all the scent of cheap incense, sandalwood; the air is dim, because the curtains are drawn, and because it is full of dust and smoke. A silent television in the corner puts a fretful blue light against the wall. It is all so wholly out of keeping with Helen—with her neat unadorned clothes, her smooth graying hair and swift calm gait—that I daresay you're taken aback. But if you open the door along the passage—there, to your right: white-painted, plain—you would see a room, which is also white-painted, plain. A narrow bed, and a dressing gown hanging from the back of the door. A small plain desk, and a small plain chair; a narrow wardrobe, in which a modest number of modest outfits hang, and beneath them, three modest pairs of shoes. Here Helen sleeps, eats, and studies: perfects her transitive verbs in German, attempts to master the fifteen patterns of Czech declension. She does not listen to music. The walls and the mattress are bare.

In the dim hall she sets her satchel down. "Helen? I said, is that you?"—and there is her companion, waddling on bowed legs, the joints of her hips worn down, splayed and weak like those of a baby; dependent these days on an aluminium frame, which catches against the carpet and in doing so is volubly cursed. She is in black, this woman, many layers of it, the layers containing the detritus of a week's meals, and the scent of sandalwood, talc, and sweat. She is decked in garnet, in cheap black chips of it, on her ears and fingers, and in a brooch on her breast which glitters like a smashed black plate. This is Albína Horáková: ninety years old, malicious, unkind, devoted to sentimental opera and Turkish Delight. Helen takes in a breath and says, "Yes, it is me. It is always me, and never anyone else. Have you eaten?"

"I have eaten." The women survey each other with a depth of dislike plumbed an inch deeper each day. Helen—rootless, not permitting herself the comfort of a home—had ended one brief tenancy in a dreary room in a stranger's house, and sought another. Karel had said, "There's Albína Horáková, I suppose, always looking for a lodger. They only ever last a month or so. Dreadful old bitch—nobody can stand her, except Thea of course—but quite entertaining in her way, and keeps herself locked away up there with her soap operas and her cakes." Then he'd given Helen a look of calculating appraisal, which was amused, but not unkind, and said, "Perhaps it might suit you, having a cellmate you don't like." A slip of paper was handed over, the call was made—*and now, here we are,* thinks Helen. Albína has seeped into the fabric of the apartment like a stain. Her scent is in the teacups, in the laundry powder, in the leaves of the dictionaries on the shelves. Helen endures it all as she endures every discomfort, every hard thing: patiently, and as her just reward.

"Well, then," says Helen, awaiting some jibe (regarding the drabness of her clothes, possibly; the narrowness of her life, or her idiotically poor Czech), but none is forthcoming.

"Well, then," says Albína, retreats into her own hot, dense little den, and slams the door. Well! Reprieve, and a quiet evening, and in her satchel the Hoffman document. Helen hangs her coat, places her boots beneath it, and makes a pot of weak black tea. This she carries into her room, and sets on the desk beside the sheaf of paper. She stands for a long moment alone on the small square of oatmeal carpet, by the light of the naked bulb. Is she uneasy, now? A little—a little: the flesh on her forearms grows chill, the hairs there lift, there is a slight dropping sensation in the cavity of her chest, as if her heart has paused before a hasty beat. It is as if she feels a pair of eyes fixed on her, unblinking, calculating; she turns, and there is only the dressing gown on the hook, the satchel on the bed. Karel's disease is infectious, it seems: she recalls, with a little quickening of the heart, herself as a child, as a teenager, certain that she was in some way marked out—feeling, as the young so often do, that she could not possibly be as ordinary as she seemed. (There is something else, also, swiftly suppressed: the memory of a cold gaze passing at the nape of her neck, when she did what she ought not to have done.)

She sits at the desk and takes out the manuscript. That minute copperplate seems already familiar—appears, as she takes her reading glasses from their case, actually to dissolve upon the page, the ink reshaping itself into plainly printed English: sans serif, twelve-point type. She takes a sip of bitter tea, and begins to read.

The Hoffman Document

My name is Josef Adelmar Hoffman. This was my father's name, and the name of my father's father. I was born in 1926, in a village east of the River Eger,[1] in the independent state of Czechoslovakia. The country of my birth was older than me by only eight years: had it been a child, it might have had trouble tying its shoelaces.

My father had been born a citizen of the Lands of the Bohemian Crown in the Austro-Hungarian Empire, and it was a source of great bitterness to him that his son was denied this birthright. He regarded the Great War, and the breaking up of the lands of his birth, as a personal slight. He would drink from whatever he had to hand, and tell me: "Do not forget that your blood is in the soil, and the soil is in your blood!"

We lived in a small house not far from the river. It was a region famous for its glass, and the Hoffmans had been glassmakers for five generations. From the window of my mother's kitchen I sat and watched the butcher's boy go by, and Herr Schröder, who was

---

1 The Eger, as I knew it then, has lost its German name, and is marked on the map now as the Ohře. An old joke goes: the Ohře must surely be the only warm river in the Czech lands, since *ohřát* means "warm," but when I swam there as a boy I always came out shivering. It runs to what is now called Terezin, but which I knew as Theresienstadt.

injured at Verdun and taught twenty boys in the village school. We knew his shrapnel scar far better than the Latin verbs he taught us. As I think of it now, it is as if I look into a cupboard full of objects, some of which remain forever shrouded in dust, but some of which I see quite plainly: a forest glass vase in which bubbles were suspended, and in them the breath of some ancestor of mine who'd lived in the Bohemian woods; a single Moser champagne flute, beautiful and useless; my mother's sewing box; the coral ring on which I cut my teeth; buttons cut from the tunic of a captain of the cavalry; a moldavite[2] in the form of a green glass chrysanthemum.

I suppose my parents loved me, as parents must; but no jury would convict, and no judge pass sentence, on any evidence of love that I might put before the court. I cannot praise them as a good son should. My mother's mind was confined to daily purchases in the village stores, and excursions to small towns with women she professed to dislike. She cooked diligently and I was at all times neatly dressed, but I do not recall her undertaking any activity which was not strictly necessary. She did not sew

---

2 In 1786, at a meeting of the Bohemian Scientific Society, a curious object was introduced to general knowledge. A green translucent kind of stone found solely in the Moldau valley, it was named the *moldavite*. Because it looks so very like green glass, they thought perhaps it was caused by forest glassmakers throwing broken pieces in the river a thousand years before. But science has done away with this story, and tells us these stones are shattered pieces of a meteorite that struck the Nördlinger Ries fourteen million years ago. The finest specimens are bright, transparent, and have a fern-like form resembling hoar frost on a window. The Moldau being now called the Vltava, the stone is more properly known as *vltavín*. I prized mine above any other possession, and lost it when I was thirteen.

flowers on pieces of linen, as I'd seen the mothers of other boys do; she did not sing *Lieder* as she peeled potatoes; she did not make sketches of the river running past the lindens just beyond our door. She talked a great deal: her knowledge of the activities and scandals of villages ten miles along the Eger in each direction was exhaustive, and delivered without wit. I was fond of her, because I was her son. My father, meanwhile, was a man made up of the parts of other men: the achievements and eccentricities of my grandfather, and my great-grandfather, and great-uncles, and so on, were his sole source of pride. I think of him now as a piece of mirror hanging on a wall: empty, unless another man walked past. At eighteen he'd been wounded in an accident in a glass furnace. The resulting deformity fused two fingers on his right hand, and exempted him from military service. It was a source of great shame to him: I believe he almost thought that if he could have served his country with the famous Hoffman valor, the dice of war may have fallen in his favor. Before my birth, in the years of the war, he would dress in the uniform of some ancestor of ours—red breeches, blue jacket pleated over the buttocks, a hat with a gold cockade—and parade drunkenly up and down the village square, rapping the hilt of a dead man's sword on the doors of homes with lost sons, offering congratulations. It is rare for a son to see his father as his neighbors see him; but I did, and I hated him, and I despised my mother for consenting to marry him. Indeed, in later years I have come to set aside a portion of my guilt and shame, and lay it at their door—for they meant no harm, but did no good. I came into their hands naked and helpless, my mind an unwritten slate; what might I have been, in the hands of their betters? For I heard nothing in that house but my mother's prattle, my father's vanity; I do not recall their reading literature, or catechizing me on the doctrines of the church, or even standing me beneath the stars and teaching me to know Orion from the Great Bear; we possessed no musical instruments, no images save that of a deposed emperor. Might I have done what I did, if I had heard "Ode to Joy," and known by heart the words of Schiller's hymn to the divine spark—if I had read Augustine's *Confessions*, or watched Faust enter into his contract, and wished that I could beg him to stop? They were dull, and they made a dull boy duller.

My father's injury excluded him from being an artisan, but he had a good head for figures, and when I was nine years old he was offered a post at the Moser glassworks in Carlsbad.[3] Nothing could have given him greater pleasure. My mother took walks to show off her new dress, which had covered buttons and a stiff underskirt; my father threw fistfuls of noisy coins in the collection plate when we attended church. The Moser name was more

---

3 Charles IV, Holy Roman Emperor, born in 1316, called Wenceslaus in honor of that one Good King, chanced on a hot spring while riding in the Bohemian Forest. Finding the waters there beneficial to an old wound in his leg, he caused a small and beautiful city to be built there beside the springs for the good of his court and companions. It became a glittering city on the banks of the Eger, with Art Nouveau colonnades many metres long where ladies walked between high white pillars. Great men came and took the waters: Beethoven, Gogol, Paganini; also Purkyně the anatomist, who discovered the gland that secretes sweat, and who once, having taken nutmeg, hallucinated for days. Water poured steaming into bronze bowls from the bronze mouths of sea serpents; in the colonnades were clocks like the clocks in a city railway station, and bronze plaques bolted to the floor declaiming the temperature of the water in degrees Celsius. All these remain; the great men are gone. In maps and on road signs the name is gone also, and we must call it Karlovy Vary.

sacrosanct than that of God. Did I know, my father said, that the Holy Father himself, Pius XI, possessed a full set of Moser glassware for use at the Vatican? Did I know that at the close of each day the master glassblower inspected each bowl, each glass, and smashed as many as eight out of every ten, for some fatal flaw no other eye could discern? It had always been assumed that I, too, would grow up to be a glassmaker, and by the age of nine I could recite the formula for the famous Moser crystal as a devout boy might have recited the Nicene creed: knew to combine silica, soda ash, potassium and limestone; to melt it at 1460 degrees. But I did not excel at school, and showed no aptitude for any skill or subject. I had no ambition of my own. I was content, always, to eat the dish that was handed to me.

It was at about this time I first began to show symptoms of an inherited disease. So, at least, I have always thought of it; but it seems to me now that in terming it thus I exculpate myself, when more properly I should think of it as a garment I was given, and wore unthinkingly, when I could easily have taken it off.

On his first day returning from the Moser glassworks I heard my father say to my mother: "They are Jews, of course; but the good kind. The kind any man might trust." I heard this without surprise or censure. One of the few books I possessed was called *Beware of the Fox*, and I vaguely understood it was a warning against the Jews. That one might readily discern them by their sulphurous scent seemed to me quite natural, for had they not, in centuries past, poisoned the wells of Christians, and desecrated the host? Had they not stolen away Christian children in the night, for purposes I could not guess at? That the Jews I saw now and then in Carlsbad seemed indistinguishable from Christians did nothing to straighten the crook in my mind. Though I do not recall my parents having ever tutored me in bigotry, in the course of ordinary conversation they would often turn to the Hilsner Affair,[4] which each remembered—with the particular pleasure the unintelligent have for the ghoulish—from their youth; and I suppose this contributed to my own loathing.

One incident alone from that part of my life I recall with perfect clarity. My walk to school took me on a narrow track past a field of wheat, where often I saw the farmer picking stones by hand in winter. Now this farmer had a habit of leaving out some form of seat in the field, which I never once saw him use. In winter, a wooden crate; in summer, a bale of hay. I even once saw a small dining chair set out in the harrowed field, but he must have been admonished by his wife, for I never saw it again. My curiosity at that time was sluggish, my intelligence mean: a thousand other wonders must have passed me by, but this one thing puzzled me. Encountering him one morning on the path, I screwed up my courage and asked what purpose these empty seating places served. "Why, it is for *she* of course," he said. He looked for a time at the stack of logs placed against the wall of an outhouse twenty yards from where we stood. A handful of jackdaws were pecking at the soil. Then he gripped me by the shoulder, and I could see a milky quality to his eyes. "It is for the Wanderer," he said. "For the Witness—for she who is

---

4 Anežka Hruzová, a young Catholic seamstress of only nineteen years, was found on April Fool's Day in 1899 with her throat cut. There was blood pooling in the forest where she died, and blood on the stones around her, and on her clothes, which were torn. Leopold Hilsner—a young Jew, a wanderer with a child's intellect—was arrested on hearsay. At a show trial it was insinuated that the girl's murder was part of a Jewish conspiracy to kidnap Christian children, and use their blood for obscure and devilish rituals. Sentenced to death, Hilsner was able to hear from his prison cell the carpenters building his gallows. He was pardoned in time, but never forgiven.

cursed to walk from Jerusalem to Constantinople, from Ireland to Kazakhstan; she who is eternally lonely, who is excommunicated from the grace of God and the company of men; she who watches, whose eyes are upon you in your guilt and transgression, from whom God has withdrawn even the respite of sleep!" He spoke like some mad preacher who goes from door to door with pamphlets in one hand and a tin cup for begged coins in the other. I left him with the idea that some damned soul required that he should leave out for her a resting place, in case she should happen by; and that he'd glimpsed her once, as a boy, and lived in terror and hope that he might one day see her again.

Later that same day I lingered after school to speak to Herr Schröder, and ask if he too had seen that single chair set out in a harrowed wheat field. It was just an old myth, he said, and one he was surprised I did not already know. "It is nothing but a story told to children to keep them in line," he said. "Did your mother never take you on her knee, and tell you that Melmoth was watching?" My mother had never told me any stories, I said. "It began like this," he said. "You know, as your bible has taught you, that a company of women came to Jesus's tomb, and found it empty, and the stone rolled away, and right there in the garden they saw the risen son of God. But among them was one who later denied that she had ever seen the resurrected Christ. Because of it she is cursed to wander the earth without home or respite, until Christ comes again. So she is always watching, always seeking out everything that's most distressing and most wicked, in a world which is surpassingly wicked, and full of distress. In doing so she bears witness, where there is no witness, and hopes to achieve her salvation." Could he have said all this to me, a boy with whom he'd never exchanged more than a handful of words? I think so, for I remember it well, and how he ran a finger in the furrow of the scar that ran from ear to collarbone. "Well, that's the legend," he said, "and this is her name: Melmoth the Witness, or Melmotte, or Melmotka, depending on the town where you were born. But what you must remember is this: that she is lonely, with an eternal loneliness which will end only when our world ends, and she receives her pardon. So she comes to those at the lowest ebb of life, and those she chooses feel her eyes on them. Then they look up—they see her watching—and she holds out her arms and says: *Take my hand! I've been so lonely!*"

I shivered then, and asked what became of those who take her hand. Herr Schröder laughed. "Nobody knows what happens," he said, "because she isn't real. If she were, I suppose one might go with her, if life had become intolerable. Put it from your mind, young Hoffman. You are too old for fairy tales."

Calamity came to my family in 1936. The Moser factory, whose frail glass bowls and flutes were no match for factory-made glass, laid off many staff and my father among them. He came home that day with a red bowl wrapped in pages of the *Prager Tagblatt* and hidden in his winter coat. It had a flaw on the rim, but he'd saved it from the master glassblower's wrath, in what was I think the sole act of individualism and courage of his whole life. Loudly he bemoaned the mischance that led him to place his fortunes into the hands of a Jew. I suppose we may have fallen into poverty had not my mother's brother died childless, leaving her the sole beneficiary of his will. He had owned a shoe shop in Prague, a city I'd never visited and to which I'd never given any thought; and so by the close of that year we had left behind the Eger and the lindens and Herr Schröder's school, and become part of the little group of ethnic Germans living at that time in Prague.

I recall how large and light the shop and its apartment seemed; see quite plainly now the apartment with its old oak floor, and how downstairs were many posters of ladies' ankles in high-heeled shoes, always with the suggestion of lace or a satin hem. There were two large windows filled with glass cases, displaying shoes on lengths of cloth, and I cleaned these every Saturday with white vinegar dabbed on worn-out handker-chiefs. My father turned his mind to the accounts; my mother fitted schoolgirls and grand German–Czech dames for shoes. A brighter child than I might have found himself living in bewil-derment and delight, for in place of a modest village and a single church, I had within arm's reach the city of a thousand spires, which glittered on the banks of a great river: of staircases steep as mountainsides, and buildings plastered and painted in the colors of girls' dresses in spring, and Prague Castle which rose up from the Vltava seeming black and terrible. But two impressions alone have outlasted the years: the motorcars and trams which seemed barbarous to me as they thundered past the open windows, and a building on the Old Town Square painted like the Wedgwood plates my mother had been given as a wedding gift and never used since. I made myself invisible among the boys at school, and every afternoon stood behind the counter with my mother wrapping in brown paper the sandals and slippers she sold. I turned eleven, then twelve: acquired breadth of body, and none of mind. No school companions invited me to their homes, and I never thought to invite them to mine. Our only visitor was the policeman whose beat included the shop. He was a childless and fatherly man whose mother had been German, and who was delighted to speak to my mother in the language he knew better than Czech. She called him Polizist Novák, as if they'd met on a Berlin street, and not Rotný Novák as the Czechs did; and though I dimly understood that this was a small act of defiance I could not comprehend why it gave my mother such pleasure. I grew fond of him because he made my mother laugh, a feat which lay far beyond my father. His wife was Catholic, and very devout, and I understood this to be a great trial to him. He did not speak to me with kindness or condescension, as people so often speak to children, but as if I were a man like him, and like my father. "Seen anything interesting lately?" he would say, leaning on the counter and eating one of the pieces of cake which he seemed always to have about him. "How's work going? Are you keeping well?" So we went on, my parents and I—dull, unspeaking: three oxen trudging in their furrow, not once looking up at the changing weather, which rolled in very low and very black from the east.

At last something penetrated through that atmosphere of foolish indifference into which I had been born. One property on our street had evidently been empty since long before we'd come to live nearby. It was a much grander shop than ours with two red doors covered with curlicues of iron, and two curved windows papered over with old newspapers. One morning—September, I suppose, for I wore new school shoes that pinched—I was astonished to find the paper taken down and the windows clean and shining. A sign swung above the door on a wrought-iron bracket: it read *BOOKS AND MAPS*, and the paint was wet, and red. Concealing myself in the doorway of the grocer's shop I looked for a long time at the new shelves that clad the walls from floor to ceiling, and the new glass cabinet where antique books were set on blocks. Two children stood laughingly directing a woman as she pinned up a map of Bohemia in a fine brass frame. I watched the light striking their sleek fair heads, and thought the woman very beautiful, so unlike my own mother: tall and plump, with strong legs in fine stockings, her hair set in fashionable rolls. Then one of the children turned and his blue intelligent eyes picked me out in the gloom where I stood and met mine with a sensation like the touch of hand on hand. I had the bewildering feeling of inhabiting for a moment that fair and shining countenance. For just as I saw him—how straight he stood, and how the sun picked out the whiteness of his shirt—I saw also myself. It was as if I'd been without warning placed before a mirror. I saw my lumpish face, and the rough hair my mother cut; saw the downturned mouth and greenish eyes that had no gleam to them. Was it then I hated him, I wonder? Or was it later, when I saw how often he laughed, and how fondly his mother put her hand on that sleek blond head? For certainly I must confess that yes: I hated him, and the hatred lodged in me as though I had swallowed a stone.

Within three days I knew the name of the boy and his family. He came into the shop one Saturday afternoon, not wanting shoes, but wanting me. He spoke to my mother and he charmed her more than I ever had. He said, "Frau Hoffman, may I introduce myself to your son? I am new to Prague and I should make friends." He was German, it seemed; and I knew this would please my mother, who had only sufficient Czech to sell a shoe, and thought it an ugly language. He bowed to her, and as he did so he looked at me with a conspiratorial look so that I would know he was my ally, and not hers. He stuck out his hand. "I am Franz Bayer," he said. "Look outside! That's my sister, Freddie." I shook his hand, and waved at the girl beyond the glass: another creature of white-blonde hair, and direct blue eyes. I could not tell how old they were: they were tall, and had a confidence I knew I would never have no matter how long I lived; but their

white clothes and buckled shoes would have suited younger children. "I saw you move in," I said. "You have a lot of books."

"We never read them." He had his hands in his pockets and
looked at the glass case where my mother had displayed a pair
of shoes. Suddenly I saw how ugly those shoes were, and what a
poor job I'd done of cleaning the glass.

"I'd much prefer this," he said kindly. "My father thinks I
should read at least some of the books we sell but I bet nobody
wants you to wear those shoes. Look at them! The ribbons! Oh
look, Freddie wants us." The girl tapped on the window; she
smiled, and beckoned.

"Look here," said the boy. "Come and see what we've got! It was
our birthday yesterday, you see, and we've got a radio, and nobody
to show it to." He did not look embarrassed, but said, with a frank
shrug: "Our mother teaches us at home, so we don't have friends."

I didn't want to leave the dreary shop, and my dreary parents,
where my own dreariness passed without notice. But my mother
smoothed her dress in a manner so strange and coquettish I
would have liked to kick her. "Of course he'll come and play,"
she said. "Won't you, Josef? I can spare you an hour or two."
Franz took my arm. I don't believe that anyone had ever taken
my arm before. I could not suppress a sensation of pleasure—
and then of course I hated him again, for that.

Freddie did not look very like her twin. The resemblance was
there in the gestures and the ease, and in the unwavering looks
she gave; but her face was quite different. I recall it now as I have
recalled it every day since: the freckles across her nose, only eight
of them, and the deep bow to her lip. Her fringe was cut very
short, and showed her eyebrows—how dark they were, and how
odd they looked below her white-fair hair. Her hands were large
and capable, and around each bright blue pupil a dark blue line

was drawn. I loved her as readily and without reason as I hated her brother.

I found they had as much to say to each other as grown siblings who have been apart for months and have family business to discuss: they criticized their mother, who fussed; and castigated their father, who let her. They deplored the rooms they'd been allocated, which were cold; they didn't like Prague, having much preferred Hamburg, but were prepared to give it the benefit of the doubt. They liked their lessons. They did not like marzipan. They were looking forward to winter. They needed a cup of coffee, and didn't I?

"Here we are," said Franz. At the threshold of the shop he actually bowed, in the manner my father sometimes had when more than usually mindful of the Hoffman name. His mother stood with a customer turning the pages of a book with marbled edges. Behind the counter a door was open. I could not see much of what lay beyond it, only an impression of light striking polished wood, and perhaps of flowers. "In we go," said Freddie; and I was drawn between them through the shop, and towards that open door. Franz kicked it shut. The shop vanished, and I found myself in a room of a kind that I had never seen before. I suppose it was not, really, so different from the ones where I had lived: there was a table against a wall, and four chairs with tapestry seats; a clock above the mantelpiece, and a rug. But everything in it was so affectionately chosen that it did not seem furnished so much as inhabited. The table was rosewood, and the grain of it shone with beeswax that had the scent of honey; the tapestry on the chairs had been done by hand, and each was different, and showed game birds and their green and amber plumage. The walls were freshly papered, and the paper was green with fern fronds and stems so lifelike I would not have been surprised to see them stir in the draught from the open window. There were books everywhere, tossed on the seat of an armchair with their spines broken and their pages folded. I could see the remains of the birthday: paper chains cut from newspaper draped over picture frames, and cards on the mantelpiece. Someone had left a pot of glue on the dining table, and the glue had run down from the lip of the pot and dried on the lace mat which was there, and nobody seemed to mind. There were flowers in a glass bowl set in the empty grate.

I was bewildered and resentful. What right did they have, to bring me here, where I could only look even more drab and more dull than ever? I looked down and my brown leather shoes against the scarlet carpet shamed me. I was thirteen years old. I did not know what to say, or how; I hardly even knew how to feel. Then Franz said: "What do you make of this?" They were standing now in front of an oak sideboard, obscuring something from my view. "There!" said Freddie, and with a funny little bow showed me a radio set on a green velvet cloth edged in gold brocade.

I'd seen radios before, of course I had. They were readily for sale in Prague, and even in our village on the Eger the pastor's family kept one, and listened to broadcasts from Austria. But I'd never seen one so close, and certainly not one so grand. They showed it to me as if they were parents of a new baby: didn't I love the dials, and how smoothly they turned? Wasn't the case enormous? Oak, of course! Would I like to see inside? There, what did I make of that? I wanted to remain aloof, but I could not, because concealed behind a panel were the valves, and they were glass, and I couldn't help touching them and saying they'd been cast in a mold, and not blown. This fragment of knowledge delighted them disproportionately. How did I know? Had I ever seen glass blown—had I even done it myself? I confessed that I had, and suffered their delight. In that case: would I like to try my hand at unscrewing one, and taking a better look, or was that unwise? Very well, it was unwise: they would leave me to replace the panel, since I knew what I was doing. How bewildered I was! They did nothing but flatter and charm, and with each word I felt myself diminish in stature. I suddenly thought of my precious green moldavite, which had been the one beautiful thing I'd ever owned, and which might have pleased them; but it had been lost on the way to Prague, and its loss left me a pauper. Then they turned the radio on, and I heard cabaret music.

The room was hot, with the close fragrant warmth of a well-heated home, very unlike the dour chill I was used to, and I became drowsy and slow. I could smell the glue drying in its pot, and the white flowers in the grate. Freddie danced, but not in the decorous fashion we were taught at school, counted diligently out: it made her white skirt lift and show her bare thighs, and the pale downy hair that grew above her knees. She spun and spun, laughing, and I saw once, very briefly, the hem of some pink satin garment which seemed obscene under her childish dress. I didn't want to look because it made me feel sick—or so I thought, though I know better now what it was. Then the decadent music gave way to something martial, and Franz took my arm and marched me up and down. Freddie, petulant and suddenly bored, curled up in an armchair and began to read.

Franz said, "Well—what do you think?" Proudly, he put his hand on the curved case of the radio, then turned a dial to make the music bloom and fade. It shocked and repelled me to think that this tall bright boy was seeking my approval. What right did he have to ask anything of me, when I had so little, and he had so much? "It's all right," I said, and shrugged. If his face betrayed the shock that comes when a plea for kindness goes unanswered I didn't see it, because I was looking down again at my scuffed shoes on the carpet. Their laces were dirty and had begun to fray. "Oh," he said, and seemed to be casting about for some means to persuade me that he'd given pleasure and I'd taken it. Then Frau Bayer came in. She wore a pleated blue dress with a full skirt, and over this a kind of white cotton apron. Her shoes had a wooden heel, and fastened with a narrow strap. She wore a string of pearls, and they were not like my mother's pearls, which often broke and scattered: they were knotted between each bead, and they glowed. Her hands were like Freddie's hands: large and strong, the nails very short, and her wedding band was loose on her finger. "Ah!" she said, and clapped twice in satisfaction. "Splendid! Are you Franz's new friend? He told me you were coming."

"I am Josef Hoffman," I said, and could say no more.

"He didn't think much of the radio," said Franz.

"Then you must choose better music," said Frau Bayer. She stooped to pick two or three dying stems out of the glass bowl in the grate, and held them to her nose. "The smell goes very sickly, at the end," she said, and wrapped them in a sheet of newspaper.

Freddie had returned the book she was reading to the shelf. "Can we have coffee?" she said. "We are absolutely dying for some. Aren't we, Josef?" I had never liked coffee, but the way she said it made me feel that after all perhaps I did.

"Such sophisticates!" said Frau Bayer. "Since your friend is here, I'll close early. Don't tell your father: let it be between us." She tapped her nose, and again I had that curious sensation of being wanted out of all proportion to what I could offer. She went to lower the shutters of the shop, then went out to the kitchen, and I heard running water, and the rattle of cups on saucers. She began to sing.

Franz disconsolately turned the dials on the radio. I felt ashamed
of myself, and then angry with him, for making me feel shame. I
asked if I might try, and he brightened a little, and said that of
course I should. I passed by the cabaret music and the Beethoven
and found the crisp bland voice of the news. Freddie turned it off
and said she'd heard enough of all that. Then Frau Bayer poured
me coffee with milk and sugar, and it was sweet and consoling.
For an hour we sat at the table, and I do not recall what was said,
only how Frau Bayer sometimes patted the heads of her children,
and lightly slapped Freddie away from her third biscuit; the ease
of it, and how readily they laughed. It grew dark. The curtains
were drawn and an oil lamp was put on the table and I watched
the narrow flame rise up from the white glass cover. Then Franz
said to me that perhaps I should go. Of course it was not that he
wanted me to; only that he'd promised my mother (he said "Frau
Hoffman" very courteously) that I wouldn't be kept too long.
He asked me again what I had thought of the radio, and I said I
thought it very good, very clever. His pleasure shone out of him
then and I despised him for it. They said goodbye with a kind of
formal affection that felt somehow like mockery: I was the sole ugly
object in that room, and they treated me like something precious.
"You are always welcome here, Herr Hoffman," said Frau Bayer,
as though I were a grown man who'd come on business. Freddie
said, "Next time I'll show you the books I'm not supposed to know
about," and ducked her mother's admonishing hand. Then Franz
took my arm, and conducted me formally through the dark shop.
"Good of you to come," he said: it was stiff, and formal, as if it
were something he had been taught. I had disappointed him, of
course. Well: he had got what he deserved, and now they'd bother
me no more. Then he unlocked the great scarlet door with its iron
cladding. "Goodbye," he said, and receded into the darkness of

the shop. There was a moment when I heard nothing, but knew he was still there; then before the door had quite swung shut he said, "Come back, won't you?" His hand appeared through the gap between door and frame: he waggled it humorously, then held it out, and waited. I looked at it—at the white cuff of his shirt, and the narrow wrist, and the long fingers which had glue drying beside the nail—and I hated him then as I had hated him from the first. I turned my back. I never spoke to them again.

Outside, the road was noisy with trams and students and offices emptying, and I walked alone watching my feet on the cobbles, thinking of the pale hairs gleaming on Freddie's skin as she danced. I went on in this way until I reached our shop, and when I looked up I saw that it was altered. The lights of the shop were out, and so was the single bulb that shone above the side door where I was to enter. This side door was set back in a little porch up a flight of stairs, and the porch was in darkness, and I stood on the pavement reluctant to make my way up in case I stumbled and fell. As I watched, the darkness began to deepen. It was as if it were not merely absence of light but a gap into which every bad thing was being slowly sucked. It pulsed. I saw it: it widened and narrowed and widened again, as though it were gasping for breath. It suddenly seemed to me that all that is worst in the hearts of women and men—all the things that I had simply never thought of before: the deceits and vanities and cruelty—had substance, and were massing there like a swarm of flies. Then the substance of it changed: it was like lengths of fine black silk hung there in the doorway, stirred by a breeze; then those lengths grew, and spilled like ink down the steps. There was no sound from anywhere: the street, which ought to have been all hustle and bustle, was empty save for a great black crowd of jackdaws seeking out places to rest. I knew then that I was watched. My body strained towards my watcher—my skin broke out in gooseflesh, and I felt my eyes adapt to that sucking blackness with a painful pulling of the tissues. I was terribly afraid, but there with the terror was something else, which was very like the sickness I'd felt as I watched Freddie dancing while the cabaret played on. It was a kind of frightened longing, like a man who sees a lover he has hopelessly longed for, and in his lover's hands a noose; and I knew beyond doubt that my watcher was a woman. Very slowly I turned. Nobody was there.

Then the light came on and I saw my mother on the step. The color of her dress, which in fact was drab and dull like all her clothes, seemed to me as bright as the flowers Frau Bayer had placed in the grate. The blackness dissipated. My mother said, "Up you come: don't dawdle down there, when food is on the table." I went up the step and put my arms around her waist and rested my head on her shoulder. She was warm and solid and smelt of soap and vinegar. She patted my shoulder stiffly and said, "What's this, then? Eh—what's all this?" Then we went inside. My father had already begun to eat.

In the months that followed I often heard music playing as I passed the Bayer shop on the other side of the road. Sometimes what I heard moved me painfully. It seemed indecent that I could walk past in good spirits and be brought to tears by a violin; or that I could scuff by on my way to school, and find myself walking more briskly at the tantivy of the brass. Confusion and desire and envy lodged low and heavy in my stomach. I knew it did me harm. I didn't care.

One morning in March I woke late, and though my room was drearily familiar I felt a change of air. In the room where we ate our meals the window had been left open, and I could hear a kind of thrumming on the streets, and now and then a man's voice raised in a yell which was not distressed or excited but somehow matter-of-fact. It was cold, and a little rain had blown in. I called for my mother but she was gone. Drawn down by the sounds of the street I went out and found my parents standing in a crowd that gathered on the pavement. My mother had covered her hair in a bright scarf I'd never seen before, and wore a cardigan stitched with flowers that fastened at the neck with woollen tassels. In her left hand she held a handkerchief which she pressed to her face while she wept. Her right arm was raised above her head, the hand flat and held palm down. I was astonished. I'd never seen her show such emotion, nor could I understand why she would give a military salute. My father was also weeping, though he could not cover his face, because his right arm was also raised, and in his left he held the Hoffman sword. Then I saw coming down the street a column of men. Some drove motorbikes with sidecars covered in tarpaulin; some rode bicycles that rattled over the cobblestones, and others were on foot. They all wore winter coats that looked too large, and carried long thin objects over their shoulders, and I remembered how the farmer back in our village by the Eger had shouldered his hoe and rake as he went out to work the fields, but these were the barrels of guns. Then the crowd drew back from the pavement and we all fell silent as if with respect, and a tank rolled past. A man stood buried in it up to his waist: he waved, and caught my eye, and waved again. Then the tank moved on, and the crowd closed behind it, and I thought there was a slight change in the noises all around me, as though excitement had been tempered with something else.

Hours it took for the men to go past, coming east over the bridge. All that day they spread and thinned throughout the city, as though they were particles in a dense black fog coming off the river that made its way into the alleys. The atmosphere was by turns subdued and hectic: often I saw women weeping and had no way of telling whether out of fear or jubilation. Despite the small crowds that gathered here and there the streets were quiet, and when I looked into apartment windows I saw faces that seemed fixed and gaunt. In the window of the Bayer shop a printed notice promised they'd return tomorrow, and I imagined Frau Bayer in a good silk dress saluting like my mother, while Franz and Freddie turned the dials of their radio until they found a jubilant, military march.

It seemed Prague had come under occupying forces, but it was all somehow quite ordinary and hardly worth a column in the newspapers. Already white signs had been fastened to lamp posts: *in prag fahren wir auf der linken seite.* What danger could there be from an army that politely adhered to the Prague custom of driving on the left? Where was the gunshot—where the fires set in the streets? I'd seen no heroism nor cruelty: only weeping housewives, and boys in uniforms that didn't fit them yet. It seemed the world, as I had long suspected, contained little in it of interest.

That night my mother put flowers on the table. They were cheap gaudy ones with no scent and already the leaves were dropping. Her eyes shone and her cheeks were flushed, and I understood this had something to do with what I'd seen that day.

"Sit down," she said. "Sit down—it's been a good day, don't you think? The best day of your life, I'd say. Sit with your father."

My father sat very upright in his chair. The Hoffman sword lay on the table beside his outstretched arms. He looked happy, with a kind of hectic gleeful happiness I didn't like. "Here," he said, and slapped the seat beside him. "See what your mother has made."

The oven door was open and I smelt burning fat and red cabbage stewed with vinegar and apple. My mother set a large oval platter on the table and spilled thin liquid on the blade of the sword. She had prepared a roulade of beaten pork rolled around mushrooms that lay soft and gray in the pork fat. She set about it with a carving knife and gave first my father, and then me, portions of meat which turned my stomach. "Eat!" she said. She reached over and patted my belly. "Eat up! Don't you know what happened today?"

"Not him," said my father, with a kind of fond contempt. "Never taken any notice of what's beyond his shoelaces, that boy, eh? Well, Josef?" He cuffed my ear. It hurt, and I did not show it. "What do you make of it?" He chewed at the pork, and grinned at me.

"I suppose the city has been invaded," I said. "Those were German men—but why were there no Czech soldiers? Where was Polizist Novák?"

"Invaded!" said my father. I could not tell if he were outraged or amused. He thumped the table, and the Hoffman sword quivered. "We are saved, boy. It is returned to us: everything that your grandfather and your great-grandfather knew, and everything that I lost, will be yours!" I had no idea what he meant. What had I lost? I slept, and ate. I spoke the language of my mother and my father. I could distinguish, because my schoolmasters taught me, between adjective and adverb. What use did I have for pride? I expected nothing, hoped for nothing, looked for nothing, asked nothing, gave nothing.

My mother leaned forward and whispered. "They say by the week's end he himself will give a speech from Prague Castle. Just think of that! We shall go. Perhaps there will be tickets for sale."

"We shall most certainly go!" said my father. "They will wish us to be there: a family of an old German name. Ah Josef, to think I have lived to see you inherit what is yours!" It disgusted me to see that my father's eyes were wet. I had always disliked strong emotion of any kind. I could eat no more for the remainder of the meal, but my parents paid me no mind, for they'd opened a bottle of good wine and were toasting, in swift succession, a long line of Hoffman ancestors of whom I'd never heard.

Here ends the portion of the document that Karel Pražan gave to Helen Franklin. She is weary. The ink on the page thickens: begins, it seems, to seep towards the margins, as if it might very well drip down and stain her clothes beneath the desk. But what is there here to account for Karel's altered appearance, his gaunt cheek? She ponders that name which has become familiar in the passing of an hour or so: Melmoth, or Melmotte, or Melmotka; ponders a woman questioned by men, and refusing them; ponders the justice of the sentence meted out. It is easy enough to summon up this watcher, this witness: to imagine, say, a hag, black-clad, stooped, unblinking, baleful; to summon up also the pricking sensation of an implacable eye fixed on a bare neck. She finds herself unwilling to raise her head to the window, as if she might see beyond the glass a face with an expression of loneliness so imploring as to be cruel. (And since *she* will not look, *you* must—there, beyond the railing—no, a little further still: between that parked car and this—wait, and grow accustomed to the dark; and yes, there you have it, do you not? Against the beech hedge with its burned leaves, something unmoving, and yet distinct; the night's fabric thicker. A figure in—yes!—black; slender, and not tall; looking steadfastly at the bare bulb burning five floors up.)

Meanwhile Helen closes her eyes, and sees behind the lids a boy—stocky, fair, unsmiling; eyes cast down at his boots; in shorts perhaps; seeing little, saying less. There is movement behind her—very slight, only the shifting of fabric on fabric— and at once the imagined boy lifts up his head and looks directly at her. *She is watching!* he says; and at the nape of Helen's neck the hairs lift. Slowly she turns in her chair (laughing at herself a little, of course, that she should be so fanciful)—and there is a woman in the doorway, steadily watching: Albína Horáková, who has draped upon her many layers yet another: black silk, green-stitched, velvet. She holds a plate. "I have treats!" she says. "Sweet things for a sweet girl, eh?" She swings and shuffles across the carpet, grunting; places a plate upon the desk. Half a dozen small cakes, the icing gleaming pink as a wet fold of flesh. "Sweet Helen," says Albína. "Eh? Eat, eat! Think it's poison, eh? Well, well. Perhaps it is. Perhaps it is." Wickedly she smiles down at Helen. "Not hungry? Never hungry, are you? Thin. Look: thin, nothing there. Won't eat. Won't sing. What's this, here? Nothing on the walls, nothing on the bed. Ugly everywhere, ugly like you." From deep in her gullet: a noise of disgust. "Eat, eat, eat." Then she turns—slowly, like a ship's hulk adrift—murmurs to herself, in Czech, incomprehensible. The scent of the sugar, of the moist and half-baked dough, rises from the chipped plate, and Helen's stomach contracts. It would be well, she thinks, to eat one now: force down thick sweet paste, and swallow. But her habits of self-denial are inescapable. She never intended this— cannot recall, when plotting how to expiate her guilt, how best to achieve redemption; does not remember having said: "I will take no joy in food, merely let myself live." Yet here we are, she thinks: butter, and sugar, and so I cannot eat. Nor can she recall when Albína first observed her rituals of discomfort: the uncovered mattress, the unheated room, the bitter tea. But she did notice, as she notices all things: slyly, from the corner of her black eye. Quietly Helen takes the plate into the kitchen; quietly sets it deep within the fridge. From Albína's room, music: violins sweet as cake, and as spitefully intended to sicken. Helen pauses, and places a hand to her side, and presses, as if the music's source is there within her kidneys, her spleen, and may be suppressed at a touch. Then she returns to her room, exchanges her clothes for a nightdress resembling the coarse shift of a penitent, lies on the bare mattress, sleeps well—though the small hours are punctuated by dreams that come in startling flashes, as if seen through the window of a train that's running late: green tiles in a corridor and an antiseptic scent; wasted limbs under a sheet; scarlet flowers seeping over a dirty windowsill; and her own hands, very steady, when they ought to have trembled in fear at what they were about to do.

And since she sleeps well, and deeply, you may step quietly onto that plain square of carpet, and look again at that characterless room. Where is the evidence of who she is, this Helen Franklin: small, insignificant, having about her an air of sadness whose source you cannot guess at; of self-punishment, self-hatred, carried out quietly and diligently and with a minimum of fuss? If you kneel (be very careful, very quiet) you'll see beneath the bed a cardboard box. It is gray, and the lid torn at the corner; there is the remains of a label at the end, and a pair of shoes drawn on it. Bring it out, put it where the street light shines, and lift off the lid. Here is what is kept inside: a cassette tape, and a picture of a young man, black-haired, laughing through green-rimmed sunglasses, on a city balcony. Folded and pressed, a handkerchief in a stiff shining fiber you've never seen before, its scalloped edges stitched with pink. A small book, hardback, clothbound, blue: the poems of Rilke, not translated. A plastic-wrapped packet of tamarind seeds rolled in sugar, the lyrics of a sentimental pop song decorated with pencil in the margins. A string of very small seed pearls, pale pink, the string yellow and loose between the beads, and earrings made of abalone shell. A ticket for what might perhaps be a tram in a foreign country—a letter, in a language you do not recognize—a bottle of perfume from which the liquid has long evaporated, but which has a sweet strong scent. Two lipsticks: greasy, pearly, violet-pink. They are well-handled, these things: the box has grown fragile from being withdrawn and concealed, pored over, held. Touch the letter, and it will fall apart in your hands. It is a whole life contained in twelve inches by eight by six; buried, as if beneath six feet of English soil; begun, forty-two years before, in a pebble-dashed house in Essex; and ended, twenty-two years later, by an act of will.

Helen Franklin had been born to a family constrained by lack of money, and by the mistrust of change which is the mark of a certain kind of English family. Her parents were small, anxious, punctilious, polite; her father occasionally bad-tempered, if pressed beyond the limits of what was comfortable, her mother occasionally unhappy, if given glimpses of a life less limited. They went each summer to a hotel where the breakfast could be relied upon, amended their Christmas card list on the first of December without fail, and never neglected to bring the begonias indoors over winter; they grew fretful if asked to drive to unfamiliar towns, ate swift quiet meals at precisely six each evening, asked guests to remove their shoes on the doormat. That Helen, early on, showed signs of an aptitude for languages which drew attention from her teachers, caused them a great deal of unease—to pass without notice, and without asking or requiring attention, was their sole ambition for themselves, and for their daughter. When she was accepted into a grammar school her mother wept, because she could not reconcile maternal pride with her feeling that she was now marked out among the neighbors—had transgressed, somehow, and would in due course be punished for it.

Helen, meanwhile, seethed. Certainly she looked like her mother's daughter—her face was narrow, sallow, pointed at the chin; she was short, and thin, and her hair lay too flat against her scalp—but there, she ardently felt, the similarity ended. It seemed to her impossible that nothing lay in store but a job in local government, with sufficient salary for a mortgage, and adequate maternity leave. Sometimes, when walking home from school with her satchel bumping on her hip, she felt watched. It was not the stern benevolent eye of an all-seeing divinity keeping a general look-out, but something more personal, more attentive; almost, she felt, the eye of a lover, who expects a great deal of their loved one. Sitting in school assemblies, cross-legged on the parquet floor, Helen looked at five hundred other girls and knew that something awaited her that would likely pass them by. In her room at night she papered her walls with cheap prints of the Pre-Raphaelites and dressed, at the weekends, as nearly like Ophelia as the local shops allowed. She listened to unfashionable songs with obsessive attentiveness, and dreamed she dwelt in marble halls with vassals and serfs at her side. She took off her clothes and stood in front of the mirror by lamplight and imagined that after all she wasn't small and thin with spots on her breastbone, but sumptuous and dark. She saved her pocket money and bought a bottle of jasmine perfume, and trailed the scent behind her in the corridors. She read Rilke, Rabelais, Neruda; formed ardent friendships on a whim, and broke them as readily; pitied those ordinary girls for whom life held nothing more than what it had offered their mothers. That she looked so ordinary, and could pass so entirely without notice, only pleased her more. She was, she felt, in disguise.

What you have in your hands, then—in that shoebox with its worn-out lid—is all that remains of the time when Helen

Franklin lived. Everything before it was prologue: everything after, a footnote.

Eight days pass, and Helen often thinks of Josef Hoffman. A certain disquiet now attends the day, though she'd be hard pressed to account for it. It is not that she expects to encounter, in the corridors of the General Library or in the aisles of supermarkets just as trading ends, Melmoth the Witness; it is something less readily cast off. Reading Hoffman's document has been like hearing a confession, and she finds herself unequal to the task of confessor, being herself unabsolved. She is sufficiently unnerved to find herself avoiding the library, unwilling either to encounter desk 209 (would she see the marks where Hoffman's dying hand had gripped the leather?) or, it seems, Karel Pražan, for all that he's her friend. Nine days pass, of small spiteful gestures from Albína Horáková (a fragment of cake ground into the carpet at the threshold of her room; the burning in the small hours of cones of incense that leave an acrid fug in the over-heated flat), of thirty-nine pages of German translated into English, and likewise six pages of Czech. On the tenth day it occurs to her that never has Karel been silent for so long a stretch, and so she sends a message. *I haven't seen you in a while. Are you well, or did you catch the cold I said you would? Say hello to Thea—see you soon.* It is precisely calibrated between care and carelessness, and entirely fitted to their friendship. A day passes, and another message, warmer by a fraction of a degree: *Hope all's well with you both. I ought to give you back this manuscript—perhaps I'll drop by later?* It would not do to confess that she thinks often of Karel not singly, but as part of a larger whole—as part of Karel-and-Thea, and of the meals had at their dining table, which glowed with beeswax and spilled wine, before Thea's blood tried to kill her; of the evenings in which very faintly she had felt herself unbending. That morning she at last attends the library, and is pleased to find that she is able to pay no heed to the plaster babies descending from the ceiling shrieking in distress, or to the precise position of desk 209. She looks for Karel: he is not there. At the close of day she puts her work in her satchel alongside the fragment of the Hoffman document, and resolves to pay a visit to her friends. It is sufficiently out of character for her to wonder at herself, as she passes beneath the stone arch where a man in a ticket booth catches her eye (he knows she cannot be importuned to hear light opera sung in deconsecrated churches): an uninvited visit? She? Well—she tightens her belt, which has a habit of working itself loose—why not. She has something which is not hers, and she will be passing the owner's door: it is merely good manners that compels her. It is a white evening, with snow drifted up against bicycles and litter bins. None presently falls, but all the same the air contains, you might almost think, the dust of opals ground against a stone. Music both sacred and profane meets above the awnings where valiant men sit on sheepskin-covered chairs and shiver delightedly. "This is it!" say the English: "Real winter, like when we were young, and on the doorstep birds pecked right through the foil milk-bottle tops." They pay over the odds for bad beer, and think it cheap.

Karel and Thea live just beyond the Old Town Square, where Helen slips through unseen and largely unseeing. She is more or less immune to the effect of the façades, which have a quality of impermanence, as though they might at any moment be drawn back like a curtain. She reaches her friends' apartment out of breath, discovering that she has walked a little faster than she generally does, as though she heard against the cobblestones the rapping of a follower's feet. Down an alley, beneath an arch—stooping, though the curved stones clear her head by inches—and there is the yard onto which four apartment buildings look out, and there the familiar door, much snow banked against it. She pauses, and puts her thumb beneath the satchel strap, which has begun to press against the bones of her shoulder. She makes a swift calculation. Either they have remained indoors for—let's say, twelve hours? More?—or have left, and not returned. She steps forward, and at that moment the single light set beneath the arch goes out, and the yard and all around it is dark. Each of the thirty identical windows set above their identical sills is merely a pane of black in the blackness, and the effect is of a total emptiness, as though no lamps were ever lit there. The sole light is that which comes weakly in under the arch from the distant Old Town Square—weakly, as if very distant indeed; as if Helen has gone twenty miles from there, and not twenty paces. She stands very still. She listens, and it is her whole body that strains within the silence. What does she listen for—the drag of long skirts against the snow, the tread of boots—or of bare feet, perhaps: feet which have walked over continents and are indifferent to pain? She listens, and of course there is nothing, save for the distant skirl of Bohemian *bock* piping away in the dark. Then the arch light returns, some loose wire finding its fitting perhaps; and Helen blinks against it, and sees now what she did not see before: that the familiar door is open by barely the width of a forefinger. She surveys that long black ribbon between the door and its frame. Manners forbid the crossing of a threshold uninvited, but it seems to her that something is awry. "Karel?" she calls. "Thea? It's me. May I come in?" There is silence. My mother, she thinks, would have said: "*Cooee!* Karel? Thea?" But again, nothing; she puts her hand against the door, and goes in. She stands in the little hall with its umbrella stand, its coat hooks, and listens. The silence is something more than the absence of noise. If it is possible to hear silence, Helen hears it: a thick, soft sensation against the drums of her ears. She reaches for the light switch, and the hall and everything in it is precisely as she remembered, save that the air is altered: it contains nothing, nothing at all—not a speck of dust sifting through the light, not a thread of scent from the lily in the vase. It is as if Karel and Thea had been removed not hours before, but at their conception: as if they are not here, nor were they ever. She moves forward, noting as she does the remnants of the familiar—the stripped pine floor, against which the ramp with its gritty gray surface sits so poorly; the cabinet with its burden of glass; the prints, each mounted in white, taken from volumes addressed to the student of botany—and pauses where the ramp descends to a door. This, too, is not quite closed, and Helen puts out her hand, observing with interest that she is trembling. Then she is arrested by a sound which comes from the room beyond, and which seems only to approximate the human. It wakes Helen from what has been, until then, a kind of detached courage: she feels instead a rising up of fear which has the effect of valor. She shoves at the door and with a sharp hard action turns on the light. The long room is instantly illuminated as brightly as an operating theatre. White light pours down from fittings concealed within the white ceiling, and presents to Helen a familiar picture, of a long table on which spring bulbs have been cajoled into bloom, and of books heaped in an inviting fashion. There is beneath her feet a rug brought north from Turkey, and in front of her a range with the six hobs which Thea had declared essential to any dinner worth the name; there is the evidence of Thea's recent history: the painted box where her barrister's wig is kept, the scarlet-bound copies of *Archbold Criminal Pleading, Evidence and Practice*. But here too the air is empty: there is no scent of food or wine, or of candles burning in blue glass bowls. Even the hyacinth on the table gives off no smell, as if all its white flowers were pieces of plastic; and propped up on the windowsill the convex silvered surface of Karel's telescopic mirror distorts the room. At the head of the table there is a wheelchair. It is not large, or fitted with devices to aid movement: it is merely an aluminium-framed chair on wheels. Seated there is Thea, with both hands curled in her lap, and her feet on the footplates turned in like those of a child sick since birth. Her head is thrown against the black leather back of the chair. Her lipsticked mouth is open, and her chin hangs as if a bolt somewhere has been loosened. Her hair is neglected, long: red-gold hanks of it drape across the rubber-clad handles which extend behind her. Her gaze is fixed upon the ceiling, and it is possible to make out beneath their lids the wet gleam of the whites of her eyes, and the green paint on their lids. On either side of her, drawn back from the table by precisely the distance required to allow the seated to rise, are two wooden chairs. There are three wine glasses on the table and they have all been drunk dry. Then there is again that noise—call it a grunt, for certainly there are no words contained within the sound, no sense worth reaching after. For a moment it is not possible to discern the source, then it comes again: a wet sighing sound which acquires the feeling of something more human than animal. Helen moves closer, and as she does so Thea's jaw is snapped upward, moves swiftly in a circular motion, then falls again to the accompaniment of what is unmistakably a snore. It is loud enough to wake her, this one: her curled hands clench, and her head slowly rises. She opens her eyes—closes them—reaches up to knuckle fiercely at them, so that the sleeve of her dressing gown falls back and reveals a soft wrist-splint fastened with straps.

The relief that comes to Helen is of the kind that sweeps away all past fear and apprehension: it is not merely that her anxious creeping along the halls seems now absurd, it is gone from her memory. "Gosh," says Thea, her voice as it always was: cultured, in a fashion that makes its origin (which in fact is nothing so grand as her self-command, her style suggest) impossible to guess at. "Helen? What are you doing here?"

"Thea!" says Helen. "*Thea!*"—and delivers, to their equal astonishment, a slap across her cheek. The other woman slowly shakes her head, and regards her from beneath heavy, slumberous lids. They gleam green in the lamplight. "Have they gone? That is"—Thea looks from left to right, waking sufficiently now to acquire a puzzled, querying look—"has he gone? I think he's gone, you know. I thought he might. I said: in the end, you'll go." She is silent a moment, then frowning says: "Tell me—is there a woman here?"

"I am here," says Helen. "I am here; but Karel isn't. Thea, have you been ill—ought we to phone for help?" She waits, for Thea dislikes silence, and is generally minded to fill it. But she does not—merely goes on turning her head from side to side, with a vague, dazed expression, as though still in the borderlands of sleep. Helen, Englishwoman that she is, briskly pats the table. "Well, then: let me put the kettle on, and we'll have tea." There is then the performance of the sacred ritual: two pinches of the leaves brought from home; the warmed pot; the teacups reverently set down. All this Thea observes passively. "Thank you," she says, cradling a cup between two hands, which is how she takes her tea, these days. "Thank you." And then, restored within two sips: "Turn off those damn lights, would you? Find a candle, anything, my head hurts." Obediently Helen turns off the lights, and strikes a match for a candle melting in a blue glass dish. Sighing, Thea says, "Better. God, my head. What has happened—I don't remember any of it—"

Helen watches. She listens, and finds no new slurring in her speech, though certainly the scarlet lipstick is inexpertly applied. Not another stroke then: nothing so readily explained. "Then drink up, and wake up, and tell me what you can—but first, let me call Karel. Let me do that." And she does, three times; and is three times unanswered.

"I thought so," says Thea. "Yes: I thought so." What is this calm, thinks Helen? It is eerie. Where is the lover's anxiety, the partner's irritation? There must have been some bitter and final row. The prospect of Karel-and-Thea being snipped at the join is too unpleasant to be countenanced, and she pours more tea.

"Tell me what you remember—look, here: three glasses, and all the wine gone. Was there a guest?"

"A guest?" Thea fumbles at her cup—sets it down—ignores the spill. "Oh, we have had a guest for weeks, let me tell you! It has been three of us since that damn document entered the house: he and I, and this—specter!" With a sudden show of spite she swipes at the cup with a splinted wrist. It breaks against the floor. "Has he told you about it—about her?"

"About Melmoth?" says Helen. The name, said aloud, astonishes her. One might as well say Peter Pan, she thinks, and expect a green boy to come flying in. (But doesn't she look up, all the same—at the closed door, the fastened windows?)

"Melmoth," says Thea. "My God! He comes home with this stinking folder some mad old fool left him—I could smell it, the moment he walked in, an animal smell, like the leather was rotten—and everything changed. Oh, it was changed already, everything between us, you know it—you have seen it: the light went out when I did." Helen does not do what is polite: remonstrate, and soothe, and say that Karel's love, his admiration, did not falter the moment his lover pitched forward into her dinner and became a cripple. For it did, it demonstrably did: it became strained, attentive, very careful—it was performed diligently, and the performance had its limits. Instead, Helen does what her mother taught her—clears up the broken porcelain, the spilled tea, and pours more. "Go on," she says.

"I don't see him. He does what he can't avoid—reaches cupboards I can't, lifts me when my hands won't hold the rails by the bath. Kisses me, even. Sometimes puts his hands here, where he used to." Comically, Thea gestures to where the velvet collar of her dressing gown crosses her breast. "Not even a stroke could diminish me in that respect, you understand. Then he puts me to bed, but I remember I've forgotten this drug or that one, and I call him, to save myself the effort and pain of fetching it myself—oh, Helen, the *humiliation* of it, it will kill me long before my body does; he puts me to bed, and it is as if he can live then, with me out of the way, with the old woman out of sight. Then all night he sits up reading over his manuscripts, making notes, bringing home books and letters. Sometimes he'd say: 'Melmoth the Witness is watching me!'—making a joke of it, for my sake. 'I've been a bad boy!' he'd say, and laugh. But it's hardly unknown, is it, to laugh most when you're most afraid?"

Watch Helen: something alters. Until this moment Melmoth has had less currency than fairy tales, for she is newly acquired. Cinderella, Bluebeard, Peter Pan: these are bred in the bones, and accepted without hesitation. Melmoth has not had this luxury, but must instead announce herself to the imagination; must rap three times upon the door. And it is now—as Thea rests her head against her chair, as somewhere beyond the window a man calls for his dog—that Helen at last hears the rapping on the door, and opens it, and Melmoth walks into the room.

"I saw him at the library," says Helen, reaching for her scarf (she has grown cold). "Photographing books, like he always did. Wasn't it research, for some paper he had in mind?"

"Some paper!" Thea laughs, and attempts to reach for notebooks and sheaves of paper half-concealed beneath a pile of novels (Helen tilts her head, and reads: *The Rider on the White Horse*; and on another book, in rubbed gilt type, *-ERT MATURIN*), but her arm falters midway. There is a small frustrated cry cut off before it could meet sympathy. "Get those, would you? The notebooks, the papers—take a look, go on." She gives her friend a look which is very like the shifty, not quite pleasant smile with which Karel handed her the Hoffman document. Does Helen pause, then? Oh, a little, perhaps—there is a certain slowness, a certain reluctance you might say, in the extended hand. "I will," she says: "But you haven't told me yet what happened tonight: who was here, and where Karel has gone."

Thea frowns. "It's hard for me to say. My tablets make me so drowsy . . . and we had been cross with each other: I wanted to go out—I said I could walk a little, if he'd push me as far as the square. I could hear the *bock* piping and I wanted to say hello to old Master Hus. And Karel wouldn't take me! He'd found something, he said. Something about a watching woman: in Essex, of all places. So then I had wine, which I shouldn't, and I said: 'If I am losing you to some other woman you ought to tell me about her, at least.' And he did."

She stops then, and raises her head, which is for a moment as it always was, in the old days when she stood naked on the banks of Mácha's Lake in winter and jumped in. "I can tell you," she said. "If you like."

"Yes, tell me," said Helen, for what she wants above all else is to restore, even if briefly, the Thea who could command a room for thirty minutes as if she'd never left the courtroom.

"Another cup, then, and light a candle—and you're certain, are you, that nobody else is here—not out in the hallway perhaps?" Another cup, and a candle obediently lit; and Thea's voice grows faintly louder, as though to address jurors sleeping at the back.

"You know the legend by now, I should think: that a group of women went to Christ's tomb to anoint his body—but as any good Sunday School child will tell you, the stone was rolled back, and he was gone. Women being what we are, they ran at once to tell the menfolk, who thought it all idle gossip, as well they might. And among those women was the one they now call Melmoth, or Melmotte, or Melmat, and I suppose any one of a dozen names; and she flatly denied what she'd seen, and said her friends had cooked it all up between them. So she was cursed not with death, but with deathlessness: to wander the earth until Christ returns— one hopes, for her sake, in a forgiving frame of mind—condemned always to appear where all's most cheerless, dark and deadly."

"Cruel, if true," says Helen lightly.

"Well: that's the Almighty all over, isn't it?" Thea contemplates her empty cup; then looks beyond Helen down the lamp-lit hall. Then she says, "Karel told me all this the day that Hoffman died, and he brought that document home. We laughed and said: isn't it strange, that we never heard the story as children? But after that, he left earlier for the library every day, and came home later every night, collecting books and papers that had nothing to do with his usual line of work—look, see for yourself! A letter dated 1637, a novel nobody's read, a journal by some artist neither you nor I ever heard of! Then he stopped going out at all, only sat here poring over his books. Once I caught him stroking the pages, murmuring at them, as if he thought they might answer him back! He wouldn't eat. He smoked until he was sick and he drank in the mornings. Then—would you know what I meant if I said: it was as if he longed for what frightened him most?" Helen thinks of Karel seated with her in the café, shivering in his blue silk shirt— of how he'd flinched at each opening of the door, but had also worn a yearning look. "I would," she said. "Yes, I'd know what you meant."

"He'd sit hunched where you are now, but with a habit of looking up all the time—up at the windows, up at the door. Then today came, and we fought, because I wanted to go out, and he wouldn't take me; and I made him tell me what he'd learned, late at night, whispering at the papers spread out on the table."

Helen says nothing. She is conscious of standing for a moment between realities, and neither appeal: on the one hand, a life which, though dreary, is dreary in the manner of her choosing; on the other, regions of confusion and darkness for which she's been given no map. The candle gutters in its blue glass dish. The tea is cold. She says, "Go on."

"It is all vague—I am a hopeless witness!—but I know he took my hand, saying, 'Hoffman was right, you know, the old fool!' All the while his eyes roamed all around the room with a kind of longing frightened look. There were accounts of her all over Europe and the Middle East, he said, and it's always the same: a woman in dark clothes seen just at the very corner of your eye, slipping from view when you turn your head. It is Melmoth the Witness, wandering the earth until she's weary and her feet are bleeding— in some countries they leave out a chair, just in case she happens to pass by. And she's lonely, and she wants a companion, so she goes to cells and asylums and burned-out houses and gutters—and she whispers, and croons, and always knows your name. Or she'll follow you down paths and alleys in the dark, or come in the night and sit waiting at the end of your bed—can you imagine it, feeling the mattress sink, and the sheets move? When she turns her eyes on you it's as if she's been watching all your life—as if she's seen not only every action, but every thought, every shameful secret, every private cruelty ... there, Helen, you shivered! Don't you worry, we're only children telling tales by the fire—"

But it is quite impossible not to turn, slowly—to look, with a shameful prick of fear, at the window, and see that it is fastened. Helen says, "But if she's been watching all their lives—watching, since they were children—are they damned, then? Is there no hope?"

Thea frowns. "I've surveyed the evidence," she says, gesturing at the papers on the table, "and I do not think it quite the case that *some are born to sweet delight, and some are born to endless night*, as Blake has it. Sometimes she is seen once, and never again—though of course after that you'd look for her in every dark alley, in every shadow, and be minded to keep your nose clean."

"So we have free will, I suppose." (Helen looks again: the window is fastened, and on the sill a jackdaw is pecking at the glass.)

"More's the pity. I always thought it would be rather relaxing to have one's life organized by the Fates. If Karel was always going to leave me—if I was always to get old, and sick—there'd be no sense railing against it, and no use seeking out someone to blame."

"What then?" says Helen. "What then, when she sits on the end of your bed, or waits for you in a stairwell at midnight? What does she do?"

"In every legend, in every account, it's always the same. She holds out her arms, and says: *Take my hand—I've been so lonely!* It would be tempting, wouldn't it, if you felt no other hand would ever be offered, to take hers, and go wherever she took you? Others, like Hoffman I suppose, expire on the spot— would you hand me that bottle? I'll make do without a glass." She cradles the bottle in her lap, because it is too heavy to lift.

Now Helen finds she cannot lift her eyes to the window (though she could not, if you asked her, say what she thinks might regard her from beyond the glass).

"So does she come only for the most wicked of us—for people beyond all hope of redemption?"

"I think not," says Thea. "There is a story, there, in Karel's papers, of Melmoth coming to a prison cell. But the prisoner has done nothing wrong, carries no burden of guilt. She is merely in despair—but all the same, Melmoth was watching."

"Then is nobody safe?"

"Nobody, I think, who might be tempted—even if it's just because they're lonely—to take her hand . . ." Thea, fumbling, puts the bottle on the table. Wine drips down the neck. "So," she says: "Last night Karel told me all this, saying he knew it was all fairy tales—but I wasn't fooled: I could see that he was afraid, in an odd, excited way. And then we drank, and it made me dazed, and someone was here—I'd swear to it in court: someone in black, who came to the door—or had been here all along—look—another glass, you see? Three glasses, three chairs . . ." She is distressed: her leonine head droops over weak, half-clenched fists. Helen stands, and busies herself at the table: cups decently cleared, scarlet rings of wine wiped with a cloth. When she returns Thea is herself again, or as much herself as she can be, these days. "I remember Karel talking softly and cozily, as though to an old friend—I remember feeling sleepy: it was like walking down into a pool of warm water. Then, my dear Helen, I was aware of nothing until you saw fit to give me, a woman of indifferent constitution, a good hard slap."

She laughs, which permits Helen to laugh also, and say: "Yes, I'm sorry about that. Hardly the manners my mother taught me." She sits again at the table, and surveys Thea, lightly clasping her hands. "Maybe she came for Karel," she says, because it is of course a ludicrous notion (Karel Pražan, his hand in that of Melmoth the Witness, tramping the lands of the Bohemian crown in his excellent tan leather shoes!); and because it would be so infinitely preferable to his having merely tired of his lover.

"Oh, certainly, certainly," says Thea. The wine has caused her to flush, and to look well. "That is likely to be it. She would not have had to watch him long to catch him out in a sin." She pauses, grows serious, and says: "Go on. You've got some of the Hoffman document. You may as well take the rest." She fumbles with the nearest paper: photocopied sheets from a paperback book. "Though let me keep this—I've not finished reading it yet. But take the rest—don't you think I want them out of my house?"

Helen stands, and lightly touching her shoulder in passing, begins to gather the notebooks and documents disordered on the table. Karel's handwriting is mercifully neat—indeed, almost troublingly so: it gives the effect of a student working without pleasure and in fear of failure. There are photocopied excerpts from seventeenth-century works in German and in French; there are newspaper clippings from the *Daily Express* dated 1953. There is also a single typed sheet entitled *Melmoth the Witness: Primary Sources*, to which Helen is immediately drawn. "Seen this?" she says, and sets it before Thea, in the light of the burned-down candle, so they can read together:

Melmoth the Witness: Primary Sources

Dr. Karel Pražan, February 2017

1. "The Ballad of Wheal Biding" [collected 1921 by Cecil Sharpe, Cornwall]
   A woman with bloodied feet seen "watching ever waiting" by the sole miner who survived the collapse of the Wheal Biding copper mine in 1823 (NOTE: consult Hansard??)

2. *Der Schimmelreiter* (The Rider on the White Horse) [Theodor Storm (1888)]
   One supposes the Rider to be an iteration of Melmoth (?male, not travelling on foot, &c.)

3. Letter from Sir David Ellerby to his wife Elizabeth [29th September 1637, original in National Trust archives, UK]
   Persuasive account, if second person only (useful comparison w/ Foxe: see Ridley, Hooper et. al.!!!)

4. The Hoffman document [J. A. Hoffman (2017): personal collection of K. Pražan]
   Elaboration unnecessary.

5. *Melmoth the Wanderer* [C. R. Maturin (1820)]
   Melmoth rendered as male (differs in key respects incl. Faustian pact/no qualities relating to bearing witness.
   NOTE: the author's poverty, isolation &c. —telling?? Had

C. R. Maturin himself encountered the Witness?! Likely if
not probable. Consult eg letters, remains &c????)

6. *arod jnice v Zeleném Lese* (The Witch in the Greenwood)
   [Janá ek (1899)]
   Incomplete opera depicting a witch dwelling in the Moravian
   forest and spying on sick children. Never performed
   (NOTE: Consult diaries, &c)

7. "The Testimony of Nameless and Hassan," in *The Cairo
   Journals of Anna Marney*, 1931 (Virago Women's Life
   Writing Series, 1985, ed. C. Callil)
   Elaboration unnecessary.

"Elaboration unnecessary," says Helen, frowning; and it is fondness, not contempt, that makes her laugh and say: "What nonsense is this—primary sources!—a failed opera, a folk song, a novel nobody reads?"

"*Watching, ever waiting*," sings Thea, gruffly, as some Cornish balladeer might do; then she laughs, too. "Maybe she's got him though, Helen, eh? Came in through the window on her bleeding feet and whisked him off to a tin mine." Her laugh falters; she says, "Well. I hope she brings him back. Listen, Helen: I feel sick."

"I should think you do," says Helen, briskly. "You must go to bed."

"I can't go to bed without Karel. I can't get in."

Helen surveys her friend. "Have you tried?"

Thea is petulant. It does not sit well on her. "I don't want to try. Why should I? He shouldn't have left me! I shouldn't be alone!"

Helen, with swift indifferent movements (it would hardly do to let Thea dwell on the humiliation of requiring help, when she has only ever given it), neatly piles the papers and notebooks, clears the wine, blows out the candle.

"Since I'm here," she says, "why don't you see how far you can walk?" There are three jackdaws on the windowsill. There is nothing curious in this—nothing odd in their watchful blue-eyed gaze—but it seems to her, as she stands and crosses the room, that six blue eyes go with her. "Just see what you can do alone," says Helen, "then you know what help you need. Think of it as gathering evidence."

Thea is mollified. "Very well." She stands. The wheelchair rolls back. She is on her feet. She says: "Give me your arm."

"No." Helen will not unbend. "Use the table, the back of that chair."

"Then bring these, at least"—Thea gestures to a pile of papers on which is written: *The Testimony of Nameless and Hassan*—"don't ghost stories make the best bedtime reading?"

Twenty uncertain paces and Thea is on her bed. She shakes with the effort of it, she is breathless, but she cannot quite conceal her pride.

Helen kneels. She removes Thea's slippers. "If you can get in," she says, "you can get out." The air between them is uneasy, but she will not allow her friend to slide into helplessness. The climb out, she thinks, will be impossible. She puts the manuscript on the oak cabinet beside the bed.

"You need to bring my medication." Thea fumbles at the belt of her dressing gown, at the turned-down quilt; gives instruction, briskly, as to which packet, which bottle. Then Helen is alone for a moment in the empty kitchen. It is possible to summon up, if she closes her eyes, the memory of evenings there, in which she ate little, and drank less, but allowed herself nonetheless to take the pleasure she did not deserve. How was it possible that these things could be lost: that Karel could have gone, and taken with him his love, his companionship? When she returns with a glass of water and a dish of tablets, Thea has contrived to slide beneath the quilt. She has wiped off her lipstick, the green glaze on her eyelids; she is flushed and weary; she might be a worn-out child. She is already reading the document (Helen leans forward and reads: *Altan Sakir his father was a tailor . . .*).

"Thank you," says Thea. She is grateful and ashamed.

"I will come back tomorrow evening," says Helen. "But sooner, if you need me." She pauses. Then with a careful diffidence she says, "If it seems you need help, we can find it, I'm sure." Thea's hand is on the cover. She has taken off the splints that strengthen her wrist, and the skin there is very tender. Helen touches it. She says, "Sleep well. I'll close the door. Let's not let Melmoth in," and Thea laughs, and feigns fear.

Before she goes home, Helen puts in her satchel the remainder of Josef Hoffman's document, feeling that she ought at least to follow that dour unlikeable boy to whatever end awaited him. Then, feeling pleasantly as if she transgresses, she takes a notebook in which Karel has transcribed, in that eerily neat hand, a letter from a man named Ellerby to his wife Elizabeth. The jackdaws on the window are gone; the snow still falls. From Thea's room, the long shallow breaths of a sleeper. Helen Franklin turns out the light, and leaves. In the Old Town Square it is quiet: only Master Jan Hus, awaiting the flames of his martyrdom, cannot sleep a wink. But—no, it is perhaps not only Master Hus; for if you are a diligent witness you might see, concealed in the courtyard which Helen is now leaving, a figure dressed in black: patiently waiting, patiently watching, patiently biding its time.

The following morning it is not sound that wakes her, but sensation. Coming out of the half-death of sleep she grows conscious of the rough uncovered mattress against her shoulder, her buttocks—of light shining through the closed lids of her eyes so that she sees in them a fretted network of veins. She rises up through all the accumulations of memory that must be sifted through before the day begins: Thea in her chair; the spill of bright hair across the rubber handle; the one light shining in the dark above her door; the clean snow drifted on the step. She is conscious of a feeling of unease which is not the usual morning anxiety of *I am still alive, it seems*, but of something more immediate. Her skin pricks: she feels all at once alert, awake, as if she has been doused in icy water. She cannot quite open her eyes—they are weighted with worry— it seems to her inescapably the case that she is not alone. *She has come*, she thinks, drowsily: *she has come for me*; then there is the sudden shaking off of sleep, and with it the lessening of unease—it would not do to let nightmares follow her beyond the dawn! She opens her eyes, half-smiling at herself—and finds that, indeed, she is not alone.

Seated in the small chair at her desk is a woman in black. Hard light from the east causes a blurred brightness all around the figure, as if she herself is the source of light: the image is indistinct, but all the same there is quite clearly the long drape of black silk fabric against a thigh, the movement of a white hand. Helen's heart rises and sinks—she feels it move, feels the panicked slamming shut of valves, the hectic coursing of her blood. Then the woman speaks. "No wonder you look so bad, eh?" she says. "Didn't know about Melmotka, is that it? Didn't know and only just found out and now you think she's coming. Ha! Stupid Englishwoman. You think she'd come for you?"

It is not after all the drape of fine silk, but of Albína Horáková's dressing gown—black, certainly, but made of some cheap stuff that (Helen sits up) smells distinctly of cooked meat.

"Look at this," says Albína. She has sheets of paper in her hand—holds them at arm's length—peers scowling at the poorly copied manuscript. "*Sir David Ellerby to his wife*," she reads, with the special contempt she reserves for English, which she considers a language best confined to its miserable little island. "*I make a true relation of what has befallen thy husband*—Ha! Ha! Now there's a liar if ever I heard one!"

"How dare you?" says Helen. She is grateful for the clarity of outrage. Albína, magnificently, shrugs; in doing so the garnet pin on her breast glitters. "Ah, don't mind me. Just a nosy old woman, you know? I wanted to talk to you."

"How dare you open my bag?" says Helen, who will not be disarmed. "Those are not yours to read."

"Nor yours either. Not this man's wife are you, eh? Not any man's wife, thank God! Ha!" The idea evidently amuses her beyond endurance, and she begins to laugh. It is a delighted childish chuckling which might have been contagious had she not all the while dribbled a little from places where teeth were missing.

"What do you know about Melmoth—about Melmotka?" Helen is conscious of feeling envious, as if the legend is something she has personally acquired, and not common currency. How dare this vile old woman—graceless, ugly, smelling of fragments of food and stale smoke—take part in it?

Albína clucks, clasps her hands across her stomach, and surveys Helen with a look of pity. "Never got told stories when you were a girl, then? Could have done with it. Might have made a difference. Too late now, huh! Ha! Not at your age!" She smooths the sheet of paper on her lap. "Maybe you better not have this. Maybe it's not for people like you."

"Put it back," says Helen, very calmly now, and thinking: *really it would be preferable to wake and find the devil incarnate tapping a cloven hoof.* "Put it back, and go away. Let me dress."

"Ah, well." Albína Horáková shrugs again, and Helen envies, for a moment, her majestic rudeness, her ironclad self-worth. She stands, throws the document on the desk with a sound of disdain, and walks slowly, grunting, past Helen to the door. She pauses. She leans against the doorframe, and patting at her hair with a coquettish gesture says, with something astonishingly like shyness,

"Day after tomorrow: my birthday. Ninety-one! Ninety-one years! Twenty more than God promised, eh!" For a moment the shyness vanishes behind spite. "You won't live so long, little weak ugly Helen, but I did, yes! I want dinner."

I certainly hope I do not, thinks Helen. "Dinner?" she says.

"Dinner, idiot! Wine. Napkins. Don't you think I should celebrate?"

"Where?" Helen feels herself tugged in a current she had not foreseen.

Again, that quick patting of her hair, which is dyed black, and through which the pink dome of her scalp gleams. Shyly, she names a café on the river, overlooking the National Theatre. "I booked seats! I phoned up! You think I don't know how to use a phone?"

"You want me to come?" Helen is astonished.

"You, the cripple, the other one. Come! Why not?"Albína Horáková is astonished. "I never hated anyone! Not anyone, not even when I might have done! Hate! Haha! I bake you cakes! Don't I? Stupid girl!" It is not entirely convincing—indeed there is a glint in her eye which arouses in Helen a corresponding light: it would be useless, she thinks, to protest. Worse, it would be bad manners.

"All right," she says. "No Karel, though. He's gone away for a while."

"Gone, you say. Melmotka got him, I bet. Walking him till his feet bleed, till there's nothing left of him, showing him the hell we've made." She stands a little straighter, with a motion which is somehow courageous: for the first time it occurs to Helen that every movement of her splayed hips, her swollen feet, must cause her pain. "That's the trick," she says. "That's what she does. Looks at the hell we've made and goes on walking through it." She waves, and shuffles down the corridor, to her own little dark domain of doilies and dolls and candles left to burn down to greasy stumps. There is silence, then the sound of the television and radio played both together.

The whole encounter strikes Helen as so funny and so bizarre that she falls back against the mattress and laughs up at the bare bulb hanging from the ceiling. "All right then," she says. "You win, Albína Horáková. Dinner."

It being Michaelmas, and all the churches of the Parish made ready for the feast of St. Michael and All Angels, I have made an end to my Business, and having obtained an afternoon's repose, I here make a true relation of what has befallen thy Husband, in whose honesty and good faith I hope thou mayst still rely, having made an end of my Report.

It so happened that upon passing within the bounds of Lavenham I made fast my horse that it might drink at the trough, and there spied a poor woman lying amid the hay. It seemed some passing person had taken pity on the creature, for she had beneath her head a fragment of a woolpack, with which to keep her from the ground, which was much wet with rain. I was at that time alone, having disposed of the greater portion of my Goods to the satisfaction, I trust, of our creditors, and having disposed also of our servant Ezra, who was desirous of staying for a time in Essex, that he might there attend his family. Upon seeing the woman, therefore, I was at liberty to indulge alike my curiosity and my Christian Duty, to vouchsafe to all God's children the pity to which we are exhorted in the parable of the Good Samaritan.

Seeing no other fellow close at hand with whom I might converse, I bent to attend her, seeing that she was much advanced in years. Her garments were rough, and much mended, and she wore no shoes, her feet being greatly cal-loused, and somewhat filthy, bearing testament, as I supposed, to many months wandering about the country, at the mercy

of the seasons. Her eyes were closed, and I might have supposed her to have already passed into the presence of He to
whom we must all give our Final Account, had it not been
possible to see the passage of blood in the arteries, which were
made the more visible by the frailty of her complexion. I confess it, that I wished thou hadst been present, that thou mayst
have guided my tongue, for I fear that in seeking to discover
whether I might offer succour, I spoke too plain, for at my
voice her eyes were opened. They were very bright and wide,
so that within the lined countenance, they had the appearance
of a full moon spied through branches. She spoke to me, yet
in scarce above a whisper, so that I must needs bend close. She
had about her, not the stink of disease, but rather of hyacinth,
or of the jasmine flower. I beseeched her to speak again. She
said, DID YOU SEE HER? and put her hand upon my own,
and grasped it, and said again, DID YOU SEE HER? and it
seemed to me, though I have little understanding of the minds
of women, that she spoke both in terror, and in love, though I
heretofore had not thought these two sensations of one piece.
I looked about me, and saw the square deserted, save for my
own horse, and for two men making war with words over a
woolsack, which one sought to obtain from the other, at one
shilling the yard less than market value. I said, No woman is
here, whereon the creature closed her eyes, and began to weep,
indeed, it seemed to me that within the minute her whole body
was wet with tears, which flowed without ceasing from her.
I saw then that her right hand, which rested upon my glove,
was marked with a scar, in the shape of a cross, the flesh there
much raised, and somewhat corded. She said, I am alone then,
I am all alone, and I said, Indeed you are not. I asked her if
she were hungry or thirsty, mindful that forasmuch as we give

comfort to the least of God's children, we give it also, to his
only begotten Son. She made no reply, and I perceived upon
her lips that unnatural hue, which signals the approach of
death. It is the greatest offence to God and man, that any of his
creatures, sinners though they must surely be, should die with
naught for comfort but a bale of straw, and naught to drink
save rain, and thus I looked about me, and perceived a lamp
in the window of an Inn, which selfsame Inn is now my place
of residence. Having made no small Sum from the sale of our
goods, it seemed fitting to me, that I should share the good
fortune with which we have ourselves been lately blessed, and
I bethought myself to take this poor creature, and convey her
to the Inn, where I might implore the innkeeper, in exchange
for due reward, to give her the care which we may all hope to
receive in our extremities. I carried her thence, which was no
great effort, since she weighed less than does our little Jessamy,
and indeed it seemed to me, that there was no greater substance
to her, than had she been the bones of a chicken which I had
eaten, and wrapped in a napkin. The innkeeper was one of that
sort whose good offices may be obtained more with coin than
conscience, and, having first exclaimed that he had no room for
so miserable a being, was soon entreated, by means of a small
Sum, to procure for the woman a Room, being somewhat spare
but clean, so that I was able to leave her on a pallet, in the care
of a serving girl, whose good nature was evident, since I saw
how she tended the poor creature, chafing her feet before the
fire, and raising her head, so that she drank a little milk. Being
myself wearied, I gave my leave, first advising that a priest be
sought, that she might enter into the presence of His glory confident of her Salvation. I slept a while, though I found my rest
not easy, for I bethought myself often of the words of the old

woman, DID YOU SEE HER?, and in my sleep it seemed to me, that indeed I did see HER, though what SHE might be, I could not guess at, nor why I should tremble, to think that SHE might indeed be present.

Shortly thereafter, the night far spent, though the day not yet at hand, I was roused by rapping on my door, which I opened, and there found the innkeeper, and the serving girl, his daughter, bearing a candle. They begged that I attend the woman, who had refused the attendance of a priest, but nonetheless beseeched that I come to her. I confess it, that I was displeased to be thus disrupted in my rest, but as thou knowest well, I am beset by curiosity, and thought that peradventure I might learn the history of this woman, and all that had befallen her. To that end I dressed, and made haste to her room, whereon I discovered the old woman in clean apparel, resting upon the bolster, her eyes illumined yet more brightly, by means of the candles which the innkeeper had caused to be set about. She greeted me right warmly, and besought my name, which she did bless. Her own name, as she did tell me, was Alice Benet, and one hundred years had passed since the day of her birth, 50 miles hence in an Essex village, named Brentwood. She told me, that there was vouchsafed to her but one day yet remaining on this earth, and that she would not depart it, until she had confessed to me her great sin. I asked, what sin is it? and she said, It is that I gave not my body to be consumed, then began to weep, and begged that the innkeeper's daughter make up the fire, for she was cold, and then depart, so that I might hear her Testament, and she give it, to no ear save mine.

It is this Testament, which I now set down, and which I cannot feel but will be met with thy censure, Elizabeth, or indeed with thine horror. Yet I must set it down, for it is as though I had been condemned, and put in the press, so that the bones break beneath the weight, and I must cause them to be lifted off, lest I perish with her.

Her name, as she told me, was Alice Benet, and she was born in Brentwood, in 1537, the daughter of a butcher, and yet no ordinary butcher, for this man was much educated beyond his stature, and in his religion a Dissenter, who kept John's Gospel in the common tongue, and moreover taught his sons and daughters alike their letters, that they might read this same Gospel, and such tracts and pamphlets as attended their devotions. Alice herself, shewing that wit and understanding which is not (saving always thee, Elizabeth) the preserve of her sex, was able, as she told me, from her earliest years, to match any priest point for point, with scripture appended thereto. In her 18th year, being commended in the parish for her beauty, humility and virtue, a shadow was cast across the land, that shadow of which you and I have so often read, in the works of Mr Foxe, and casting it most darkly upon the Benet family, and upon all of the Protestant religion, in any degree beyond the cursory, for Mary Tudor attained the throne. Now this man her father lacked prudence to conceal his Lollardish tendencies, and continued preaching in the highways and byways, negligent of the safety of his wife, or of his children, and escaped arrest, on more than one occasion, only by reason of his being swift of foot, and conversant with hiding places of the village, which the Queen's men were not.

But it so chanced that Alice Benet was tending to her mother, this woman being taken sick, when the Queen's men, being alerted to their presence by such in the village as were of the Popish religion, came to the door, and demanded, with violence and much contumely, that they be let in. Alice, in all things meek and obedient, greeted the men, and said to me, that she held in her hand an earthen jug of water, with which to give her mother to drink, and might have brought it down hard on the head of such men as laid hands on her, but forbore to do so, that she might bear more richly the fruits of the Spirit. Being yet stood within the hallway, in sight of her mother's chambers, one of the Queen's men questioned her, as to her father's whereabouts, and as to their religion, not least, as to whether she submitted to the faith, which Her Majesty demanded of her subjects. Alice said that she did not, moreover answered the man's interrogation, and making plain, in the words of Martin Luther, that she sought salvation by faith alone, and not by the ringing of the coin, in the coffers of the church of Rome. Being much perturbed by her response, the Queen's man snatched up a candle, and passed it back and forth across her hand, in the shape of the cross, until the skin blistered, and the very tendons cracked, yet she did not cry out, nor submit to their demand that she play the coward, and give up alike her conscience and her soul. Her father being yet from home, and her mother insensible, she was conveyed to the Guildhall, and there kept, in a condition in which I should shudder to keep a pig, there being much dampness, such that her joints ached, as though she were old, and no place to rest her head, and little to eat, and no means by which she might determine the passage of the sun, and mark the day from night. A Priest, tasked with restoring the whole lands of England to that apostate faith from which we had been so lately delivered, catechised her with much threatening. It was demanded of her, that she take the Latin Mass, and that she consent to repent her Protestant faith, and moreover give word of such other companions in the faith as she might name, that they too might be brought under arrest, and under condemnation. It was of all things the most repellent to her, that she should give up the Bible in the common tongue, for it seemed to her the sign and symbol of her own mind, that is, that she might obtain for herself its meaning, without the intervention of a mere man, to whom, she said, she owed neither fealty nor overmuch respect. WAS NOT HER MIND HER OWN? WAS NOT HER SOUL? These things the old woman spake to me, with much tears and pleading. At last, having secured from her no recantation, it was determined that she be put to death, by means of burning in the town, publicly, and in company of four others, who had shewn like courage. The Priest, in making his last visit, did point to her hand, and to the cross burned thereon, and did urge her to consider such pain as she had already endured, and indeed the very smell of the wound, and to consider how much greater pain was to come, with flames consuming her, from bare foot upward, until her whole body was naught but a bundle of sticks, with her head not yet consumed, so that she remained sensible of it, and indeed might look, and witness for herself, how fire doth wreck the flesh. Yet she did neither bend nor break, and said that it was better to endure the flames for hours only, than for a lost eternity.

So much though mayst believe, Elizabeth, for so much thou hast read, in the works of Mr Foxe, but I have more with which to test thy patience, and thy belief in my own integrity. For on the night which was to be her last upon this earth, Alice Benet, confined within her miserable cell, which, as she recalled it, was so small, that she were not able to lie upon the floor, and stretch, and which had within its walls no slit or window, through which light might enter, woke. She perceived within the cell a plume or drift of smoke, which caused her much terror, for it seemed to her, that some spark had entered beneath the door, and set the fire with which she was to be burned, though the appointed hour had not yet come. Yet there was no flame, nor warmth, nor any thing visible, save this plume of smoke, which seemed as it were far distant, as it were on some horizon, and yet could not be, for the cell was small. Believing that the terrors and shocks of those days past had caused her to run mad, she closed her eyes, and commended herself into the care of He to whom all things are possible. As she prayed, the cell filled with a divine smell, as of lilies-of-the-valley, or of the dog roses which grow in the Essex hedges, so that, confident of the Grace of God visited upon her, she opened her eyes. And there beheld, to her great astonishment, that she was not alone, for that which she had supposed to be naught but smoke, was revealed to be a woman, clad in some thin black Stuff, the like of which she had never seen before, since it seemed that the cell was full of wind, which moved the woman's apparel. Now this same woman was tall, so that perforce she must stoop beneath the cell roof, and she wore no cap or hood, so that her hair was loose, and seemed also as it were to move, as did her apparel. There was that about her, which shifted, and moved, as does a candle flame, her skin withal both light and dark, and her eyes, which were very large, having about them the manner of ink, which has been dropped into water. Her feet were bare, and it seemed that she must needs have waded through a charnel house, for they were bloodied, to the very ankle, and there was upon the stone the

prints of them, scarlet, marking where she had stood. Greatly
afraid, and bewildered, Alice cried out, and cried out three
times, and yet none came, nor did the woman move, nor raise
her hand, nor speak, until she had ceased her crying out, and
fallen senseless upon the floor. When she woke, it was her
ardent hope that it had been naught but a dream, but there was
beneath her head something soft, and something soft also upon
her arm, moving, as it were a hand stroking her. She heard also
the sound, which as she said to me, was as a woman speaking
without words, which is to say the crooning of a mother to a
child, and this crooning, though much soft, pierced her
through with a hot terror, so that she lay unmoving, and
insensible. Then spake the woman thus: My child, my Alice,
my beloved, whom I have longed for, from whom my eyes have
never wandered, at last I am come, as you had known I must!
The Almighty vouchsafing to Alice such courage as was
desirous, she stood, having been cradled in the woman's lap,
and said, I do not know you. Madam, give me your name. The
woman said, Surely it is I, Melmoth, who has watched, yea,
even from the hour of your birth, who knows you, as none has
ever known you, and is come now, that you may be delivered
from such torment as has been made your sentence! Alice said,
Nay, I do not know you, nor have I ever heard your name, nor
do I seek deliverance, for God has promised it, that she who
honors Him, will He honor! Then said the woman, Ah, but you
do know me, and have always known me, for it was I who
watched, when you did what you ought not to do, and I who
knew, when you thought what you ought not to have thought,
and it is I alone who loves you, in all that is most secret and
most sinful in your soul! Alice said, Nay, again, for does not our
Father in Heaven, in whose image we are made, know us, and

yet love us? Then the woman, whom we must, as I suppose, call Melmoth, laughed, with a terrible laughter, such as is the laugh of those who have run mad, and are cast out into streets, where they might indulge their madness, as the dogs indulge their lusts. Then Melmoth stood also, so it did seem she filled the cell, and that indeed her hair, and her clothes, and the very smell of her (being, as Alice told me, like lilies set all about a dying man) reached into the furthest corners, as does a shadow. Then said Melmoth, I have seen with my eyes what is the cost of the love of God, and it is a dear price, such as will leave you a debtor, and your debt paid, not in coin, but in the mud and bones from which you are made! Then this same Melmoth reached for Alice, and embraced her, with the embrace of a lover, and with such a smell of lilies, that it seemed to her a stink, as of a pestilence, so that she fell into a swoon, and could not resist, nor keep her head from resting against that breast, upon which the black stuff of her apparel moved. And in her swoon there passed before her eyes as it were a parade, of the most grotesque torments, such as in her innocence and grace, she had never seen or imagined, and indeed, she marked that moment, as the very end of her youth, as if that veil with which we are all born, which keeps us from gazing upon all that man has wrought against man, was rent asunder. She saw two men, bound at the waist with chains, and supported thereby against a wooden pillar, and at their feet faggots of greenwood. And the one consoled the other, as the torch was applied to the flames, and bade him have courage, for if their breakfast was sour, their supper that night would be sweet, and soon he died. But the other, in great terror, did not burn, nor was he consumed, for the wood was green, and scorched him, so that in his great and lengthy pain, he did beg those standing by, to heap the fire upon him, that he might burn more fiercely, and thus meet his end. Again he entreated, and called upon God for His pity, and cried out, More wood! Of your mercy, sirs, more wood! And fully one half-hour passed, and yet he endured, until at length a man, not fearing for his safety, took a billhook, and banked up the wood about him, so that the flames burned more hotly, and the man died. And again, she saw another man, much advanced in years, bound to a stake, it being dawn, and skylarks all about, and a great crowd gathered, as it were at a country fair, in much excitement, for there are those among us, who have an appetite for cruelty, as does a thirsty man for water. And this man burned fiercely, with his eyes fixed heavenward, and silently, and the while beat against his breast with his right hand, indeed until the hand was consumed, and he beat on with his arm only, such as remained of it, until the fat dropped out the end. And again, she saw a woman, in years scarce older than herself, and this woman wore about her neck a bundle, and wept and pleaded that her mother be told none of what was to pass. And again the wood was green, that the flames would be scant, and her torment all the greater, and indeed she burned slow, so that she seemed to dance about upon the faggots, and to writhe indecently against the chains, which sight caused much entertainment amongst those who watched, and in the men who spake against her in their lusts. At last, calling upon her Saviour, she bent herself to the flames, so that the bundle about her neck was lit. And this bundle, having been fastened about her by a kinswoman, was filled with gunpowder, which caught, and thus ended that portion of her life which is not eternal. These things Alice Benet saw and heard, as though indeed she had stood at the pyre, and born witness to the flames, so that it caused as she said a rupture within her, within which were all the terror of the world, brought close at hand. Then said Melmoth, You see what lies in store? Is it not fit recompense for your pride and folly? Yet I will not have you suffer thus! I would give you my companionship, and deliver you from thence, that you may walk with me all your days, and that you may see what I have seen, and hear what I have heard, and yet be not dismayed! Then said Melmoth, seeing that Alice in her horror understood not what was at hand: Do not think me an agent of the devil, for I am not such. I am naught but a poor woman—lonely, as you are lonely! Condemned, as you are condemned! Then might we not together share our condemnation? Behold the door, whose iron bolts could not keep me from you: will you not depart thence with me, that we might wander together all the days of your life, and seek solace in each other?

Then Alice said, I know not what you are, save that you tempt me, for indeed my heart fails me! And yet my Saviour did not falter at the last, when he sweat as it were great drops of blood, and sought that the bitter cup would pass from him, yet drank deeply, for love of all whom he had chosen!

Ah! said Melmoth, and spake yet more softly, Then you are elect?

Indeed I am! said Alice.

And once elect, may you be lost?

That I may not be, for before the foundations of the world, my name was writ in the Book of Life!

And was your name writ there, because tomorrow you pass through the flames?

My name was writ there by grace alone, and none of my doing.

Then surely, child, is it not mere pride that guides you to the pyre?

It is not pride! It is faithfulness, for to recant would be a sin!

What were the punishment, were you to escape the fire?

I should fall upon the mercy of God, for my cowardice and sin.

Then was it your hand, that built the Mercy Seat?

It was not my hand!

Was it you, that lit the Shekinah Glory?

I have done nothing—I can do nothing—I claim only the promise of God's grace.

And who most knows God's grace?

Why, the sinner.

And whom is forgiven most?

She who sinneth most!

Then Alice—my dear heart, my friend!—would you not sound the deepest depths of God's love? Would you not sin much, that you may be forgiven much? That being forgiven much, you may love yet more? Then Alice fell, for the weariness in her bones, and indeed in her soul, and in her mind, for she was much taxed, by the horror which had passed before her, and which awaited her. And this same Melmoth pressed her mouth against her mouth, and her breast against her breast, in an embrace most unholy, and yet most chaste, and said, Alice, my dear one, my longed for, whom I have watched, who hath never left my sight! Alice, do not consign your flesh to the fire, but rather your soul to the grace of God. Sound the depths of that grace—would you not be forgiven much, for sinning much? Alice! Come with me! Take my hand, for I have been lonely!

• • •

All this Alice Benet told me, with much weeping, such as I had never before seen even a child weep, and would say no more. Oft-times she raised herself against the bolster, being yet weak, and would be watchful at the window, with a fixed watchfulness, as of a man seeking out his lover, nay, of a man whose debt is great, fearing the bailiff at the door. I gave her to drink from a cup, and she placed her hand upon mine, that hand which had been branded with the cross. Then at last she ceased her weeping, and asked that I commend her to God's mercy. At dawn, as the cocks crowed, she spake her last, which was this: Sir, have a care, lest her eye be on you, for her loneliness is terrible, and she will not withstand it. Thus she passed into Judgement, and all was silent.

My dear Elizabeth, I am desirous that I should return to thee, more swiftly than thou hast anticipated, being much disturbed in my rest, and on occasion certain, that a pair of Eyes are upon me, and that these Eyes, are not as thine and mine, for they perceive not my actions alone, but my thoughts, indeed my very soul, down to its blackest depths! Five days yet remain, until that day, when I am safe with thee—pray God that I keep safe—for I am certain—that when I lay down my pen— and turn for my bed—that I shall see—as it were a plume of smoke—burning far distant—though in truth my chamber is but small—and there is about me—very sweet—the scent of the lily-flower --------------

Look! It is evening now, and no snow falling: the cobbles on Charles Bridge and in the Old Town Square are glittering and treacherous and every minute someone somewhere stumbles. Master Jan Hus in his winter cloak looks silently over the crowd: you might think, were you so inclined, that he is recalling how once he wore a paper hat on which painted devils danced, and walked to where the fires were banked to burn him; but perhaps after all he is merely watching the mice dining well from the bins at his feet. Stalls strung with lights sell ham on the bone, and disks of potato cut thin as paper and fried in oil; the astronomical clock strikes seven times. In the National Library of the Czech Republic (you recall its pale bell tower, and the ghosts of the Jesuits praying in the aisles) Helen Franklin finds she is unable to complete her work. It is not merely that she sees on the page not a leaflet in German cautioning against the onset of cataracts and blindness, but the final words of Sir David Ellerby; it is not merely that within arm's reach there is desk 209, where Josef Adelmar Hoffman wrote his life and met his death. It is not even (though you're certainly right to think of it) the notion that somewhere among all the backs turned to her—the many bent backs of students at their books—there might be, silently waiting, Melmoth the Witness, making notes in the margin of a document entitled *The Sin of Helen Franklin*. It is not quite these things that cause Helen's pallor, her look of unease. It is this: she is being followed. On her walk that morning—brisk, purposeful, all documents relating to legend and myth decently stored at home—she saw, at every pause by traffic lights and on street corners, a figure at her heels. The figure is dark, slight, swift—moves as quickly as she sees it; slips behind passersby, behind cars, behind kiosks selling tickets for the tram. Sometimes it seems to her that it is singing, so quietly that it is impossible to make out the words, or whether it is a man or woman so diligently at her heels; sometimes it has a way of walking that she half-remembers. It arouses in her a kind of dread which Melmoth has not yet—not quite—been able to evoke: a feeling that she ought to drop her satchel, her papers, and bolt. But where would she go? It seems pinned to her coat like her shadow.

It is no use. She cannot work. Overhead the plaster babies yawn and gape. A librarian stands and with authoritative tread crosses the library floor, scowling at a boy who is drinking a bottle of water, and flings open a window. Cool sharp air comes in and with it the sound of someone singing. Helen flinches as she always does when she hears music and is not guarded against it. Night is coming. She imagines her follower sitting cross-legged beneath the window, singing perhaps, waiting patiently. She is saved from further reflection—from the rising tide of memory which laps about her feet—by three messages in quick succession. It is Thea, fumbling at her phone: *Come n. Come now. Helen come now please.*

"Karel!" says Helen, aloud, and receives from all sides looks not of censure but amusement. *It is Karel*, she thinks: *either he has come home, or Melmoth has taken him!* This last thought is cheering, because it is so absurd. She gathers her papers; the singing beyond the window has stopped. *He's come home,* she thinks. *Thank God!*

Reader, witness, here is what you see: a woman so nondescript as to almost vanish. All Bohemia around is vivid and bright—a gold serpent painted on a crimson wall, a woman looking in wonder at an owl on her arm, a man in green silk robes imploring passersby to stop and drink beer in a lamp-lit den. There are jackdaws on high ledges and doorsteps: courtly jackdaws, nodding their gray-cowled heads; above the river a flock of swans flies north. Among all this Helen Franklin passes without notice, but it is best to look, and go on looking. For there behind her (she has stopped to adjust her satchel strap) is a watchful figure in a dark hood. You cannot see, from where you stand, what face is concealed within the shadow—cannot make out the shape of the body in the coat. But certainly there is something there which is very attentive, very fixed; whether benign or malignant you cannot guess, but all the same: don't you think it might be kind to take Helen Franklin by the arm, and guide her back within the library walls?

Thea and Karel's home is hardly ten minutes distant—down the lanes, across the Old Town Square—but all the same Helen hurries. It is noisy in the evening in the tourists' thoroughfares: everyone is hectic, happy; there is the sound of pop music from an ice-cream parlor and a child crying merely because he is excited beyond endurance. All the same she is certain that there is a kind of echo to her footfall—that with each step her follower takes another, that with each pause her follower pauses. Schoolboys in yellow vests come winding down the lanes hand in hand, herded by watchful teachers: they block her path and make it necessary to stop at the foot of curved stone steps leading up to the door of a church. It is not quite deconsecrated, but God isn't there so much these days. On the children come, rather solemn, carrying small meals in plastic boxes; across the road a woman in furs is staring with the ardor of a jilted lover at a case of garnets. It begins—again, as always—to snow. The waiting crowd presses up behind Helen, impatient, waiting for the children to pass. In among the bustle of German, French, Korean, Dutch, she picks out very clearly and with a cool hard piercing in her heart the sound of someone singing. It is low and soft and might be either a man or a woman, and the melody is one she hears at night while sleeping—which she sometimes wakes half-singing and must instantly suppress: *I dreamed I dwelt in marble halls, with vassals and serfs at my side . . .* It is foolish, sweet, wistful, and its effect on Helen is like that of a blow to her back. She stumbles, as if jostled—grasps at the coat sleeve of a man who rebuffs her with a curse, thinking himself at the mercy of pickpockets; she rights herself, and finds she cannot look behind her. *And of all who assembled within those walls*, she hears, and her eyes grow very wide, very startled. On the schoolboys come, and they seem to her malevolent now, summoned up from who-knows-where to pin her back against the church steps, in earshot of the singer behind her (. . . *that I was the hope and the pride* . . .). The children stop, clutch hands, look at her one by one: there is in each plump face a look of censure and distaste, as if they've seen through the belted coat, the colorless hair, to what is kept inside. A boy with dark hair brushed back from his dark placid eyes surveys her for a long while and begins to acquire a knowing lascivious look— he winks, very slowly, and without smiling. Then the teacher gives a signal—slowly, reluctantly, they look away; slowly they walk on. *I dreamed that one of that noble host*, hears Helen, and it is closer now—very close—seeming at her ear; the dark-haired boy turns and winks again—then looks behind her, to where she supposes the singer must be, and he grins, showing all his sharp young teeth; he nods as if in recognition, then moves on. The steps behind Helen are littered with flyers for a concert, with receipts, with sticky paper napkins that once held cakes—she stumbles blindly up towards the door and blunders in. It is a heavy door, studded with iron, and beyond it velvet curtains are hung against the chill. They have the smell of incense in them, or of funeral flowers, as if the church was still put to the use for which it was intended. They enclose her deliberately and with malicious intent; the heavy fabric wraps around her shoulders, her legs; causes her to stumble again, and fall prostrate as a supplicant on the cold stone floor. Then the cloth releases her, and she finds she has come into a concert. Seated on red velvet chairs men and women in winter coats have all turned at the sound of her heels on the hard floor and seen her pitch forward out of the curtains and onto her hands and knees. Then they look away, out of decency, and because in front of the altar a woman has begun to sing. She is wearing a pink dress in stiff nylon that rustles as she moves: there are hard pink rosettes on the hem and shoulder, and the hem is frayed, and under it there are layers of cheap petticoats gone gray with washing. Helen, kneeling, sees the woman nod with practiced hauteur at the waiting pianist, then she begins to sing, and it is the kind of music that most disgusts her: a sort of melodious form of hysterics. The singer gapes and trembles. It is unseemly. Coming slowly to her feet, rubbing herself where she aches, Helen makes for the nearest chair. The song is a punishment. She has so long avoided music of any kind—taken this alley, and not that, to dodge a busker; learned which cafés will not torment her with their radio—that to be compelled to submit to it now is intolerable. Pressing a palm to each ear for respite she looks about her, and sees the mottled surface of silvered mirrors on the ceiling and on the walls, the gilded organ pipes with their look of a ribcage cracked open to reveal the heart. A pair of angels above the singer exchange dubious looks, and each holds an empty scroll. The music grows still louder, still more hysterical—then abruptly, mercifully, stops. The singer extends a hand to the pianist, smiling very sweetly indeed; the pianist returns the tribute; both bow. There is desultory applause. Helen's knee is bleeding. She looks at it, and as she looks a gloved hand appears, and somebody says, "*Geht es Ihnen gut?*" and then, shyly: "Are you all right?" Her accent is neither German nor English, nor is it Czech.

"I am fine," says Helen. She presses her hand to her knee and looks without surprise at the blood in her palm: she is bleeding through her clothes. "I'm fine," she says.

"I have something, here." The gloved hand moves, is gone for a moment, and returns with a packet of tissues. "Press hard for a minute. It will be all right." Helen looks up, and sees a young woman with soft hair growing thickly to her collar. She wears a white shirt, well starched and pressed, and a small gold cross on a silver chain. She smiles, and it is, I think, a very appealing smile—somewhat hesitant, very warm. "Sometimes you don't want anybody to see when you fall over, I know."

"It was the curtains," says Helen. Her fear of her follower is taken over for a moment by her indignation that she should have made a disgrace of herself. "I caught my ankle, and fell." She takes a tissue and presses it to her knee. Concertgoers stand and gaze at the ceiling, the floor: there is much discussion regarding the organ, which Mozart is said to have played. A pretty girl adjusts her fur collar in front of a gilded mirror and accepts a kiss from a friend.

"Did you enjoy the music?" The woman in the white shirt places both gloved hands in her lap and looks placidly at Helen. She seems unmoved by the organ, the many mirrors, the angels with hard gold feathers weighing down their wings: she has the air of someone to whom all this is too familiar to be noticed.

"No," says Helen.

"I always think," says the young woman, "that it's a little—undignified, somehow." She removes her gloves. She wears no wedding ring. "You are still bleeding. You may need a stitch or two." Her voice, which is soft and quiet, grows a little brisker here, with a kind of professional disinterest.

"I don't think so," says Helen; but the tissue is wet. Silently the woman hands her another.

"Have you far to go?"

"Not at all. Just by Jakubská." Then, keen to demonstrate to this young woman, who is really hardly more than a child, that she is not so helpless as she seems: "I am visiting my friend."

"I am walking that way too." The woman stands, and draws on her gloves. They are of a fine gray wool, and could do with a wash. She is large-boned, a little ungainly, rather tall; she wears a pleated skirt over tights and stolid shoes. The extreme plainness of her clothes suggests suddenly to Helen that she may be a nun. "Perhaps we could walk together?" She flushes. "Only it's easy to fall when the snow freezes, you see."

It occurs to Helen to reject, as has always been her habit, this offer of company. But in everything the woman says—in her shy uncertain smile, her way of offering help—there is an appeal which is very hard to resist. Somebody turns out the light, and the gleam of gold on her small plain cross is gone. "That's very kind," says Helen. "I'm Helen, by the way."

"Adaya," says the woman. She removes her glasses—wipes them—returns them to their place. Behind them her eyes are unremarkable, save for a very steady gaze. "Are you able to stand, do you think?" Under her gaze Helen feels young, and rather foolish: she would like to say, *You must understand that I am generally the one who remains on her feet when others take a tumble.* "I think so. There's not much blood."

"Well then"—the woman offers her arm. She is no longer shy-seeming, but has instead a kind of practiced kindliness. It occurs to Helen that she is not, of course, a nun, but a nurse, if perhaps one called to the vocation by the Almighty. "Well then—take my arm: I'd be glad of your company. Only you must tell me if your knee is sore. The patella is a tricky bone."

Certainly a nurse, then! Helen thinks of Thea—of her weak uncertain gait, her saucers of tablets, her clumsy hands. She briefly takes the woman's arm, stands (she is, after all, a little dizzy), and releases it. "I'll be all right, I think; but if you are going that way anyway—" At the door, the woman holds back the heavy curtain, with a small gleaming smile, as if to say: I will keep you from peril. Helen believes it. What danger can come to a woman in such very sensible shoes? She looks back at the dark church—at the silvered mirrors, and the angels with their empty scrolls—and sees a jackdaw on the windowsill outside. It inclines its head in the gentlemanly fashion of its kind; Helen inclines hers in return.

The snowfall has been thick and swift. Prague seems sleepy now beneath its freshly laundered eiderdown. The bustle of tourists is thinned to clusters of bright coats on the thresholds of cafés, and all the beggars have packed up the tools of their trade. Adaya—in a long coat of navy blue which conveys more than ever the effect of a nurse on duty—says, hesitantly, as if unwilling to trespass: "You live here?"

"I have lived here almost twenty years."

"Do you like it?"

"It seemed the most suitable place at the time." Helen pats her knee, but the bleeding has stopped as if her blood has frosted over.

"Are you happy?"

"Is anybody happy?"

"Ah, well. It is not a happy city." This startles Helen, who is accustomed to feeling that she alone is not swept up in Prague's merriment, its beauty. "Look over there," says Adaya. Her gloved hand gestures down towards the river. "Did anyone ever tell you about the priest who took the queen's confession, and would not tell the king her secrets, and was tortured for it over many days? They drowned him, in the end."

"Still," says Helen. "It got him a sainthood, at any rate."

"Yes: and a crown of gold stars, as they say. And then over by Wenceslaus Square, you know, Jan Palach burned himself alive in political protest. Do you think he meant to die?"

This melancholy company is curiously consoling. It is restful to be exempted from the obligation to find, in every spire and pinnacle of the mother of cities, reason to wonder and delight. "Oh—look—" Adaya pauses for a moment. She gestures with the toe of a well-worn shoe to a place on the pavement which has been cleared of snow. "A stumbling stone." These are familiar to Helen, who has seen them shining among the cobbles many times before: brass plates that mark places where men and women and children were taken from their homes to be murdered in the camps. She looks. The inscription is very small, and somewhat rubbed, and she is not particularly minded to stoop and read. Adaya removes her glasses. She says: "*Murdered in Theresienstadt, 19th of August 1942*. And only just sixteen. I wonder, when God permitted us to fall, if He knew we'd fall so far."

"Sixteen," says Helen. It is so melancholy, so beyond her comprehension, that she is chastened out of indifference. She bends (her knee aches) to read the name, and when she has done so she takes in a breath which is so sharp and so cold it seems to deposit a coating of hoar frost on her tongue.

"Is it your knee?" says Adaya. She holds out a steadying hand.

"No," says Helen. "No, it's only that I've seen that name before." She steps back, and looks at the windows behind the stumbling stone. It is a shop, rather handsome, and the blinds are down. It is all as she thought it would be.

"Ah." Her companion hesitates. "Well, you have looked, which is all that could be asked of you now. Let's go on." She holds out her arm. "Let's go."

Thea answers the door on her feet. She is drunk, in the perfectly calibrated fashion of the expert drinker: voluble without indiscretion, witty without cruelty. She wears a dressing gown in scarlet brocade with collars and pockets of grass green, and a green cravat is loosely wrapped around her throat. On her head: a large and shapeless velvet cap, such as a Tudor page might wear; in her hand, which very slightly shakes: wine in a gilded Moser glass; around her neck: a green moldavite on a silver chain. Her small feet are white and weak against the pine floor; the left turns in somewhat, the toes curled back towards the sole. Everything about her is both grand and disordered—it is evident it has taken time and effort to dress, and that in many respects she has failed. The cord of her dressing gown is coming loose, and there is nothing under it.

"Helen Franklin!" she says. It is necessary for her to lean against the wall if she is to give her customary embrace, her usual double kiss with its smell of green leaves, and as she does so Helen looks instinctively behind her, down the dim hall with its cabinet of glass, for the wheelchair. It is there, on the ramp. It is tipped on its side, and one wheel slowly spins. "You have brought a friend?" This is delivered with a formidable scowl intended to convey that there is nothing Thea likes better than an uninvited guest.

"I am Adaya," says the young woman. "How do you do?" Shyly she holds out her hand. Helen observes how she takes in the flesh-colored splints on Thea's wrists, and how unevenly they are fastened. The eyes behind their thick lenses rove down the lamp-lit hall and take account of the toppled wheelchair, the gray ramp.

"Absolutely delighted to meet you," says Thea. "Thrilled you felt you could come by. Did you bring anything to drink?" She contemplates her glass, which is empty. "Pleased to have company, actually. I have had nightmares. I am a maiden in a nightgown: there is something squatting on my chest."

"I don't think you should be standing," says Adaya. "You ought not to be standing. Won't you take my arm?"

"I do not need your help!" Then she overbalances—reaches for support—encounters Adaya's offered arm. "It is merely the drink, you understand," she says, allowing herself to be guided down the hall. The velvet cap has fallen on the mat. Helen picks it up, and puts it on the cabinet of glass.

"I quite understand."

"A very good Tokay, as it happens."

"I have never had it, myself."

"Have you not? What a terrific shame! I shall give you a bottle." Then Thea takes in her visitor's muddy tights, which gather and sag at the ankle; the shabby open coat, and beneath it the heavy skirt and plain cloth of her blouse. "What can you be wearing? Extraordinary ensemble! Helen, where did you find this young person?"

Helen watches. Adaya—with that curious combination of hesitancy and professional skill which is so appealing—contrives to deposit Thea in an armchair, and having done so claps her hands together with the satisfaction of a job well done, and smiles. She looks briefly very young. It might have amused Helen, were she not still seeing, shining at the toe of Adaya's shoe, the stumbling stone set in the pavement, and the name that was written there.

"I fell over," she says. "I fell over, and hurt my knee, and Adaya happened to see me. That's all."

"Where? Where did you fall? I don't believe it."

"A concert, in the mirror chapel," says Adaya. "Do you know it? It was Dvořák—*Song to the Moon*."

"A concert—Helen? Dvořák? Now I know that you are playing tricks, and I in my dotage, and dependent on the kindness of friends. Be serious, now."

"I need to sit down," says Helen. "Thea, may we at least turn on the light?"

"Illuminate, by all means," says Thea; and then the room is warm and bright, and almost as it has always been: the white walls obscured by a lifetime's accrual of prints, etchings, paintings, and tapestries; the Ercol table on the scarlet rug; the pair of armchairs set side by side, one of which is empty. All the same, there is the air of a home dispirited—a peace lily in a porcelain bowl has gone too long unwatered and there are plates of lonely half-eaten meals scattered about. Thea has taken her barrister's wig from its box, and it is now huddled, as if frightened, beneath a chair. On the table, there is a pile of books and papers: a document entitled *The Testimony of Nameless and Hassan*; a lined notepad on which is written, in Thea's shaky hand, *Melmoth— Evidence for the Prosecution*; a clothbound hardback with *Melmoth the Wanderer* written on the spine.

"How are you coping?" says Helen, with that diffident manner which seems to her best suited to Thea's pride.

"Aren't I dressed? Aren't I fed?"

"You look wonderful. But, all the same"—Helen gestures to

a teacup which has acquired a skin of mold—"I wonder if you could use help, now and then. I was so grateful for Adaya today." She makes a show of rubbing her knee.

"You have muscular atrophy and peripheral neuropathy." Adaya has removed her gloves and coat and is watching Thea. A steel watch is pinned above her narrow breast. She speaks mildly, but with authority: it is not quite possible to recall her old shy manner. "You have foot drop on the left, and your balance is compromised. Have you applied for state social support?"

Helen watches Thea attempt to be affronted, but it has wearied her—the valiant absurd attire, the walk to the door, the Tokay in its gilded glass—and she leans against the armchair acquiring, it seems, a decade in a moment. "To be honest," she says, "I don't know what to do." It is very unlike her, this moment of defeat. Helen recalls all at once the messages that brought her here: *Helen come here now.*

"What has happened?" she says. "Is it Karel?" A look of such childlike sadness passes over her friend's face that she attempts a little levity. "Did Melmoth get him in the end, huh? Has she taken him away?" She closes her eyes, and sees behind her lids a woman—tall, severe, unspeaking; guiding Karel Pražan by the hand; down on the banks of the Vltava perhaps, or some miles distant already: long gone north, until the Vltava ran into the Elba; to Wittenberg and Magdeburg and Hamburg, bleeding through his lambswool socks.

Thea looks swiftly at her uninvited guest, who says, without the inflexion of surprise or query, "Melmoth."

"Just our little game of make-believe," says Thea. "Nothing to worry about. Sit down, won't you? You're making me nervous. No, my dear Helen. Turns out it's not Melmoth's fault. Turns out I have only myself to blame." She reaches into her pocket—it takes effort, this, and Helen and Adaya each for a moment look away—and withdraws a postcard. It is torn at the centre by only an inch, as if she has attempted to destroy it, but lacks the strength. She hands it to Helen. It is cheap, and evidently not chosen with the recipient in mind: an orange stein of beer, very badly drawn, perched among the castle spires. It was posted from Prague. "Read it," says Thea, and Helen does:

> *I am at the airport. I don't know where I'm going, but I've gone. I'm sorry. Everything is different now. I am not myself, you are not yourself. For a long time I thought SHE was coming for me but it was only ever shadows on the floor. I'm sorry. I loved you.*

"You will note, no doubt, being yourself a student of language, the tense." Thea's valiance in the face of defeat moves Helen almost to tears: these, she stems, as she has taught herself to do. "*Loved*, he says. Well, things fall apart, don't they? All things tend towards entropy. I thought, when we met: I have fifteen years on him. It will not last. But Helen"—Thea's courage fails her—"he may have gone, but I am still here, and now what am I supposed to do with all this love?"

"I think perhaps you shouldn't drink any more," says Adaya, with a watchful eye on Thea's hand, which moves towards the wine bottle.

"All right, dear child. All right." Helen is startled to see that Thea, by no means the most biddable of women, returns her questing hand to her lap.

"I am sorry," says Helen. What more is to be said? Karel has gone—Thea is left alone—she is sorry for it: these are the facts.

"So am I! So am I!" Thea begins to cry. Adaya surveys her.

It seems she has caught her tears by sitting close by: they shine behind her glasses. Then she stands, and begins to gather the moldy teacups, the plates on which crusts of bread have begun to curl.

"Do you think," says Thea, turning to Helen, "that if he really is gone—if he never comes back—I'll stop loving him, too?"

"Probably not," says Helen.

"No. Probably not. Well"—she wipes her nose on her brocade sleeve—"perhaps Melmoth will come for me, eh? Think she can manage a wheelchair?"

"I expect so," says Helen; and it may seem to the observer that she is a little distracted, a little cool. The fact is that her mind is elsewhere. Lovers' tiffs are not of great interest to her, even when concerning her friends: she has so long left behind that part of her life that she might as well be asked to summon up enthusiasm for children playing games in well-tended gardens. She is fond of Thea, she is fond of Karel, she wishes them no ill—she is moved by Thea's tears, her weariness, and hopes Karel will return. But what is all that to the follower whose footfall she thinks—even now, as Adaya pours a glass of water on the dying peace lily—she hears in the hall? What is that to what she saw on the stumbling stone in the street? What is that to her own guilt, which weighs her down, and will one day break her back?

"She's right, you know." She gestures to Adaya, who has gone now into the kitchen, with the bustling, contented air of a woman for whom strangers' kitchens are familiar ground. "You ought to contact social services; or perhaps hire a private nurse. I wonder if we might perhaps ask Adaya—"

"I don't want charity, and I don't need staff!" Thea is affronted.

"All the same," says Helen. "You do need a little help. For example: I wish you'd tie your dressing gown tighter." She smiles to show she means no ill, bends beside Thea's chair to tie the cord. There is a smell about her that she recognizes—a body unwashed, growing stale from disuse; it summons a memory which is instantly suppressed.

"So then: what about asking her?" says Thea. She watches Adaya return with a cloth, with which she wipes the table, the sideboard. "She seems to be some sort of nurse—she may know someone."

"She does, doesn't she?" Helen touches her knee through the tear in her trousers. Her flesh has sealed over in a scab. "I thought she might be a nun. I wonder why we don't ask?"

And why don't they ask? It is curious, this placid acceptance of the woman's presence, as if she'd been expected all along. She disappears with the cloth—returns without it—sits beside Thea with her hands folded in her lap. "What time do you take your medication?" she says. The lenses of her glasses are occluded with mist: she has been washing something with hot water. Thea gives Helen a quick, baffled look—*what business is it of hers?*—but says, "With an evening meal, generally, or I feel sick."

"And have you eaten?"

"I don't want to eat."

"I really think, you know, that you should." Again, that baffled look from Thea to Helen—again, the acquiescent response.

"I wouldn't mind some toast."

The woman hesitates then, and looks down at her folded hands. It is as if her apparently professional interest in them both—in muscular atrophy, in knees requiring stitches, in the necessity of taking distalgesics with food—has faltered, and she has realized that she has imposed herself on strangers. Helen pities her. She is young, and uncertain of herself: she has merely tried to be kind. She says, "I think that would be a good idea." She raises her eyebrows at Thea—*Why not? Why not let her help?*

But it is not Thea's habit to accept help without seeing to it that the balances weigh even. She looks, with kindly disdain, at Adaya's muddy tights, her scuffed shoes, the cheap gold cross on the silver chain. "It seems to me," she says, "that you could do with a job."

Adaya looks up, and Helen watches a flush of pleasure cross her cheek, and it occurs to her for the first time that perhaps she, too, is lonely. "You would like me to stay? I already have work," she says. "But I have time for more. Yes: I would like it very much."

"Well then!" Thea is triumphant (but the postcard is clutched in her right hand). "Well then! We shall see to it. Your yoke will be easy, and your burden light. Two rounds of toast with honey, please, and all the Naproxen my constitution will allow." Adaya stands without speaking—still more briskly, still more at home—and returns to the kitchen. There are the consoling noises of a kettle filled, and of a knife against a board.

"Well then," says Helen. She is relieved. Now that help has been acquired, and far more competently than she might have been able to provide, she is able to see Thea once again as she always was: merely her friend. "I am so sorry," she says. "About Karel—about all this." She gestures around the room. For all the neatness instigated by Adaya, it has a dreary, half-empty look, like the windows of a shop gone bankrupt.

"Ah, well." Thea's courage fails her: she unfolds the post-card, and clumsily wipes at it with her thumb. "There are worse things." In Adaya's absence, it seems possible to return to the matter at hand. She nods at the documents on the table. Her face alters: there is again that mischievous, not quite pleasant look which Karel had worn as he first showed her the scuffed leather folder with its gilded monogram. "What have you read?

Have you read the Hoffman document? Horrid little boy, wasn't he?"

"Only the first part." (Again, she sees the stumbling stone.) "This morning I read Sir David Ellerby's letter."

"My God! That one!" Thea shudders. "I will never have lilies in the house again."

"Even though it can only be legend—even though it is only something made up of fear and rumor and guilt—you almost think, don't you, that one day you might look up and see her there?" (Again, Helen hears the footsteps of her follower.)

"Last night, after you left, I fell asleep reading the story of Nameless and Hassan. When I woke it was three in the morning and there were no lights outside, not even the courtyard light, and my own room was as black with my eyes open as it was with them closed. But all the same I could have sworn there was a movement in the corner of the room—somehow very far back, too far, as if it wasn't against the wall but behind it, actually behind it—moving like a swarm of flies, or like the shadow under a tree." In the kitchen, Adaya begins to sing. "The strange thing is that I wasn't only scared. I wanted something to be there—I wanted to see something waiting for me—do you think you can long for something that scares you half to death?"

Helen considers this, carefully, as she considers all things. "I sometimes think that one great emotion is never very far from all the other ones. Best to avoid them entirely, if possible."

Adaya returns with a plate. There is the scent of honey and melted butter; there is fragrant tea in a pot. There is also, in a plastic box designed for the purpose, a handful of tablets of various kinds. She sets these on the table, beside the pile of books and documents: they nudge a sheet of paper, which drifts to the floor. She stoops to pick it up. "*Melmoth the Witness: Primary Sources?*"

Both Helen and Thea feel embarrassed at the quiet, querying look that comes from behind the young woman's glasses. "We are . . . researching, that's all." Thea has the faint hauteur of the mildly ashamed.

"Oh yes. Melmotte. Doesn't everybody know?" Adaya is unperturbed.

"Not us," says Thea. "Not until recently."

"We know, of course," says Helen, "that it's only a legend."

"Ah!" Adaya's shy smile grows teasing. "You don't imagine she is watching you? Perhaps your consciences are clear. Now, Thea. Please: eat."

Helen stands. She is tired. There is a dull ache in her knee. "I must go," she says. "But I will see you tomorrow, I think—Thea, have you had a call from Albína Horáková?"

Thea laughs. "A veritable royal summons. Dinner, and then—heaven help you, Helen, heathen that you are—the opera." She cradles a teacup, which trembles in its saucer.

Adaya surveys Helen. "You don't like music?"

"I did once." It is useless to explain, and equally useless to protest. Albína Horáková is, she has learned, as immovable as Prague Castle. She buttons up her coat. "Thea, shall I come tomorrow—will you be all right?"

Adaya and Thea answer together: "Oh yes," they say. "Oh yes: everything will be all right now." The young woman stands beside Thea's chair. Steam rises from the teapot in her hand; the lamplight shines on her thick fair hair, and on Thea's ruddy mane. She looks, in her brocade gown, not frail and compromised by sickness, but like a queen who has acquired a courtier.

• • •

Walking home, Helen listens for the echo of her follower's footstep, but there is none. Is it merely the muffling of the snow, which has not yet been cleared from all the paths and alleys? Perhaps. But Helen is almost minded to think the arrival of that shy, competent young woman in her thick brown tights marks the end of the matter—the end of unsettling dreams in the night, of blue-eyed jackdaws and their knowing winks, of watchful schoolboys in the street. Josef Hoffman has merely died, as all men must; Karel Pražan has merely turned tail, as many men do. But climbing the stairs to her apartment, submitting humbly to the additional pain (the well-deserved pain) that comes from her throbbing knee, Helen thinks of the name on the stumbling stone. Certainly Melmoth the Witness may be discarded as a tale told to keep children in line, but not all things can be so readily set aside. Two hours remain of the day, and she resolves to devote them to what is left of Josef Hoffman's manuscript.

Her apartment is silent. There is no fitful television light, no muttering from Albína Horáková's room; there is not even the musky scent of incense cones burned in dishes to ward off the evidence of cigarettes. But Albína has been at work, all the same, for there on Helen's bed (you recall the bare mattress under the bare bulb) is a pile of dark and flimsy fabric. It is a dress, very old, very fine, almost disintegrating at a touch: it is embroidered with fronds of fern, and beaded with small birds. There is also a woolen wrap, cashmere, reeking of camphor; a pair of buckled shoes; and a handful, carelessly tossed down, of garnet jewelry glinting bloody in the light. There is no note. None is required. Helen pictures herself in an opera box, a brass eyeglass raised to the stage, trailing scraps of beaded net, and laughs. She hears, very distantly, a corresponding laugh, and this one is delighted—comes, it almost seems, from the cardboard box beneath the bed. Then she tosses the glittering pile to the floor, takes the Hoffman document from her desk, and lies on the hard thin mattress to read.

The Hoffman Document

And so Prague changed, but no more (it seemed to me) than a door is altered by a coat of paint. Red banners with the black swastika appeared on municipal buildings and the German boys filled out their uniforms. One night a synagogue caught fire, and the fire wardens let the whole temple burn down; but I knew nothing of this until long after the war was ended.

Often when I passed the Bayer shop I heard the radio. Each time I thought of Freddie spinning in the warm room as flowers died in the grate and saw Franz extend his hand towards me through the closing door; each time I felt again the weight of desire and dislike.

One January night, when I was fourteen—it was a Friday: I know this beyond doubt—I walked home late from school. All along Viktoriastrasse lighted windows showed citizens of Prague and soldiers of the Reich sitting amiably over coffee and cake. Jackdaws had come away from the river and were seeking out ledges for the night, and the tram bells sounded like sleighs at Christmas. Everything was as it had always been and would always be, but when I turned into our road I saw Polizist Novák on the doorstep of an empty shop. He held his hat in his hands and he was weeping. It wasn't done for show but seemed as private as thinking. I said, "What is it, Polizist Novák? Have you lost something?" I recalled, as I often did, my lost moldavite, and put my hand in my pocket as if I might feel it there. He said: "Josef, isn't it? How tall you are. I hardly knew you."

I sat beside him on the step. There was beer on his breath. "I only ever tried to do what is right," he said. "What can we trust, if we cannot trust the law?" I had no answer and hoped none was expected. He plucked the fabric of his uniform coat. "I wake up naked, and I'm a man. But then I put this on, and I'm the law, and there is only the law, and the law is right. All my life I put my faith in it like my wife puts faith in her rosary. Who will I serve if it turns out my gods are false—what will my life have been then?" He went on in the rambling way of a man who relies on drink to loosen the tongue. There were laws, he told me, whose wisdom he doubted. "Now there's a list of things Jews can't have. Skis, for instance. What harm did skiing ever do? Bicycles, radios, gramophones, and so on." What was more, they were no longer allowed in the public baths. He supposed it was wise (he knew the Jew to be sly as a fox, and one must protect the chickens in the coop), but all the same . . . he jerked his thumb towards the windows of the empty shop. One pane was cracked. "An optician, this one," he said. "And a decent enough fellow. But three times now I've caught him coming home past curfew from his fifty lengths, with his towel rolled under his arm! I said: you'd better sharpen up or there'll be trouble for the whole family. I might as well have said: 'Karl, you've got something on your coat.' He just went on sorting index cards into boxes. Then I came by this evening and found the whole lot gone."

I asked where they had gone, and he said, "Away from harm, I suppose." I understood then that his intellect was like mine: slow-turning and deliberate, reaching its conclusions with great pains and by small degrees. He said, frowning: "All I've ever known is that I am the law, and the law is right. But now I wonder if there is what is right, and there is what is good, and these are not the same."

It was late and I was restless but something in me changed. It was as if, having only ever looked down at the shuffle of my shoes on the cobblestones, I began to lift my head. Memories I hardly knew I'd acquired appeared clearly to me then: I saw a man lying in the doorway of the place where my father smoked with friends, and this man's arm was raised, and his hand dangled backwards against his wrist, and swayed loose as a tree branch broken by wind. I overheard, on a street corner as I was sent to fetch tobacco, a man crying because his son had been arrested and had never come home. I saw boys missing from my class, because they'd gone away on holiday, and not come back; I heard young soldiers in their winter coats pointing at our neighbor Anna, saying very quietly: "Pig. Pig."

We looked at each other. I think each saw in the other's eye a kind of fearful reluctant wakening. The snow went on falling, but it began to change. It was no longer fine, and white, but began to drift down in huge and filthy blots. Then there was a deep thrilling sound from above the clouds, and I saw that it was pieces of paper, thousands and tens of thousands, tossed out from planes that flew above the city. Novák picked up a sheet and held it under the light of a lamp. Then he came and stood beside me in the shelter of the optician's shop, and showed it to me, and I read: VELKÁ BRITANIE ESKÉMU NÁRODU— GREAT BRITAIN TO THE CZECH PEOPLE!

"What does it mean?" I said. "What else does it say?" What did Britain have to do with us—a boy and a man in a doorway in Prague? Novák shook his head in anger and disbelief: "*Czechs! The world Democracies are watching in admiration and sympathy your wonderful struggle against oppression!"* A child was sitting laughing in a snowdrift, gathering bits of paper. Were we oppressed? Did we struggle? "A few little rules and regulations," said Novák. "To keep the people safe—and they talk of oppression! Josef: look at these lies. TRUTH WILL CONQUER!" I looked at him. All the unease we'd briefly shared was gone. He stood as straight and proud as a young soldier on parade. I understood then that he was very like my father: a spinning weathervane, which turns easily at the movement of the wind. He shook me roughly by the collar, and I understood that in seeing his weakness I had committed an offense. "Go home to your mother," he said.

So I went on my way. A few yards on I had the sensation that he was standing under the street light and watching me go—but when I turned to see, he was on his hands and knees in the snow, picking up sheets of yellow paper, shaking his head. At that moment the street lights dimmed and I saw the figure of a woman at the window of the apartment above the optician's shop. She was tall, and draped in fine black cloth that stirred as if somehow the wind blew indoors. I could not see her eyes but knew, with a kind of longing terror, that they were fixed on me. I thought of the farmer in his field by the Eger leaving out a chair; I thought of Herr Schröder and how he'd touched his shrapnel scar when he told me the cursed woman's name. "Melmoth!" I said: *"Melmoth!"* and helplessly stepped forward. Then the street lights came on and I saw plainly what had been in the window: just a coat stand, on which the optician, leaving in a hurry, had left a good black winter coat.

My walk home was arduous because of the snow, and because all around me people were gathering to exclaim over the leaflets scattered about. When I came to the Bayer shop it was closed, and the shutters were drawn down; but someone had left on the windowsill one of the stones that sometimes come free from the pavements, and it prevented the shutter from closing as it should. I put my face to the window. In the dark shop I saw that the map of Bohemia I'd seen Frau Bayer hang had been sold, and in its place was a picture of some dark landscape bounded by water. A little light came from lamps in the room where I'd once danced and drunk sweet coffee. I saw the corner of the dining table and the oak sideboard where the radio stood on its green cloth. I saw candles burning, and bread plaited like a schoolgirl's hair. I saw a back turned to me, and I knew it was Herr Bayer because of the way his fair hair grew at the nape of his neck. I saw Frau Bayer standing with her arms raised over the candle, and saw how their flames stirred as she moved. I saw her cover her face and stand for a time with her mouth moving. Then I saw Freddie stand beside her mother. She was not the child I remembered at night: she'd exchanged her white socks for stockings. She kissed her mother as if she were the older woman and Frau Bayer a frightened child. Then I saw Franz. I saw his white-fair head and saw how broad he had grown in the year since he had offered me his hand, and I rejected it. Then he closed the door.

I leaned a while against the wall beside the shutter. I understood what I had seen: my mind, always so sluggish and so dull, grew clear as water. These were the Jews against whom I'd been so often warned: who were by some alchemy both bankers and Communists, both powerful and wretched, who for two thousand years had wandered from place to place because no nation could bear their presence? This family? This girl who pouted as she read—this mother, who stood on a ladder to dust the tops of gilded picture frames, and poured cream in my coffee from a blue and white jug? This boy, who had only wanted me to praise his radio? I shook my head until it ached.

In the years that passed between then and now—as I walked the streets of Berlin and London and Istanbul with feet that ached and bled—I've allowed my past self one minute only, of an anger which is righteous and pure. I give that dull boy leaning on the wall a moment to reject what he'd been taught—to cast off the filthy coat thrown about his shoulders the day he was born. Then the minute passes, and his vanity and prejudice wins out, as it won out that day. *How they must have mocked me!* I thought. In bewildered anger I thumped my head with my fist. How they must have laughed, to have taken me in—to have made me complicit in their crime! What crime it might have been, I could not have said—I simply understood I had been made to feel poor, and drab, and foolish. It ought to have been they who flinched from me—they were the despised! They the outcasts! I was a German, and the son of a German, and it was my blood that made the soil rich, not theirs!

I pulled out the stone that held up the shutter. It fell noisily into place, so that I imagined them looking up from their rituals of bread and wine and sharing a look of alarm. Well: let them. I put the stone in the pocket of my coat. It was a poor substitute for my moldavite, but I stroked it and petted it as if I'd found my lost treasure. Then I went home, and slept—as my mother said when she woke me in the morning—the sleep of the righteous.

Reader, shall I lie? Shall I redeem myself with a story that goes like this: that I, Josef Adelmar Hoffman, woke from my sleep of ignorance and shame? Shall I say that I lived out the war in fear and indignation, alert to sorrow and despair—that I saw two women carried out of an apartment three doors down, having attempted suicide with bottles of poison meant for greenfly on the roses they grew on their terrace—that I pitied them, and knew

what they dreaded? Shall I say that I went into the Bayer shop
and coolly said that security was a concern, these days, and they
ought to fasten their doors and windows securely?

I wish I could! But if I were to lie there is one who would see,
there is one who bears witness now, as she bore witness then—I
feel her eyes on me now—implacable, as they have always been—
what use is it to deceive, when from the first I was found out?

So I go on with my confession, which is this: that I went on
as before, my eyes cast down, in my pocket that piece of stone
which I caressed and turned over and over as though it were a
sacred object. Yet Prague did not go on as it had before because
some great crime[1] had been committed which altered the city.
Jews now wore the yellow Star of David. Sometimes it conferred
a strange defiant pride (two Jewish boys with whom I'd studied
arithmetic passed me on the street with a swagger and looked
me hard in the eye), but mostly I saw a staring, shadowed look.
Once I saw Polizist Novák remonstrating with a man, gesticulat-
ing towards his lapel, indicating that he did not wear the mark

---

1 On 27th May 1942 Reinhard Heydrich—Protector of Bohemia and
Moravia, the Butcher of Prague—was wounded when waiting men threw a
grenade into his car. Himmler's own physician tended him; but his body was
full of pieces of horsehair upholstery driven in by fragments of steel. These
festered, and one week later he fell sick while eating his lunch, and died the
following day. First it was proposed that a tariff of ten thousand Czech lives
should be set against that single German soul. But this was impracticable:
who'd man Prague's munitions factories if the workforce was so depleted?
Instead the town of Lidice, a little north-west of Prague, was chosen as the
scapegoat. Military trucks took every man and boy to the village orchard,
where blossom had begun to cede to the fruit. Here they were shot in groups
of five; then, for efficiency's sake, in groups of ten. The women and girls

of shame prominently enough. Then Novák met my eye, and nodded, and I felt warmed: we'd shared a moment's weakness, he and I, and had not been broken by it.

The year I turned sixteen the Jews began to leave Prague. Sometimes I heard the trucks going from house to house and instructions in German issued and accepted and thought how ordered and polite it was. One morning I met Polizist Novák on his beat, and asked him what became of them. "Off to Theresienstadt," he said, cheerfully. He looked stouter and more benevolent than ever, well-fed on the meat of a job done well. "Pleasant little town, and you don't hear them complaining: off they go, with their papers and suitcases. Grateful to be all together I shouldn't wonder. Birds of a feather, eh?" Then he showed me his wrist. "Look at this watch. Swiss! Gold! Never short of a penny you notice, these Jews. You can pick up all sorts for a song. Sergeant Svoboda got his hands on a gramophone: they say his wife's never been happier."

We had come to the corner of our street. It was spring. The trees were not in leaf but had a kind of green mist on them. Overhead the scarlet Bayer sign hung on its bracket. In my pocket the hard cold stone called for my hand. I touched it. I could hear music. I said, "They take things from the Jews, and give them away?"

---

were sent to the camps. Lidice's orchard, church, homes and outhouses were burned to the ground and their remnants ploughed into the soil. When after the war a handful of the living returned they found nothing but a levelled field on which grass had begun to grow. (Once the war was ended, some German villages were awarded the same treatment. It is for this reason that I cannot return home to the village by the Eger where I was born, for not a stone of it remains: there are only the lindens on the riverbank, and somewhere in the soil, I daresay, the moldavite I lost.)

"Nothing's free in this life, little Hoffman. But ask the right questions in the right places and have the right sum in mind, and you'd be surprised what might come your way."

The music went on playing. I saw the curved oak case of Franz and Freddie Bayer's radio: saw the green cloth under it, and the three glass valves inside. How beautiful it was—how far beyond anything I ever hoped of having for myself! And how it had shamed me—how it made me diminished and small! Where was the glory my father had promised, which was in the blood and the soil, in the steel blade of the Hoffman sword, which had come over the River Moldau in iron tanks, in the hearts of boys in their winter coats? Frau Bayer crouched beside the case where the costly books were kept. She was polishing the glass with a bottle of vinegar and a white cloth, just as I did when I cleaned our shop. She was thinner than I remembered. The orchestra grew louder. I imagined Franz standing by the radio, one hand in his pocket, turning up the dial—imagined Freddie seated swooning on the floor. The stone in my pocket was cold. I said: "Polizist Novák, what should I do if I know a crime has been committed?"

Novák breathed on his watch and polished it on his sleeve. "What have you been up to?" he said.

I saw three jackdaws on the bracket where the Bayer shop sign hung. Their eyes were chips of glass and they were turned on me. They opened their beaks and made their querying cry. *Why?* they said: *how? how? why?* I looked away. I said, "Can you hear music? These people have a radio and I think it should have been taken away a long time ago."

"What do you mean?" Novák peered through the glass. Frau Bayer stood and pressed her hands into the small of her back. I could hear violins. "This is a good German family from

Hamburg. I've been in there: Herr Bayer found my wife a book she wanted for its cover."

"I don't think they're a good family," I said. Now there were five jackdaws on the sign. "I don't think they're the sort of people that should have a radio."

Novák shook me by the shoulder. "Tell me what you mean," he said. "Don't you know you can break the law as much by doing nothing, as by doing something?"

"I don't mean anything except that I don't think they should have a radio. Work it out for yourself." I had frightened myself and it made me churlish. "Aren't you a policeman? Go and do your job." Frau Bayer was on her knees again and I could see the worn soles of her shoes. I felt sick. I turned and ran home and all the way the music followed me, and with it the sound of the jackdaws: *why? how? why?* My mother opened the door to me and I was sick on the step, and for a week was too ill to leave my bed.

That night and for many nights after I dreamed of a woman. It always began with something burning in a corner of the room giving off smoke, but neither light nor heat. Then the plume of smoke would thicken, and take on the form of black silk moving in the wind, and I knew that what I saw was not an object but a feeling of despair and loneliness made incarnate, as if thoughts had substance. Then in time that dark and insubstantial thing formed itself into the figure of a woman. She was dreadfully tall. Sometimes she was thin as if worn down by time, sometimes large as if about to deliver new life into the world, and I knew that this life also, though naked and speechless, would hunt me down to the ends of the earth. Her face was veiled by gray-black hair that made me think of the jackdaws that watched me above the Bayer shop, and I knew this woman watched me too. Then I'd wake and find the sheets were wet because I'd urinated like a child in my terror, though it was not relief I felt, but loss. On the sixth day I was able to eat, and my father buttoned me into my new winter coat as if I were still very young ("The best wool, the finest, woven in the north: only good things now for the Hoffmans, eh?") and took me out for fresh air. When we came to the Bayer shop my father cuffed my shoulder and said, "See this? Those people down from Hamburg with their fine clothes and their music? Turned out they were Jews all along. Heard it from Polizist Novák: forged papers, the works. Well, off they go to Theresienstadt with the rest of their kind. The stink of a pig gets smelt sooner or later, you mark my words." Trembling, I looked into the windows of the shop. The glass case was cracked. A book with marbled endpapers lay upturned on the floor and its spine was broken. I saw an empty vinegar bottle and a bit of white cloth. I asked to be taken home.

A month later, shortly before my mother's birthday, I said to my father that she might like a radio. I said I'd heard they could be got cheaply if you knew where to look—that in fact Polizist Novák might know where one could be found. But when her birthday came her gift was a new cotton housecoat, to wear as she swept the shop floor.

So the war went on. I spoke to no one, read no papers, crossed the street to avoid Novák, could not abide the company of boys my own age. One day Polizist Novák came to the shop. He had brought a piece of cake wrapped in paper, and ate it while I wiped crumbs from the counter. "What's it like in Theresienstadt?" I said. "I sometimes wonder." I did not add: *after what I did*; but I think he understood. "Don't fret, young Hoffman," he said. "Why, the

Red Cross paid a visit[2] and what did they find? A playground, no less! Schoolrooms and washrooms. A bank. The Jews complain of a boring diet—too many tinned sardines, which can't be beaten, in my opinion, on a slice of hot toast of an evening. But you're looking thin, young Hoffman. I won't have it! Some fruitcake for you. We'll look out for each other, you and me."

The war was coming to its end and something had altered in the air of Prague. I hardly noticed it, as one hardly notices the onset of winter until one finds oneself chilled in the morning. Once when going to buy packing paper I was jostled by three Czech boys. I heard one say to the other: "Soon we'll take our clubs in hand and drive the Germans from the land!" Instinctively I reached for the stone in my pocket. What could they mean? Whose land was it, if not mine? One evening as I lay doing nothing I heard a bustle in the street below. I saw men huddled around a woman in uniform pulling her cap from her head. Her curls were pinned tightly underneath and they wanted these too and some of the men held lengths of her hair in their fists. They were saying: "Whore! German bitch!" Then they vanished as if on a signal and

2 The Red Cross sent a young man to visit Theresienstadt and make a full report. He found that all was well. The population had all it needed: a school, a playground, a court for those who fell foul of the law. But it was nothing but sauce poured on spoiling meat. They'd watched a boy run up and pluck at the Commander's sleeve and say: "Uncle, tell me it's not canned sardines again for dinner—we are all so bored of it: let us have something else!" and watched him rewarded for his pertness with a silver coin, when if only they'd looked they might have seen all the teeth loosening in his starving head. The camp was not overcrowded, they said. It was not, because ten thousand prisoners had been transported away the preceding week, to Auschwitz, where there was no witness.

the woman was left in the cover of a doorway, shaking, trying to put on her hat. Two women crossed the road to avoid her. I closed the curtains. It was May 1945. I was nineteen.

Then the lights went out for the Hoffman family. I was in my room. My father was doing the accounts and my mother was in the kitchen. I heard doors slamming and my father running up the stairs, and when I went to the window I saw darkness cover the city as one shop after another and all the yellow street lights went out one by one. But in the distance other lights shone: they were red and low like many small suns rising. I went downstairs. My mother was looking at her oven. "It's gone off," she said. "It's cold. Tell your father. Tell your father it's all gone off."

That night we sat at the table. We had no heat or light. Once my father went outside, but whatever he saw on the street sent him back inside. There was the sound of something being constructed a few yards away and I thought for some reason of a gallows. At dawn someone hammered on our door and when I opened it there was Herr Becker, with whom we sometimes did business. He was tearing at his hair, and told me the Czechs had turned against the Germans, who after all had sought only to protect them. "They have taken over the radio and are broadcasting terrible things, so that we fear for our lives! Stay where you are! Tell your parents—tell everyone you can—stay where you are, until we are safe!" Later from my window I saw a barricade built at the end of our road, and Herr Becker approaching with his hands held high. The men at the barricade spoke for a long while quite calmly and amicably and then they shot him. I closed the door and returned to my parents. The candle had burned down to the wick.

I cannot tell in what order these things came: when we realized the city was burning; when we heard the German bombers over the Old Town Square; what night it was I saw a German woman lying in the street while men busied themselves with her in a way that made me think of ants worrying at the body of a spider. On the third day we ate cold mutton stew dotted with hard yellow fat, which had a rancid taste, but was all we had. On the fourth day my father began to shiver. Still nobody came. Our suffering and fear made no bond between us. My mother put all her shoes on the table and fretted over their worn laces, or praised the gloss of their polish. "What about the delivery on Tuesday?" she said. "Where will they take the order if the man can't come to the door?" One night below my window someone cried over and over with the patient tireless regularity of a ringing bell: "God! God! God! God! God!" After an hour the voice broke—I heard it break—and then for another hour there was instead a kind of wordless questioning which may just have been the jackdaws on the windowsill. My father took all this as a personal slight against the Hoffman name. "Six years!" he said. "Six years I lived as a man of German blood on German soil. Was that all I was to be given? Is my son to have no more than this?" He kept the Hoffman sword by his side. He began drinking. He remained drunk until the very end.

Often as I crept about the cold apartment in a daze of hunger and weariness I'd see a black column of smoke rising—distant, as if on a far horizon—then growing nearer, until it rose up from the floor of the room where I cowered away from the window. Each time the sight of it filled me with a kind of longing fear—as if what I desired most was also what appalled me most. Sometimes I made out a grinning mouth, a wrist, a hand—then I would reach for it and find myself saying: "Melmoth—Melmoth!"

They came for us on the fifth day. There was the sound of

breaking glass and I thought: I polished those cases as well as I could. I remember how soft the light was, and how precise—how it picked out the drab curtains at the window, and the drab blankets on the bed, and my hands reaching for the door. I recall this very particularly because it was not in darkness that Melmoth came at last to me but in the light of a May morning. One moment I was alone, and the next I was not. It was as swift and absolute as that. As I reached for the door my hand did not meet the wood, the brass handle, but HER. Fear and wonder fixed me where I stood and I could do nothing but look. Her hair was coarse and long and moved slowly as hair does under water. Her face was lovely and dreadful: her eyes were like the slick of oil on water—gray-blue, steel-blue, their colors moving—and set deep in the sockets of her skull. Her skin moved. It seemed to me like shadows on a wall: now black, now very pale. She was gazing at me with so imploring a look that I could not speak. Then she raised one finger to her mouth—*Be silent!*—and her eyes filled with tears and these ran very slowly down her gaunt cheek. Beyond the door I heard my mother shrieking, and heard her damned as a German whore. I heard my father blubbering, and heard him damned as a collaborator and a coward. I heard my mother cry, "No! I won't go! I won't!" So I moved again towards the door but Melmoth through her weeping made a sound which was like the growl of an animal you would not want to rouse. "I won't go!" said my mother, and I knew she was being taken. Then I heard laughter, and someone said: "What a brave German soldier we have here, hey, old man? Did you ever see anything like it? *Heil,* soldier! Show us how it's done!" I closed my eyes and imagined my father holding the Hoffman sword. I saw him feinting and thrusting, fumbling with the useless fingers on his right hand—saw how absurd he was and had always been—how absurd it all was: the blood, the soil, the pride, the name. Then I heard an explosion that was small, but very close by. "Leave him there," they said: "he'll get what's coming to him." There was the sound of blows landing, the clatter of boots on stairs, and they were gone. I opened my eyes and Melmoth was gone too. Her absence was so absolute I felt the loss like grief. She'd seen what I had done—seen my desire, my resentment, my envy, my cowardice—and still she had come for me. Tears poured out of me as though I were a broken bottle of water. What did I mourn—my mother? My father, whom I'd always despised? Freddie Bayer, and the light picking out the fine fair down above her knees—Franz, and his offered hand, which I had ignored? I didn't know. Somewhere in the adjoining room my father was tidying up. There was the sound of objects stacked against each other, methodical and neat. I wondered why he never called for me. Then I heard a noise like that of a starving man who has at last found food, and is incapable of eating without choking. *The old bastard*, I thought. How could a father keep food from his son? Angrily I pulled open the door. He was not seated at the table: he leaned against it, or seemed to—leaned in a dragging, weary way, like a man come home after a day of laboring. Then he slumped further in his weariness and gurgled as he did it—then further still until his forehead rested on the place where my mother would put dishes of meat. In the lucid morning light I saw then that some long, wet object reached from him to me. It was the blade of the Hoffman sword. It was bloodied and there on the steel were other fragments—of cloth and flesh, I suppose. He had contrived somehow to lodge the hilt of the sword in a place where the floorboards were broken, and brace it firm with heavy things—the cashbox which had been his nightly companion, my mother's mangle—and fallen on it, thinking himself, I suppose, a tragic figure undone by cruel fates. He was not dead yet. Blood and fluid poured from his open mouth. His eyes were very wide. Then the weight of his body dragged him still further down the sword, and I suppose that was the end of it, for all that evening I sat with him at the table and never heard another sound.

The following night my mother came home. She had been stripped of her coat, of her shoes and her stockings; she dragged one foot behind her. Her hands were swollen and rough and she pulled splinters of wood from her palm with her teeth. She sat with me at the table. If she saw my father there with his blood dried like lacquer on the wood she gave no sign of it. I said, "Where did they take you? What did you do?"

She had in her pocket a piece of bread, which she put on the table. I took it and ate it. "All the women are at the barricades," she said. "Taking them down. Early start tomorrow. Better rest." Then she lifted up her dragging foot, and inspected it. "Why did they do that?" she said. "Why would they do that?" I looked, and saw that someone had cut a portion of flesh from her heel, very precisely, measuring half an inch square. Within that neat wound was a mass of yellowish fat and fibrous tissue. I went on eating my bread.

When they came the next evening it was quietly in uniform and with sheets of paper to consult. "Josef Hoffman, father. Josef Hoffman, son. Adela Hoffman, mother." They looked at my father, and made a note. "Downstairs. Bring your papers, bring a coat." There were jackdaws on the windowsill. Nobody touched us; nobody spoke. It was all done with decency and order.

Outside the streets were busy and the atmosphere seethed: it was as if the air was composed of combustible gas and a single spark would detonate the city.

"Over there," they said: "over there." We were taken to stand with a handful of other Germans, who looked as I suppose we did: made gaunt by hunger and sleeplessness. Some were empty-handed; others clutched briefcases as though on their way to an ordinary working day. "Do as you're told," said a woman to my mother. Her head had been shaved. "Just do as you're told."

A man said: "What are you doing with us?" It was grown dark by then, and somewhere fires were burning. This man was very anxious. The back of his hand had been branded with a swastika.

"It's all official," said a Czech. "It's all decided: nothing to do with you, nothing to do with me. Only official business." Across the street a group of women gathered. I'd queued with them at the bank to pay in cloth bags of coins; I'd watched them walk home with their children. They spat at us. A white-haired woman said: "You'll get what's coming to you! An eye for an eye, that's it—I'd cut them out if they'd let me, I'd have your eyes on my knife!"

"All right," said the Czech official. He held a stick and with it he lightly switched the anxious man without malice, as a farmer might a cow. "On we go," he said; and we few Germans shuffled along the street, watched from above and below by many baleful, gleeful eyes. Beyond our street the sky was lit with an orange glow; nearer fires also burned, in braziers or in the windows of apartments which I suppose had belonged to Germans like us. Beside me my mother dragged her mutilated foot. The branded man had begun to mutter to himself with a bitter furious stream of complaint—it wasn't fair, he was only an administrator, what harm had he ever done filing paperwork, he had never harmed a soul—and I hated him for it. What good was complaint—what good had it ever been? The ant does not complain when its nest is destroyed, and we were no more than that. I had always thought so. I'd never seen evidence of grace, nobility, or courage in my fellow men. What did it matter that, as I supposed, my mother and I were not to live? We were no great loss. We'd come by then to the Bayer shop. A man in police uniform lay unconscious or dead on the threshold. Two boys had tied around his neck a thick white cloth that smelt of paraffin and they were trying to strike a match, but the matches were damp and wouldn't light. They swore, and kicked him, and tried again.

On we walked, acquiring more companions as we went: three young women so silent it seemed to me their suffering had exceeded anything I had seen so far; an elderly couple, smartly dressed, talking amiably about what a warm evening it was, just as if over the road they could not quite clearly see men stamping on the stomach of an SS officer so that in time there seemed nothing left of him there, only the fabric of his uniform on the wet cobblestones. Once we passed a broken window and paused there as the inventory was consulted, and more names were read aloud in a brisk dispassionate voice: "Reinhard Weber, Marlene Weber, Rudy Weber— good, good. Next house. Falke Möller, Franz Möller." I saw a long table carved with leaves and flowers. Here sat a family dressed for church: three girls in cotton aprons over floral dresses, their mother in a silk blouse, a man in a fine double-breasted suit and a baby in his arms. There were five wine glasses on the table—elegant and thin like Moser glass—and all but one had been knocked over. They'd drunk poison. Their mouths were open and those fine clothes were stained with blood and vomit. Only the baby looked peaceful because someone had broken its neck. I thought I saw, beyond the table, deep in the shadows behind an open door, a woman, watching—I strained to see her, and to make out the blue eyes burning. I thought: *she must be there—how could there be no witness?* The Czech official switched me with his stick and moved us on like cattle.

Then I saw a small crowd coming down the road, shouting, dragging a man on his knees. The official sighed and put his pen in his pocket: he looked, I thought, rather bored. He turned to face the crowd. "What have we here?"

A woman had taken a military jacket from a soldier and wore it over a white cotton blouse. She said: "Look at him. Collaborator! Pig!" She leaned forward, and spat in the face of the man.

"Show me," said the official.

"Show him," said the woman. The crowd loosed its grip on the captive who dropped to his knees. His head had been partially shaved. There were cuts on his arm in the shape of the swastika. He was not young. He raised his head, and helplessly I moved towards him, because it was Polizist Novák. His uniform was gone and so was his ruddy, benevolent look: he was bewildered and gaunt. I could not have said then, and cannot say now, why this policeman roused in me more pity and terror than the death of my father and the mutilation of my mother, but there was a sensation in my heart like the breaking of a twig underfoot. I said: "Novák!" but my voice was very quiet because my throat was dry, and he didn't hear me. The Czech official said, "Do you know this man? Who is he?"

Novák looked at me. He was empty as a burned building. Slowly I understood that I had his life in my pocket—that it was in my possession, like the stone I carried with me. If I called him Polizist Novák as my mother used to do, he would be damned for a German, as I was damned, and boys would come and tie cloths soaked in petrol around his neck and they would set him alight. If I called him Rotný Novák, he would be taken for a Czech, and he would be saved.

"Novák!" I said—and at that moment the morning sun was extinguished as if a great black cloth had been thrown over it.

There were no stars. Jackdaws descended from every quarter, disgorged from window ledges and chimney pots and other roosting places, all asking over and over *why? why? how? why?*, all looking brightly at me with blue eyes—and Melmoth was coming implacably down the street. She came not enclosed in a pillar of smoke but rimmed with light, with a bright, bluish light like that from a gas flame. Her robes lifted around her as she walked—thousands of yards, it seemed to me, of fine black cloth, so fine it ran like liquid into the gutters as she walked. Shadows shifted across her face and her eyes were wide and they were fixed on me. Her feet were bare and bleeding and the Prague streets were marked with footprints in blood. As she walked she left stillness in her wake: every woman and man she passed was arrested in the moment of her passing. I do not mean they were seized, like insects caught in amber—I might have preferred that. What I mean is that each went on doing precisely what they had been doing as she passed—that and only that—like damned souls hopelessly carrying out the same tasks over and over. So I saw a child in a doorway go on being struck with a woman's shoe; saw a girl go on being tormented by men that busied themselves under her skirt; saw a soldier go on being stripped of his clothes.

She came near and I smelt her then—sweet as lilies in summer, rotten as spoiled meat. I was not afraid. Had I not been waiting for her all my life—ever since I'd seen the farmer by the Eger leaving out his chair? She came slowly to me and she said nothing and then she fell to her knees at my feet. Her eyes hung in the bones of her face like spheres of smoky glass and they contained every wickedness imagined or acted on. Then she spoke and her voice was soft and appealing. "Josef!" she said, "what are you doing here—what do you think you will do?" She pointed at Novák, who groveled, and grunted, as if he might well go on groveling and grunting until the sun was extinguished for the final time. "Little Hoffman, have I watched you so long, only to leave you here in the street? Have I waited this long, only to see you burned before my eyes?"

I said, "How can I let him die? He is my friend."

"Your friend?" She stood, and she began to laugh, and I cannot say whether she towered above me or whether in my guilt and confusion I'd dwindled down until I was only an ant awaiting her heel. "Your friend?" she said. "And how do you treat your friends, little Hoffman—of what does your friendship consist?" All the inky robes trailing about her began to reach for me, as if they had a spiteful intelligence—they wrapped around me and I found I was in her embrace. Her arms were bolted iron gates. My cheek was against her breast and she was soft there and the scent of lilies was strong. She said, "Shall I show you where your friends are now? Shall I show you what your friendship does?" I began to faint against her until I was almost dreaming and in my dream I saw a railway track that ended at the gate of Theresienstadt and all around it no grass grew. I saw barracks emptied of their military men, and filled with children who had the faces of old women. I saw a boy with his head shaved for lice stoop to pick a horse chestnut from the gutter and saw him struck five times with a club for this breach of the law, and I saw a starved girl brought before the authorities because someone had heard her sing, and I knew this boy and this girl were Franz and Freddie Bayer. I saw many filthy bunks in a filthy room and in one of them the starved girl shook so that her iron bed rattled against the wall and someone brought her a dish of potato peelings to eat. Then I saw a train pulling carts like those for cattle along that railway track and I saw a hand coming out between wooden slats and the hand was bruised and I knew it, and I knew that I had rejected it and I knew hell waited where the track ended, and I knew that I'd helped build that hell as surely as if I'd put stone on stone. "Do you see, little Hoffman," the woman said, and her arms were a jail cell I have never left. "Do you see what you did to your friends?" Then I saw the girl in her iron bed and something like filthy water ran out of her mouth, slowly like rain running from a gutter pipe, and she had once worn pink satin under her school skirt and read books her mother had forbidden her and she had once danced with me as the radio played and she had liked her coffee with sugar and cream and she was sixteen years old and on the 19th of August 1942 she had been murdered not with passion or anger in the ordinary decent human way but by a great engine turning and I had been a cog in the machine.

Then Melmoth said, "Who else will know your wickedness, as I know it? Who else has seen what it is in your heart, as I have seen it? What if they knew, little Hoffman? What if they saw?"

I said, "I am damned, then."

"Damned! Oh yes: you are damned!" She released me, and began to laugh. "Don't you see what punishment awaits you?" I looked and everywhere I looked the punishments went on all around me, still burning, still tormenting, and I knew somewhere knives were being sharpened and they were knives meant for me.

"If I am punished, it would only be just," I said, but I did not feel courageous.

"Do flames burn less, because they are just? Are knives blunted because the cut is righteous? Do you think you will suffer less because of your sin?" She touched me and I felt a pain in my wrist. She had done nothing but put her forefinger on me, but it was as if my arm were pinned to the ground and someone had quietly and calmly crushed it with rocks. I discovered then that pain could obliterate everything that made me human and reduce me to something lower than an animal. I would have done anything to escape it—I would have bitten out my tongue—then she took away her hand, and the pain was gone. As I stood gasping in the street Melmoth did not tower over me any more. She was only as tall as I was tall and her eyes were cool and calm, and when she spoke to me it was shyly and quietly as if she were afraid I might turn and run. She said, "Josef, little one, little Hoffman"—she touched me again and her hand was small and soft on my arm—"Josef, don't you pity me? Have you never known what it is to be lonely? I am the one survivor of a wrecked ship adrift on a tideless sea! I am the sole star shining among all the burned-out galaxies! Who is there to bring me water when I'm thirsty? Who is there to answer when I speak?" I had never heard until then, and have never heard since, a voice more seductive, more appealing: I believe I would have hanged myself from the Bayer sign if she had asked me to. "Josef, my dear one, my heart," she said. "Come away with me now. Come away and be my companion. What is left for you but suffering? What is left but the just outcome of all your iniquity?"

I looked at Novák then. All the while Melmoth had been speaking he had simply gone on groveling there in the street—gone on bleeding, gone on sobbing, while all around him women and men went on looking at him with hard avaricious faces. I said, "But what then will become of Polizist Novák? How can I leave him here alone to be beaten in the street!"

Her voice was still more soft, still more appealing: she whispered against my cheek: "But what can you do? You are only a schoolboy—let it be! Ah, Josef, my dear, my longed for: *take my hand—I've been so lonely!*" She held out her hand and the temptation was like every hunger pang I'd ever felt tormenting me at once. If I took the hand she offered I could not say what lay in store, but it would not be this: the cruelty, the struck match, the child tormented in the doorway. I reached towards her and her face altered and I saw triumph in it, and a blue light shining in her smoky eyes. Then I put my hand in my pocket and felt the stone there. It had worn smooth from my touch and was heavy. I looked at Novák—I looked at the fires burning in the streets, and the child being struck with a woman's shoe—I looked at the officials with their sharpened pencils and their sheets of paper and I looked at the truck with its engine idling at the end of the road. I said, "No." It was the sole act of courage of my life. "No," I said. "I won't go with you. I will stay and help my friend."

Instantly she changed. All the softness and all the appeal left her and I was afraid. She was gaunt and tall and terrible to look at: her mouth was red and wide and her unblinking eyes flickered and blood pooled at her feet, and I saw how they bled from places where bone broke skin. "Stupid boy!" she said, and she was shrieking now, and jackdaws were all around her like flies around a dead dog: "Stupid boy! Do you think you can atone for all you've done? Do you think there's enough blood in you to settle the debt? I have seen your punishment—I have already been the witness!" I could not bear to hear more, or look at her—I closed my eyes and pressed my hands to my ears and when I took them away I heard a man's voice and the Czech official was impatient and he was saying, "Do you know this man? Do you know him? Who is he?" I looked. Melmoth had gone and it was morning again. It was morning, and the beaten child was toppled on the step and didn't move. It was morning, and my mother looked dully down at the wound in her heel. It was morning, and Novák was on his knees, and he was looking at me.

"I know him," I said. I ran forward and hit Novák hard and

when my hand came away there was blood between my fingers. "Traitor!" I said. I spat at him. "You betrayed your fatherland! You should hang!"

The official tapped his pen on his sheet of paper. "What do you mean? What do you mean, traitor?"

"He knew," I said. "Who lived there, in that shop. He knew they were Jews and he did nothing. Who knows what else he did?" I spat at him again. "Pig!" I said. "Traitor! Nothing but a dirty Slav!"

"Is this true?" said the Czech official. He said it mildly. Did I think Novák would look at me with gratitude? Did I think he would understand what it was I had done? The woman in her military jacket shook Novák and said, "Cat got your tongue, man? Is it true?"

Dumbly as a dazed animal Novák nodded and nodded. In Czech he said: "I am Rotný Novák. I did what I could. I did what I thought was right." The woman made a sound which was part boredom and part disgust, and released his collar. He pitched forward onto the street.

The official looked at his paperwork. He looked at Novák. He looked at the woman, and at the hard vengeful faces of the crowd. He might have been my father totting up the day's takings in the ledger. Then he shrugged and said, "His name is not here. Leave him, leave him." Then he looked at me with such contempt I've worn it like a brand ever since. "On you go," he said. So on we went, the little group of us, on to our punishment—my mother, limping, snuffling into the sleeve of her blouse, the man with the shaved head that bled from small cuts. Someone opened the doors of the truck at the end of the street. I looked back once. The crowd had begun to disperse. For the moment their anger was spent. Only one woman remained—young and very pretty, she wore a blue scarf in her hair. She stood beside Novák where he'd fallen and stirred at him with her foot as if he was just a pile of abandoned clothes. In the truck men and women and children sat quietly waiting. I was weak and someone had to help me in. There was no room for my mother. We drove away and left her there, waiting for somebody to come and tell her what to do. I never saw her again.

So in time I too was taken to Theresienstadt, where the few Jews remaining had been freed from the typhus and the squalor within its walls, and there I lived in confinement for nineteen months and thirteen days, with all the men and women who had shared my crime. At all times I wondered if I walked where Franz and Freddie Bayer walked, and if I suffered as they suffered, and considered all my sorrows and my pains little but an afterthought. But I make no record of it. Let them be the song, and I the dying echo.

Part 2

Karel Pražan
c/o John Bunyan House
Bedford

Dear Thea,

As you see, I am in England. It's cold, but not like the good
clean Czech cold. It is simply wet, as if the whole place has
been crying about something for weeks. For days I've been here
in this room with pink wallpaper you can wipe clean, and pink
curtains with a ruffle. Each morning the landlady makes toast
like squares of white wool made slightly warm, which we eat
with very thin sausages. I regret to tell you the English are not,
to my mind at any rate, pleasing to the eye. The women have
thick legs with bad circulation that makes the skin turn blue,
and all the men at every age wear jeans and anoraks. Certainly
I think you must be the best of your kind, as I have always
known.

My learned friend: I write to ask that you forgive me. I have
been mad. I should like to blame Melmoth but we both know
a man can't be sent mad by a children's story. Were you afraid I
believed she was real, and was coming for me? Maybe I thought
so sometimes. I was often drunk—I was always upset. My
friend died, Thea! And worst of all, you have gone. They say
love is not love, that alters when it alteration finds. Much as it
pains me to tell you that your English poets are wrong, how can
this be true? Love must change if its object changes. You don't
stand under a tree in winter when the branches are black and
admire its green leaves and its shade. No, I don't love you as I
did because you're not as you were. What I must know now is

whether you will let me learn to love the Thea that remains. Don't think I haven't thought of you every day. Are you taking your tablets? Write down your medicine in the notebook I kept, and all the times you take it. You are stronger than you think. You could dress yourself if you believed you could do it. Is Helen caring for you? She is cold I know but good at heart, or knows her duties, which is perhaps even a better thing.

So let me tell you what I did, and what I have been doing, and what I mean to do. When I left you I was confused and sick. What did we drink, Thea—how many bottles? Sometimes it seems to me someone was there—someone in black at the table pouring the wine and whispering terrible things to me while you slept in your chair—but of course it was only my thirst and all the Melmoth stories. I put things in my bag and got in a cab, and said to the driver: "I want to go to England." I had England all muddled up with how you once were, as if you might be waiting for me at arrivals with your collar turned up, and that smile which I'm certain is different from all your other smiles when it's only meant for me. I was sick in the cab and I had to pay him more for that. I had coffee at the airport and wrote you a card, and then I was on the plane and sick again, and the sickness cleared my head, so that when we landed I was almost myself again. It was past midnight. In England the airport was busy but also quiet and everywhere people were sleeping, so I put down my bag and thought I would sleep too, and in the morning decide what I should do. I put myself in a corner where I could smell coffee and the toilets being cleaned, and put my head on my bag and thought again of you, but then I heard a man shouting. All around me people were sitting up and looking around. Everybody is nervous these days, aren't they? The shouting wasn't angry. It was sad and hopeless and his voice was rough as though he'd been shouting for a long time, and knew nobody was listening, but all the same couldn't stop. I stood up and saw a black man with white hair walking in the way old Albína walks: swaying, like his hips didn't work. He had a chain around his waist. There was nothing around his wrists or his ankles, only his waist, and the chain went out in front of him and a white man, an Englishman I suppose, pulled him along like a dog. This man was not a policeman or a soldier: didn't have a uniform, or a hat, or a number on his shoulder. He wore a short-sleeved shirt and black trousers and a blue tie, and an identity card around his neck on a blue strap. Another man walked next to him and he had an identity card too on the same blue strap, but he had put it in his pocket. He had a clipboard and on this clipboard one sheet of white paper, which he looked at as if there were instructions written down and he wasn't sure what it was he was supposed to do. They walked quickly as if they were busy and ashamed, and they tugged and pulled at the chained man because he could only walk slowly, and because of this he shouted, "*Regardez-moi! Regardez-moi!*" The two men said nothing. It was as if they heard nothing at all, and I think what made me angry was that if they were not wearing the uniform of the police they must have been doing this terrible thing not for the law, but for money.

Thea, you know I've never been brave. I like to be comfortable and quiet—I like good shoes and excellent wine. But anger went up in me very fast and very hot, like lighting a match. How could these two men, who looked as if they had no more authority than someone come to read the gas meter, have such power? Then I saw coming close behind a group of

young people holding signs. There was a girl with a nose ring
and a pink scarf and two boys in checked shirts, and another
in a dirty coat. The signs said NO HUMAN IS ILLEGAL
and the young people and their signs looked helpless and useless. I asked if they'd spoken to the man, but of course they
had little French, and knew only his name, which was Michel,
and that he was being flown to Kinshasa and didn't want to go.
Suddenly—even there, even in the very bright concourse of a
London airport—I thought of Melmoth the Witness. I imagined her standing beside me with all her black robes winding
around her legs. I imagined I heard her breathing hard as if
she'd walked a long way to reach that place at that moment—
I imagined looking down and seeing her bare feet, and blood
under them, on the hard gray floor. All this seemed so real to
me that I was amazed when I looked up and there was nobody
there, just an English girl with a nose ring and a scarf and a
painted sign trying not to cry. So I ran forward and I walked
beside the chained man for a minute or two, spoke to him
in French and told him my name, and asked him who these
people were and what they were doing. He spoke to me quickly
as if he had it all stored up and now everything could come
pouring out. The men ignored me for a minute or two, but
then lost their patience and said, "Sir, I must ask you to step
back." I told them they were welcome to ask, but they had no
authority over me, and could not tell me who I could speak to,
and who I could not. They rattled the chain. They punished
him to punish me. He looked at me and his eyes were wide. He
lifted up his hands and I knew he was telling me that nobody
could help him now: that there was nothing anybody could
do. They pulled the chain again, sharply, like you pull the lead
of a dog that won't sit when it's told. Then I heard the English

girl shout that the police were here, and I saw two men and a
woman with weapons coming slowly down the concourse. They
didn't hurry. They looked bored. But their guns were huge and
black. So the flame of my anger went out shamefully quick.
I watched the police surround the man and he was shouting.
Then all of them were gone through a door that had no sign
on it, and I noticed there was a phone beside the door, the old-
fashioned kind with a coiled wire, and the receiver had been
taken off and was hanging right down to the dirty floor.

The young people with their signs came and spoke to me. I
liked them. They were full of energy and a kind of anger which
was somehow more excited than despairing, though God knows
there is always cause to despair. They had something I lost a
long time ago—the belief that they were doing what was right
and that if they failed this time they would win out in the end.
They asked me what the man had said. I told them he'd been
a mechanic, and that in the town where he lived he'd often be
beaten because they found out his lovers had all been men.
He was never beaten badly or until he thought he might die,
but so often and over so many years that his hips and his legs
were weak and stiff and his hands couldn't hold his tools, and
he couldn't work. He put up with it until a boy he loved had
been killed by his own mother, who was a pastor, and thought
him devil-possessed—so he came to England, but was kept
for months in a kind of jail until they told him he had to go
home. Once he had a fight with another man and because of
this he was marked as dangerous (I thought about the man in
the white shirt looking at the clipboard with its piece of white
paper), and so they pulled him through the airport on a chain,
even though he walked like an old man.

The girl with the nose ring started crying again. The others comforted her, and so did I, and they didn't seem to wonder who this old man was who patted her shoulder and gave her a handkerchief. They made me think of my students, who are so young and look at the road ahead of them happily, having no idea that the road narrows and turns back on itself, and goes through dark places, and is covered all over with things to trip you up and break your ankles. Then because they were young, and everything for them is possible and everything is easy, they took me with them to a fast-food place still open where the lights were very bright. They propped their signs against their chairs and ate fried chicken and began to plan what they'd do next. Oh, I see you laughing now as you picture me drinking Coke at a plastic table! But it all seemed natural and right. They'd mistaken me for someone good. They thought I cared, like they cared—they thought we were all of one mind. And because I have been mad, and lost—because you are gone— even, I think, because of Melmoth—I let myself be taken by the flood. It seems they are part of a student group protesting the detention of asylum seekers which (so they tell me) is neither legal nor just. Two have been handed suspended jail sentences for acts of civil disobedience; another broke his arm scaling a wall in Calais. Between them they speak Arabic and Farsi, a little German, a few phrases of French, a fair amount of Portuguese. That I myself speak four languages seems to them little short of miraculous. I asked them where they were going next, and they told me something was happening soon at a detention centre where women are kept. There would be hundreds of them, they told me, demanding it be closed and all the captive women set free. Many terrible things happened in there: girls who'd been raped as punishment in wars would wake in the night and find English men in their room watching while

they sleep, smiling or something worse. Sometimes women try
and hang themselves or jump from high places and are mocked
by the guards when they do. Often they don't understand how
it can be that they have done nothing wrong, but are impris-
oned, and this alone is enough to break their spirits and make
them mad. I thought of that poem you sometimes recited when
you were homesick for England—*Stands the Church clock at
ten to three, and is there honey still for tea?*—and wondered if
maybe the plane had taken a wrong turn and put me down in
some other country. Then I felt that anger again, the flare of
the match, and I welcomed it. It is much better than what had
been there before—just loss, loss, loss. The girl with the nose
ring wiped her eyes on the handkerchief I gave her and said,
"Come with us, why don't you?" And I said, "All right then."
There were no more trains for four hours. So we found a corner
and put down bags and coats and slept, and someone's head was
against my leg, and I didn't mind, and I didn't for one moment
think: what am I doing, Dr. Karel Pražan, on the floor of an
English airport, with a stranger's coat for a pillow?

So here I am. I can hear them talking downstairs: the landlady
asks us to keep the noise down, but we take no notice. I have
made a sign that says SET HER FREE. A coach is coming
and they say there'll be cameras and film crews waiting. Will
it be any use? I don't know. But I do know this. There is no
Melmoth, no wanderer, no cursed soul walking for two thousand years towards her own redemption—there is nothing to
fear in the shadows on Charles Bridge, in the jackdaws on the
windowsill, in the way the shadows on the wall seem sometimes
blacker than they should be (you are nodding—I know it—you
have felt these things too!). No, Thea, there is no Melmoth,

there is nobody watching, there is only us. And if there is only us, we must do what Melmoth would do: see what must be seen—bear witness to what must not be forgotten.

They are calling me down. Goodbye for now, my learned friend.

KAREL

Helen Franklin, forty-two, neither short nor tall, her hair neither dark nor fair; on her feet, shoes of patent leather with a wet cherry shine, and a garnet bracelet on her wrist. About her shoulders, a cashmere stole, very fine, very black, with camphor and lavender in its cobweb folds; falling from collarbone to foot, a dress which is too long and too large: a tissue of tulle and silk, with something of the Weimar in the ribbon about the hips, in the tarnished dazzle of sequin and jet. Garnet also in her ears, around her throat (draw a little closer and note, in the light of that one bare bulb, the oxblood gleam in the stones). In each corner of the room—crouched on the bed, say, or tucked behind her neatly hanging dressing gown—uninvited visitors. Josef Hoffman in his new school shoes, with a cobblestone worn smooth in his pocket; Alice Benet, from whose burned hand there comes, very faintly, the scent of branded skin. At the window, Sir David Ellerby in a plain cloth coat whispers to Freddie Bayer, who is pale, and thin, but all the same is singing. On the windowsill, a jackdaw paying court in the fashion of its kind; beyond the window, five floors down, a watchful figure. It stands very still, very quiet—there is about it an implacable patience which would frighten Helen, were she to look beyond the glass and see it.

There is a knock on the door. Here is Albína Horáková on her ninety-first birthday. She has abandoned her aluminium frame because it is not festive, and uses instead an ebony cane. It is insufficient: she grunts and shuffles on her worn-down hips and is breathless with the effort, but nonetheless her cheeks are flushed with a hectic good cheer and perhaps (let's say) a thimbleful of liquor. "Aha!" she says. She surveys Helen—she tilts her head, as the jackdaw does, and winks one glittering eye. "See?" she says. "Not so ugly after all, huh? You will want to thank me I know, but it's fine, it's fine, this is thanks enough, the sight of you. You like it? You like my garnets?"

They are not comfortable: they rasp at Helen's wrist and throat. "I like them," she says. And it is true: their beauty satisfies that part of her concealed beneath the bed; their discomfort satisfies her desire for punishment.

"And what do you think of me, eh?" Her left hand shaking on the ebony cane, her right hand graciously extended, Albína Horáková bows to a depth of perhaps six inches. She is in white. It is an extraordinary, a pristine white: it is the white of garments dried on rocks under equatorial suns. Her dress is certainly silk. It is heavy, and has a paper rustle. It stands out above stiff under-skirts and displays ankles gleaming in nylon above white buckled shoes. She wears, over her white silk dress, further white layers, within which Helen sees seed pearls, feathers, brooches of paste stones in silver settings. Above it all a velvet coat, snowy and thick, is fastened with buttons of ivory. What remains of her hair is clipped back with plastic pearls. Among all this her face is a walnut on a tablecloth. "Amazing," says Helen, because she is indeed amazed—it has never occurred to her that Albína possesses a single garment which could not politely be worn to a wake. She examines herself and finds that her loathing of the old woman, which has always had in it the sourness of disgust, has become merely dislike.

"Never much wanted to be a bride," said Albína. "Didn't have the stomach for it. Men, you know? Just big children pawing at you for this and for that and turning bad when they don't get it. Still"—she makes a small adjustment to this brooch, that ribbon—"it was the clothes I liked the look of; and if not now then never, eh?"

"I have a gift for you," says Helen, and takes something from the desk (in order to do so she must move aside Franz Bayer, who shakes his bare shaved head three times). "Here," she says, and passes over a bottle of scent in green paper.

"Is it that you think I smell, hm?" says Albína, having fumbled it free of its wrapping. The bottle is small. It looks cheap against the velvet, the ropes of seed pearls.

"You do, a little."

"Ha! You learning to tell the truth after all this time? All right, Helen Franklin, a spray for me and a spray for you, eh?" Helen is doused in jasmine water. The pleasure it gives her is troubling, and she is recalled to her need for penitence. What is she doing, dressed in cashmere and tulle, smelling of gardens at dusk, while rich sweet food and music is promised within the hour? She is revolted by her transgression, by how willingly she submits to small pleasures, and in contrition scratches her wrist and raises a welt on the skin. This does not pass Albína Horáková by. "What's the matter with you, eh, *myš*? Face like a bowl of whey. You don't want dinner? You don't want music? Well, no choice. Do as you're told." With the end of her cane she straightens the cashmere stole. "I know what it is. You think Melmotka's watching, huh? Why worry? What's to be done, if she's got her eye on you?"

The jackdaw on the windowsill is speaking. Helen cannot hear it, of course: these are well-made apartments, with no expense spared on the double glazing. But she can see its beak move and knows what it is saying: *why? why? how? why?*

Then: *who?*

• • •

Look—here is Prague's golden chapel, its fairy palace, sporting a gilded crown. The National Theatre, twenty feet east of the Bridge of the Legions; its pit, stage, flies and curtain paid for out of the pockets of peasants, beggars, governments and princes. High up on the gable a winged victory not dressed for winter weather bestows a laurel wreath on every passerby, while her three bronze horses hurl themselves in panic from the roof. Meanwhile in the auditorium whole pantheons of minor gods are employed to carry lamps and plaster wreaths, and in well-heated rehearsal rooms sopranos drink hot water with honey and wash their tights in the sink.

Over the road—over the icy cobbles, the tram tracks, the discarded tickets for the Torture Museum down on Celetná Street—Helen Franklin sits at a marble table and surveys her dining companions. Here is Albína Horáková, whose white garments have somewhat lost their lustre in the arduous journey on the Metro; she is pressing rouge from a tarnished compact into her gaunt old cheeks and has drunk two glasses of Bohemia *sekt*. Here is Thea, whose chair has been folded against the wall. She is sombre in a pleated dress shirt and someone has cut her curls. She looks rather young, very serious: a pageboy intent on his work; nonetheless it seems to Helen that her recent grief has lost some of its sharpness. Seated beside her, chair drawn solicitously close, is the young woman Adaya, who has made no concession at all to the festivity of the occasion, save that her blouse this evening has a faint blue stripe. (Her uninvited arrival—pushing Thea's chair, a little shyly, across the threshold; smiling, more shyly still, at Helen in her trailing dress—delighted Albína Horáková, who can sniff out a fresh victim at fifty paces or fewer. "What've you got here then, eh, Thea? Replaced Karel quick as you like, I see! She looks like a nun, eh, but one who might change her mind. *Ano, ano,* sit then,

I like your face, better than the little mouse here. I've seen enough of that, haven't I? Ha!")

The habitual surliness of the attending waiter is tempered by the sight of these four women. Albína in her white velvet coat is coquettish and voluble, making girlish requests for another candle, another bottle in a silver bucket, the dishes of food she has ordered in advance. There is brawn set in aspic and garnished with thyme, and bowls of beef broth and liver dumplings in which leaves of parsley float. Baskets of rye bread have the scent of caraway; little dishes of butter soften in the heat. It is early, but a man in a white dinner jacket is merry enough to sit at the grand piano and play, with charming ineptitude, an Austrian waltz that slides soon into familiar songs: delighted, all his nearby companions lift bottles of beer and sing. Over the road the National Theatre is lit entirely gold, as if Midas brushed it as he bustled past on his way to kingly business elsewhere.

"Well: I have news," says Thea. She looks commandingly at her companions. "It is Karel," she says.

Helen looks at her glittering eye, at her smooth brushed cap of golden hair, and concludes that Karel Pražan has not, for example, been found on the banks of some distant river, walked to his death by the Witness.

"I have had a letter," says Thea. "Karel is in England. In—and Helen alone will understand my amusement—in Bedford." Helen adjusts the garnets pricking at her neck, and cannot help but laugh.

"What's more," says Thea, "he has fallen in with a group of students, and has decided that his lot in life, for the moment at least, is to protest the unlawful detention of migrants—Helen, are you choking? You should have a glass of water." Helen drinks the glass of water that Adaya hands her. It is so absurd—Karel Pražan, with his fondness for fine tailoring, his distaste for unease, discovering a social conscience in some previously unopened compartment of his mind—that she cannot suppress her delight.

Thea tears a piece of bread and the scent of caraway rises from the table. "He says: there is no Melmoth—there is no one to witness what's done these days—and so he will simply have to do it himself."

"But why?" Adaya frowns. She flushes, very faintly, and butters Thea's bread. "What use is it? What good does it do, to watch?"

Thea loses for a moment her newly acquired merriment. "I don't know," she says. She is frowning. "But perhaps he feels he must do his duty, even if no good will come of it." Then she turns towards Helen. "You haven't slept," she says. Her breath is sweet with brandy. "Melmoth, was it?"

Helen looks up, and there is Josef Hoffman at an adjoining table, very old, making marks on his manuscript. "Something like that." She presses her hands on the marble table, which is very cool. Then she says: "Someone is following me."

"Helen," says Thea. She looks both reproving and secretly, maliciously thrilled. "I didn't think you'd fall for it like Karel did—you, of all people! Oh, it's distressing, I know, those stories, but hardly worse than the morning papers, and Melmoth herself—" she pauses.

"You see!" Helen, laughing, taps her hand (on it, Thea wears a silver ring in the form of a grinning skull on which an industrious bee is perched). "You see! You can hardly bear to say the name yourself!" She allows herself a spoonful of beef broth, and Josef Hoffman goes on writing in the margins of his document.

"No, it's not Melmoth," says Helen (though I wonder if you saw how swiftly, how secretly, she looked up at the open door?). "But Thea: someone is following me."

"Dip in your bread, like this!" says Albína, thickly buttering a slice; then raises her glass to the piano player and begins to sing.

"Come now, Helen!" Thea is amused: and really, who can blame her? Helen Franklin, buttressed on all sides against disruption, against emotion, against intrusions of any kind into her ordered days, hearing Melmoth at her heels!

"You have soup on your shirt. No, not Melmoth—of course not: do you think I can't tell what's myth and what's real?—but somebody, all the same. I hear them behind me, when I walk out of the library, when I come to see you—they wait round corners, they wear black, sometimes they sing; I don't know if it's a man or a woman or even a child, but it frightens me. I wake frightened in the night and read about Josef Hoffman or Alice Benet and in the morning they are there with me in the room." It is as much as she has ever confessed, even to Thea, whose genius for eking out confidence has been refined over two decades on her feet by the witness box. "Of course in the night I think: perhaps it's her, perhaps she has come for me, but, well." Another spoonful of broth. "We all have nightmares."

Adaya dips the corner of a napkin in a glass of water and wipes at the soup on Thea's shirt. She allows it. Adaya says, in her perfect and faintly accented English, "I once heard a mother in a playground tell her child, 'Watch out for Melmotka, she knows you took my purse, she has her eye on you.' Very cruel, I thought. I don't think Melmotka comes to take children from their mothers. She is not a monster."

"Then you know little about her," says Thea. "Leave my shirt alone! I am not an infant! You know nothing about her—she is a drowning woman who wants only to pull you under . . ."

Adaya puts the napkin down. "Don't you pity her?" she says. "Wouldn't you long for company if you were so lonely? Wouldn't you, Helen?" Her look of shy appeal reaches Helen irresistibly.

"Oh, perhaps," she says.

"I think," says Thea, through mouthfuls of bread, "we may safely say it's not a damned soul on bleeding feet that chases you through the town. Who, then?"

Albína Horáková, removing her coat, sheds seed pearls on the table. They scatter among the silver forks and rattle on the plate. "Look at my empty glass!" she says. "No manners in the young." Then she nudges Helen and says, "She's got a past, this one. Thinks I don't notice, little English *myš* with her hair like water in a ditch! Thinks I don't see how she sleeps without sheets and won't eat sweet things and scratches her wrists when she thinks I'm not looking. Made them bleed once. I noticed, yes! You hiding, Helen Franklin? You got something to hide?"

Josef Hoffman is not alone. Here is Alice Benet, turning the pages of her bible; here is Franz Bayer beckoning to someone just outside the window. One by one they turn to Helen, who closes her eyes.

"I suppose," says Adaya—gently, softly, passing Thea a glass of water—"nobody has ever lived who didn't keep something in their pocket out of sight."

"Not me," says Albína, and without warning delivers a gleeful belch. It is greeted with applause from men in suits eating pork at a window table. "This Melmoth, she'd have no interest in old Albína Horáková who never hurt a fly—yes, *milá ku*, yes: clear the plates." A waiter with white sleeves rolled to the elbow bends over the table.

"What about Thea then, eh? What about you? You think Melmotka is waiting at home, on your bed, with your name on a piece of paper?"

Helen—eyes open, Josef Hoffman mercifully gone—is grateful to feel Albína's blue gaze move on. She says, "Yes, Thea: what about you? What sins do you have to confess?"

Frowning, Thea says, "I sometimes wish that she were real—that she had come for me before all this"—she shows them the splints on her wrists—"before Karel went, while I was still myself; I might have preferred to wander alone with the damned than find I am no longer loved."

The man at the piano has worn himself out, or got suddenly weary with beer; he's leaning on the music rest, forehead on forearm, not hearing the calls from his friends. It is quiet now. Helen says, "You are not changed; not really," and she believes it because she must. She watches the table filled again with food: veal schnitzel, very fragrant and gold, with almonds broken in the crust; pieces of dark beef garnished with cranberries and cream; potato salad and milk-white dumpling fatly sliced on the plate. There are gherkins. There is more bread, hot from the oven, with yeast rising on furls of steam. The butter in the dish has melted. Helen, who has not eaten herself to satisfaction in twenty years, feels faint at the sight of it. "You don't fool me," says Thea, smiling. "And I don't think you are fooled. Illness like this—" she shrugs. "You think I'm not changed? You think it's like I used to drive a decent car, and this one has a flat tyre? It is the passenger that changed, not just the vehicle! Still"—another shrug, and this a careless valiant one. "I suppose the trick is to acquaint myself with myself."

"Do you despair?" says Adaya. It is a curious question, very direct, and asked with a blush, as if she thinks she might be violently rebuffed. Beef parts softly under her knife. She puts a piece on Thea's plate and says, apologetically, "So often, people do."

Thea accepts the plate, the question, a glass of wine. She says, as if with surprise, "No, I don't think I do. I wonder if I should."

"Enough of this talk!" says Albína. "You think you know suffering? You wait and see what time does to your bones and come speak with me about suffering then. Sometimes I hear mine grind like stones! I watched my mother dry out like a landed fish in the sun. Now her hands are my hands. Helen, eat, for pity's sake. You think you'll choke if you do?" And indeed the veal is irresistible: Helen takes a bite. (Jackdaws are convening on the National Theatre roof; musicians are convening in the pit.) "Come now, Thea," she says. "If Melmoth were watching what sin would she know—what would she have seen?" On her white clothes there is now gravy, flecks of parsley, a cranberry gleaming like a jewel on a scrap of Guipure lace.

"The very worst?"

"I expect," Adaya says, "it was when you were very young. So often it is."

"Helen, make them stop," says Thea. But she brightens and straightens with a clumsy flourish the napkin in her lap. "I didn't always have money. My mother brought me up on her own in a two-room flat on a miserable North London road. You have never seen a more dispiriting place, all pebble-dashed houses black with pollution, and I thought I should have dwelt in marble halls, as the old song goes (Helen, you're pale—have more wine, I would). She worked long shifts cleaning council offices and there was never enough to go round. By the time I was ten she looked sixty. I hated it. The woodchip wallpaper. The two-ring stove. I hated the fire with the three electric bars and the brown tiles all around it. I wanted a pair of leather boots that laced up to my knees and I wanted a white dressing gown I could wear straight out of the bath, and my initials stitched on the pocket. I wanted records and something to play them on. I wanted the right kind of clothes, not always very slightly the wrong ones." There are chandeliers overhead, and beneath them Thea is queenly, serene: her cropped hair is threaded with copper wires, the silver bee gleams on her hand. It is impossible to place her in dingy rooms with windows blackened by passing cars. "I knew that I would be all right, in the end: I had a good mind and I knew I would see to it that if I didn't dwell in marble halls it would at any rate not be a house with a stain on the ceiling of every room. But I'm not patient now and I wasn't then. I wanted money almost more than anything. Sometimes girls at school had five-pound notes and I didn't see the queen's head on blue paper: I saw lipstick in gold cases and velvet jackets with velvet buttons and hand cream that smelt of roses in a pot with a silver lid. So I began to steal. My mother kept a notebook where she wrote down everything she spent and everything she earned. She kept her money in a biscuit tin: the purple kind with flowers printed on—you remember, Helen? You got them at Christmas every year and they lasted months until they all went stale. Every day, almost, I took coins out. Just ten pence, sometimes. Once I took a pound coin. Do you know, I wasn't the least bit guilty? I acquired a conscience much later on. I simply thought: well, if you didn't want me to steal, you shouldn't be so poor. I remember always having money in my pocket. It's heavy, isn't it? The weight of metal."

Helen does not like this admission of a small, mean transgression. It would be somehow more likeable, and certainly more glamorous, if her friend had, say, killed a dog in a fit of temper.

"I wanted a suede jacket for my birthday, with fringes at the back. I'd seen how much they cost and I knew it would always be beyond my mother but I wanted to punish her for making me poor. On the morning of my birthday she made eggs on toast, and she gave me a gift—a book, I don't know what. She'd wrapped it very carefully, I know that. She had bought red ribbons. She had never done that before. I opened it and said, 'I don't want this. You know what I wanted. Didn't you listen? Don't you care?' She cried, but then she cried so easily in those days it didn't bother me. She told me she had been saving for something special, but that she never seemed to have quite enough—that she tried to make a note of everything she earned, but had made a mistake somewhere. All the time, of course, I could feel the money I had stolen in my pocket, getting heavier and heavier, because I never spent it."

"Horrible!" Albína is delighted. "Horrible child!" She eats a mouthful of beef and mops up gravy with bread.

Adaya, hands folded in her lap, says, "Do you think you have been punished?"

Thea gestures with a rare hard flash of anger to her legs, which are wasted these days beneath the fine wool cloth of her trousers—to the well-shod feet which never rest quite as they should on the floor. "What do you think? And do you think the punishment is fitting?"

"Still," says Helen. She feels a perverse enlarging of affection for her friend. She had never thought, when first meeting Thea—first seeing her competence, her expansiveness, the apparently fathomless depths of her generosity—that she, too, was a sinner. "Still: if Melmoth sought out every scheming little thief in North London she would hardly be lonely."

Adaya smiles, blushes, touches Thea lightly on the wrist. "I think so," she says. "I think we might rule you out: unless, of course, you have secrets too dark for the dinner table."

Albína, scoffing, says: "You think that's a bad thing? Listen to this. I killed a man with a hatpin. There, that put the dog among the pigeons!" There is no need, now, for the rouge that sits on the tablecloth in its tarnished case; her cheeks are flushed with wine, with meat, with delight. "You think Melmotka would trouble herself with this English mouse, this cripple? This girl with a face like a saucer of milk? When she comes, she'll come for the murderer!"

Ten yards distant someone drops a silver tray: it spins and rattles on the floor and wakes the man who slumbers at the piano.

He starts, snorts, wipes his mouth on his sleeve: begins idly to play a waltz. The many chandeliers overhead shine on the windows, so that everything beyond the glass is obscured save the National Theatre sailing adrift in the darkness. (If I were to turn out the lights, just for a moment, you might well see—there on the steps of the National Theatre, leaning on a white stone pillar—a watchful figure, seeming weary, with eyes fixed on the dining women.)

"I don't believe you," says Helen, lightly and coolly, because she has begun to feel nauseated. *Murderer*, said Albína Horáková, and the food on her plate is viscous, thick, with something of the scent of the slaughterhouse in the fibers of the meat; *murderer*, she said, and the wine glass in her hand is fragile, and would break if she pressed it; *murderer*, she said, and here is Josef Hoffman, here is Alice Benet, here is Freddie Bayer, and they are beside her on the leather seat, very attentive and very close.

"I believe you," says Adaya. Hesitantly, she brushes a fragment of meat from Albína Horáková's sleeve.

"Tell us," says Thea. "In comparison my own soul will be white as snow, I'm sure."

"Not much to tell." Albína shrugs. "You girls, what do you know? I've seen tanks coming over the Bridge of the Legions so often I forget what year, whose tanks. I heard about the Old Town Square burning while I worked a shift in the Škoda factory and hadn't had good food in months. What do you know—anything you want, you get." She snaps her fingers; a waiter comes, and is despatched with a squeeze of his arm to bring more and better wine. "You know the happiest days of my life? The day each month they let three books from the West come into Czechoslovakia. Just three! Imagine! It was always a Thursday. Up we got at dawn to queue in the cold and not a complaint between us. You think you suffer? Hah!" She chuckles without malice, and eats a piece of dumpling.

"But the hatpin?" says Adaya, in her hesitant way. She has eaten very little; there is nothing on the crisp striped breast of her blouse.

"Ah, that. My friend and I, we took a cab home one night. It was raining, hard, our shoes were new. The driver went a different way, and a different way, and a different way. 'Where are you going?' we said. He didn't say anything, went a different way again. Well, we'd heard of these things. I had a hat with a hatpin and I took it out and I stabbed him! Like this!" She prods Thea on the shoulder. "Hard, very hard! Well, it was raining: he couldn't see, could he? Came off the road, straight into a shop. It was a shop selling, you know, mops, vacuum cleaners. Funny what you remember. We were fine, though my friend's nose never looked right after, but she was ugly anyway and it didn't matter. But he broke both his legs. Got an infection, died in hospital two months later. Serves him right, eh! Now what do you make of that?"

"To be perfectly frank," says Thea, "I am disappointed. I'd hoped for a charge of wounding with intent, at the very least."

"Then"—Adaya picks one by one the scattered seed pearls from the table—"we can safely rule you out, I think? We can say: you are acquitted from the court of Melmotka."

There is another of Albína Horáková's shrugs. It dislodges a feather from a swan pinned on her shoulder. "Ah well, what life have I left to give her? A year, a month. Perhaps a day. Thea, give me your glass: we shall toast our innocence, *ano*?"

Obediently Thea raises her glass. "Now," she says. "Melmoth the Witness versus Helen Franklin, in the court of King Wenceslaus in the lands of the Bohemian Crown. Dear Helen—dear good little Helen, so calm, so considered: who never says a word out of place! What can her sin be?"

Do you see—there beyond the shining window, coming down from the steps of the National Theatre; coming over the road, the tram tracks, the gleaming cobblestones; coming closer, with a steady implacable tread, with a head withdrawn inside a soft black hood, a watchful figure at the door? Well, perhaps: the chandeliers are dazzling on the glass, the streets seethe and bustle, there are lovers on the Bridge of the Legions. Certainly Helen sees nothing, because she has closed her eyes and is looking down a corridor. It is lined with cheap green tiles. At the end, in the wall, there is a place where a door has been taken from its hinges. On the threshold there is an empty chair with a shadow on the seat; beyond the shadow, a room which is very hot, and very dark. She opens her eyes, and sees there all her companions: Albína Horáková, from whose shoulders snowy feathers fall; Thea with her pageboy's hair, the *memento mori* on her hand; Adaya, who goes on removing from the table the seed pearls that are tossed among the plates. There also is Josef Hoffman, and he is young, and he is watching Franz and Freddie Bayer as they dance beside the piano.

"Do you think you can?" says Adaya. She has a handful of pearls. "Do you think you can tell us?"

Can she? It is not fair to say that she is being asked merely to tell a secret. It is as if she is required now to excise a piece of her flesh and place it on the table, where it may be scrutinized, anatomized, taxonomized, before being returned to her body: packed in, closed up, stitch by stitch. It has so long demanded the constant mortification of body and spirit—the constant denial of pleasure, of richness, of emotion: of everything that might be said to have conspired with her to do what she did— that to tell the tale seems as impossible as a disruption in a planetary orbit.

But: "I should like to know," says Adaya, and says it with that hesitant, appealing look from behind her glasses, so that Helen—palms pressed against the cold marble table; eyes averted from Josef Hoffman's dour young face—overhears herself saying, as if from a great distance: "When I was twenty-one I left home and traveled to Manila. I'd never really been abroad before—"

The Sin of Helen Franklin

She was woken at dawn by a cock crowing on a tin roof ten feet down. This was not some country yokel strutting for the hens, but a prize fighter fitted with steel claws upon whose bad temper small fortunes were gambled and lost. On waking she dislodged from her forearm the busy cockroach nymph which had been dining on the salt on her sweat-doused skin; it bolted for the corner where it hid among the corpses of siblings dispatched with a slipper at midnight. The ceiling fan stirred the air as a spoon stirs soup. She had been in Manila a month, but felt each morning as if she'd been deposited there only five minutes previously owing to an inaccuracy in some celestial paperwork. The whole undertaking, she reflected, had been to show that she could butt up against the constrictions of her parents: to demonstrate that for all the smallness of their lives, and the smallness with which they'd assumed she would be content, she could live more widely, more intemperately. As it turned out, it had done little but create in her a longing to be back behind the pebble-dashed walls of her Essex home, with nothing more strange beyond the double glazing than a jay among the bedding plants.

Pressing idly at the cockroach bite, she stood. It was a June day before the rains, and so humid that her satchel hanging against the wet walls bloomed with mold which could never be quite cleaned off. Between the greasy slats of the lowered blind she saw the hazy sky, and against it the thicket of power lines descending from a pole to the sprawl of shacks in the shanty town below. Litter blown up from littered pavements hung from the wires like filthy laundry: black bin bags in flapping rags, colored scraps of cloth. The crowing cock met the cries of vendors in the street below, and the ten-lane roar of Aurora Boulevard in the middle distance, elevated high above the city on its concrete stanchions. Beneath it all there was the very faint sound of singing, which might have come from any quarter. She felt as unguarded then as she had on her arrival: her eyes contracting against the sun, which had a vehemence no English heatwave could conjure even at noon; her throat a little sore from the polluted pall that gave Manila Bay its famous sunsets. Eleven months remained of this—of standing beneath a shower that did not work, and had never worked, to wash with water sluiced from a plastic dustbin with a plastic ladle; of using a toilet that did not work, and had never worked, and flushing it with an inexpert toss of that same plastic ladle from that same bin. Was it a disaster? (She spied the cockroach nymph, and having no slipper to hand crushed it with her bare heel.) She could not bring herself to think so, since that would be to admit that after all she was her mother's daughter: that unfamiliar constellations above unfamiliar lands were not for the likes of her.

A month after graduating—modest library of German set texts consigned to an attic, their pages curling in the damp— she had encountered an advert in a student newspaper: *Assistant Aid Worker sought, Quezon Aid Foundation, Manila. Experience of teaching languages desirable, twelve months fixed-term contract, apply online.* Manila? How utterly unsuited she was to bolting across the globe on a whim! And yet (there was that familiar, seething, furtive sensation; the notion, never confessed to anyone, that she alone was being watched by a loving and attentive eye)— might she? That night she studied a map of the Philippines, with its look of a donkey's head composed of many small pieces; looked up its national language, with its composition of Spanish and native dialect. It seemed to her impossibly charming to find that one's senior by so much as a fortnight should be addressed as *Kuya* or *Ate*: elder brother, elder sister. The nape of her neck pricked. She felt herself like a dumb-seeming but restless sheep which had suddenly spied a gap in the hedge.

What, then, had she expected—some indolent tropical city, growing out of the stones of the Spanish colonies: palms in the garden, unfamiliar spices, men for whom her weak-tea English face was compelling? What she discovered was this: that a foreign country is both more foreign and more familiar than the traveler imagines. It was foreign, but in ways for which daydreaming in her Essex bedroom could never have prepared her: the barefoot child selling mango dipped in salt from a high chair on the street with a boil on his scalp the size of a calamansi lime, the mere fact of the heat, the shopping malls kept cool to allow the wealthy to wear their furs, the shanty towns that had a strong scent of washing powder: these things left her reeling. But in the particulars it was somehow very ordinary. The traffic was heavier in the mornings, and pop songs drifted up from karaoke machines in the shanty towns; teenage girls in plaid school skirts sat laughing on walls eating chips, and the photocopier in the charity's office jammed most often when deadlines were most pressing. It depressed Helen, who felt it proved beyond doubt that she herself was so ordinary, so circumscribed by appearance and parentage, that—even so far from home a new moon tilted at an odd angle—her life could never be anything but narrow.

Scratching the bite on her arm, and thinking nothing of it, she left her flat. Above her on a balcony her neighbor grated coconut into a plastic bowl and sang along to the radio. Helen attempted her Tagalog—"*Magandang umaga Ate! Kamusta na po ang anak nila?*—Good morning! How is your son?"—and waited, smiling, for the lengthy response, then struck out for Aurora Boulevard. She taught English to the nineteen girls that lived in the Q.A.F.'s well-appointed home, and found her duties easy. She knew herself to be looked on with faint pity (sometimes they pinched her cheeks in fondness, and found them disappointingly thin) but also with ardent affection. They admired the earrings she wore, and her long cotton skirts; they tried to curl her hair, and praised her if she sang.

That afternoon, in the long and sleepy hour when work of any kind was impossible, since the heat seemed to thicken one's blood to paste, one of the older girls flicked Helen on her elbow. "Look, *Ate* Helen, what's this, eh? You got bit and it's gone bad."

"Just another mosquito bite." But Helen looked at her forearm doubtfully. It no longer itched, but had swollen and developed a scarlet rim. It looked, she thought, as if she had acquired another nipple, as witches were said to do.

"No, no, *Ate*! *Ipis, di ba?* Cockroach! Dirty! My uncle, he had one, bit him right here"—the girl gestured to her neck—"went very bad, very very bad. You need penicillin. You got money, *Ate*? You better, *di ba*!"

Helen pressed an experimental finger against the scarlet spot. It emitted a single droplet of pus. "All right," she said. "Maybe tomorrow. Now thirty minutes' sleep, please, then we do our verbs." On her way home she bought from a street vendor a warm bag of *pancit* noodles, and ate them on the balcony, feeling her blood beating in the bite. That night she shook the small fridge in the corner to scare out the cockroaches biding their time beneath it, and killed thirty-nine with the sole of her shoe.

The following evening she discovered on her arm a swollen place the size of her palm, the centre of which had opened up, creating a small uneven cavity. It was as if the heat and the dense wet air accelerated all the mechanisms of her body so that a degradation of the flesh which in England might have taken a month had happened overnight. If she clenched her fist, pus trickled sluggishly out. In one of the alleys beneath Aurora Boulevard, she knew, there was a pharmacy: she'd seen its green light shining from her window. The accepted wisdom of the English traveler was this: keep to the familiar routes. But what harm could come from a detour of no more than a hundred yards, when her arm throbbed and ached? Nonetheless she shivered in the shadow of the great road roaring and whining overhead: here cheerful shanty towns with their scent of laundry powder and of noodles on the stove gave way to single beggars squatting on squares of cardboard, or little groups of men, in vests drawn up over sweating stomachs, that fell silent as she passed. It was all filthy, with the filth of humans and machines living an uneasy truce, and she saw for a shocked moment a broad fissure in the concrete in which someone had been sleeping. A stump of candle burned on a ledge; black cloth dripped from the gap. The heat was appalling—it was a punishment: red welts were raised on the flesh of her thighs and rubbed to bleeding with each step, and the sweat that poured into her eyes was as salty as the sea. She cradled her swollen arm against her breast, and hurried on—past a naked infant, past a squatting woman sorting beer-bottle caps and murmuring. She reached the pharmacy in tears, though the tears were not precisely about the aching bite, the naked child, the heat: they seemed to have more to do with a feeling that all her life she had tried to outrun the disappointment at her heels, and at last it had caught her up. She stood for a moment in light cast on the pavement by the green cross shining above the shuttered window, heard laughter above the remorseless good cheer of pop songs on the radio, and pushed open the door. A schoolgirl sat cross-legged on the counter chewing sugar cane. She looked wryly at Helen, who felt more than ever that she was shabby and small and ill-equipped. The girls said, to nobody, "*Americana Siya.*"

"I am not American," said Helen. "I'm English." She shivered in the thin cool air of the shop. The girl attended to her sugar cane, and hummed along to the radio; it seemed she had lost interest. Behind the counter, between cheap metal shelves stacked with paracetamol, diarrhoea medication and face-whitening cream, strips of blue plastic fabric hung in a doorway. They moved, as if someone had just passed through. In a distant darker room beyond them someone in a white shirt stood. Is it possible that Helen felt, as she pressed a finger to the wound on her arm and watched a thick green fluid rise up, that a pair of watchful eyes was on her then—as it seemed there'd been when she was young, and walked home from school, with the strap of her satchel biting her shoulder? Certainly there was that telling prick at the nape of her neck, like that of a prey animal crouching in long grass; but then the room was cold, and the air moved across her. A young man came out to greet her. His shirt was buttoned to the neck; in his pocket, a biro had begun to leak. He wore his hair rather long, and had combed it into a parting which might have given him a look of severity had he not been smiling as he came through, and had he not gone on smiling when he saw his visitor. "*Magandang gabi*, ma'am," he said, bidding her a good evening; but she felt at once that the "ma'am" was not the unearned deference which so often came her way because she was white, but was largely ironical. He shook the schoolgirl a little roughly, and said something that made her laugh, and leap down, and go out giving Helen a pert, amused look.

"Can you help me?" said Helen. "I need someone to tell me what to do." She was conscious of speaking more crisply and more slowly than she ought, and fretted that the man would notice, and be affronted; and indeed it seemed he did notice, since he responded with a swift fluidity she took as a rebuke.

"Of course! The pharmacist is not here until the morning, but I am in training, and we have everything you might need. Are you sunburned? It's often sunburn, with tourists."

"I am not a tourist!"

"No?" He took a pair of glasses from his pocket, and put them on.

"I work at the Q.A.F.—the Quezon Aid Foundation," she said, then wished she hadn't: he raised an eyebrow, and smiled, and said, "OK. That's very good of you."

There was silence. Helen looked at him, and could not remember what it was that had brought her here. Then the radio began to play a song which she recognized—it was a more than usually foolish one, and it made each smile at the other, as if to say: *it's awful, isn't it, but don't you know all the words?*

"All right then," said the young man, briskly, returning his glasses to his pocket. "What can we do for you?"

"It's this," said Helen. She came forward, and placed her forearm on the counter as if it were an object she had been carrying and was glad to set down. In the bright bluish light of the shop her skin looked sick. The infected bite had spread, it seemed, in the brief time of her standing there: it was possible to make out a single thread of scarlet extending towards her wrist.

The man grasped her wrist and drew her arm towards him. He rolled it this way and that, the better to inspect the wound; it was both intimate and absolutely disinterested, and Helen was conscious that she was holding her breath.

"Something bit me," she said. "A cockroach?"

"Sure thing," he said. "This needs cleaning. Want me to do it for you? I have hydrogen peroxide. Then maybe some penicillin. You'll be fine." He reached for a large white bottle, and held it out inquiringly. Helen mutely nodded, and watched as he sluiced the liquid into the swollen cavity. It hissed, and stung; he did it again, and she saw the cavity grow a little larger. It seemed impossible to query or resist. He sealed the bottle and said, "You probably have streptococcus. You should have penicillin. The pharmacist would say the same. Does it make you sick?"

"No, it doesn't," said Helen; then she said, stumblingly and shyly, "Thank you, *Kuya*."

Delighted, he laughed. "You're welcome! You think you are younger than me? I don't know, you seem old, because you are quiet. Tell me your age."

"Twenty-one."

"OK then, little sister! I am twenty-three, *di ba*." He laughed again. "You are the first American to call me *Kuya*. I like it! You can come back here, any time."

"I am not American—I am English," said Helen, laughing because he was laughing. Then the man frowned, as if an unseen hand had reached out to admonish him. He nodded at her arm, which still lay on the counter between them. "You must drain it, you know? Squeeze, hard. It'll hurt, but it's only pain. Throw away the tissues, or whatever. I'll give you penicillin, three times a day, seven days. Then it's just a scar, and you go home and say to your friends: see, I was in the tropics and was bitten by a snake, or maybe a lion. Excuse me." He went behind the plastic curtain and Helen stood alone in the shop. It occurred to her that her face had begun to ache, and because she had been smiling so much; she tried to be decently sombre, but found she could not. When he returned, he held a paper bag. "In here you have some dressing, some tape and lint, and your penicillin. Don't forget you must take them all, right? Even when it's better."

Helen paid, feeling obscurely transgressive for having acquired medication without a doctor's intervention, and taking the paper bag said again, "Thank you. I was worried, but now I'm not."

"You're welcome. Come back and tell me how it is, yes? We can get you a doctor, if things go bad."

"Thank you, *Kuya*," said Helen at the door.

"Goodbye, little sister! Goodbye."

When Helen Franklin walked back under the filthy shadow of Aurora Boulevard, she almost thought she saw, deep in that candle-lit break in the city concrete, a figure all in black—in long robes of black, very odd in that broiling heat—but gave it no more than a glance, because something had lightened in her, and caused her to hold up her head and walk home singing.

When she returned to the pharmacy it was proudly done, to show the young man the diminished scarlet circle on her arm, and the healing wound. In the days that had passed since her first visit she had been astonished to find that the city—even the vile black rags hanging from the sagging power lines, and the reek from the drains—had begun to charm her. At night she stood sucking the sugared flesh from tamarind seeds on her balcony and could make out, in the distance, the bloom of the pharmacy light beyond the ranks of tilting shacks. The mere presence of the man whose name she did not know rippled out across the city, as if she'd seen a precious stone dropped into a muddy pool. She looked at the blue-white flesh of her wrist, and at the tendons moving there, and marvelled that he had touched it. In comparison to that single exchange over the counter—*elder brother, little sister!*—the two boyfriends with whom she'd dutifully shared her college bed seemed nothing more than charmless children. Of course it was absurd, but no more than Rilke had promised in her small Essex bedroom, while her mother boiled frozen peas downstairs.

Outside the pharmacy, a schoolgirl stood. "Hello," said Helen, who recognized her scathing look, the way she ate her piece of sugarcane. This time two friends were with her: each looked Helen up and down, and laughed. Helen flushed. The girl relented, and said, "He's in there, ma'am. He's in there. You want to see him, right?" Her friends laughed again. Overhead the green light flickered. Helen pushed open the door. He was standing at the counter with his back to her, and at the sound of the opening door he made a hasty movement out of sight. Then he turned and she saw that in the intervening days he had changed. The neat line of his parting was awry, so that hair fell into his eyes, which were swollen with lack of sleep. He held a small leather bag, which he quickly closed and hid behind the counter. There was a long moment in which Helen stood silently awaiting recognition that did not come, then he smiled and said: "Little sister! How is it? You still have your arm, at least."

"I wanted to show you," said Helen. She went forward, and stretched out her hand. "Look! Almost gone. It got pretty bad—one night it ran all down my arm, and it smelt, it actually smelt!—but now look!"

He took her arm between his palms, which were very cool. He lifted it to the light, and made a great show of inspecting it, and said at last: "Top marks. See, you'll have a nice scar." And for a moment she saw her arm through his eyes, and saw that indeed there was something pleasing about the deep uneven dimple that remained.

Then she said, "Are you all right?" because it had never seemed to be quite the ordinary transaction of professional and customer, and it felt right that she should ask. He met her query without surprise, and released his hold on her arm. "Bad news last night," he said. "My brother Benjie is a student—law, you know? He's the clever one—and crashed his motorbike. Broken hip, broken pelvis, the nerves in his spine bruised. It won't kill him but—" He shrugged, and Helen was at once rinsed with a feeling of pity. Her hand, which was not far from his, moved towards him, and fell short.

"I am so sorry. Will he be OK?"

"Eventually. But he suffers, you know? I don't like to see it. I'm going there now." He was silent for a time, and Helen tenderly watched as he pushed back a lock of hair. Then he said—not with diffidence, as if he thought he might be refused, but with a frank look of invitation—"Do you want to come with me?"

And Helen, neither embarrassed nor taken aback, said, "I'd like that, thank you." Then she said: "My name is Helen, by the way."

"Arnel Suarez," said the young man. He smiled, and looked a little less weary. "Nice to meet you, little sister."

"You too, elder brother."

Benjie Suarez slept in a small ward on the ground floor of a shabby hospital, whose gray tiled floors gleamed wet with disinfectant. "I know someone here," said Arnel, with a pride that made him shy: "I paid to get him a room, so he wouldn't have to be over there." He gestured to a long bright room in which many beds with identical frames of white-painted iron were set in columns against bare walls. It was noisy, so that Helen doubted how ill its residents were: in a far corner three men in day clothes were gambling with beer-bottle caps on the lap of a patient who'd long since fallen asleep. The room where Benjie rested was by contrast small and sombre. There were three other patients, all of them elderly, and there was in the air the unmistakable scent of bodies which would not outlast the year. The windows here were coated with plastic, which diffused the harsh light, and made soft shadows on the floor. One sloped half-open, revealing the clotted scarlet flowers of a bougainvillea. Turning fans in wire cages faintly moved the air.

"Benjie," said Arnel, and approached the bed. The young man stirred, and revealed a soft, fleshy face, which was rather like that of his brother, but which Helen at once disliked. He was pale, and as he stirred he moaned and grimaced. A plastic bag of saline hung from a steel hook above the bed, and his body beneath the thin cover looked overly large, with proportions all awry. A clear rubber tube extended from beneath the sheets and ended in a large glass flagon with a small handle; beads of blood collected in the tube and gathered into a stream that fell into the flagon and the inch of scarlet fluid at the bottom. "Benjie?" said Arnel, sitting on the single stool beside the bed, placed his leather bag beneath it. Helen watched him, and found so much to admire in his slight frown, and in the movement of his hand on his brother's arm, that she was startled to find both men regarding her. Arnel looked fondly at her, though with amusement; the patient meanwhile scowled, with the petulant open dislike of a child. He said something swiftly to his brother, and Helen understood the meaning, if not the words—that she was unwelcome, and

nothing much to look at besides. All the ease and comfort she
felt in the company of Arnel vanished: she became conscious of
the sore welts raised between her thighs, of the spots on her chin
which bloomed scarlet in the heat. "*Magandang umaga*," she
said, hoping to impress or mollify; but the young man smirked,
and then—arrested by pain—turned his head against the pillow
and cried out. It was not necessary for her to understand the
words he used: it was the disbelieving railing against pain which
has never needed a translator. It struck her that pain was as intimate in its way as pleasure: she said, "I'll leave you with him,
Kuya—maybe I'll go find some water," and went swiftly out. She
could not turn left, since there was only that vast ward, imper-
sonal, inhuman, seeming more of a jail than a hospital; instead
she turned right, where the corridor seemed at once to narrow
and grow darker. Here the windows were concealed behind lowered blinds. The scent of disinfectant dwindled, and the floor
was gray against the skirting boards; there were no fans, so that
the heat and humidity intensified, making each indrawn breath
a mouthful of dank warm water. A nurse passed by, harried and
ill-kempt: he held three files of paper, which he scrutinized as he
walked, so that he did not see Helen pressing anxiously against
the walls. At the end of the corridor there was a doorway from
which the door had been removed. Its broken hinges glittered
in the faint light coming from beneath a lowered blind. It was
all very quiet, but not with the tranquil quiet of empty spaces.
Helen leaned against the wall, wondering how long she should
wait, and as she waited a sound entered the silence. It was not a
human voice, or the ordinary interruption of footfall on the hard
floor, but a kind of rooting, scratching sound. It was swift and
frantic, rather like the sound of an animal scrabbling in earth,
but with the high unmistakable note of fabric against fabric. It

stopped, and then began again, still more frantically, and then it was accompanied by a voice. It was not a cry of pain, but a kind of rhythmic wordless grunting almost lusty in its fervor. Helen's heart began to thrum—she moved forward—there again was the scrabbling, scratching sound, and above it a grunting that gave way to a moan. She crept forward, towards the empty door-frame, and saw on a hard chair just beyond the door a woman who slumped as if very weary. She wore long, loose black clothes, and it seemed that in this room were many fans blowing against the heat, since the clothes moved about. But she was very still, and could not have been the source of the noises, and Helen stepped forward once more. Then the seated woman began to raise her head—very slowly, as if it caused her great effort to do so; the fabric that draped across her feet lifted, and Helen saw that they were bare, and bleeding. *She must be injured, and waiting for someone to see her,* thought Helen; but the thought did not console her: she became terribly afraid of what she might see when at last the slow-moving head lifted and showed the woman's face. Turning away, she heard her own name called down the corridor—"Helen? Little sister?"—and went gratefully towards it, breathing swiftly as if she'd been running, and not merely standing mute and still beside the wall. Arnel stood at the doorway beckoning her in. His brother was sleeping now, and a pink flush had spread across his fleshy cheeks. He looked like a very small child, with curls clinging to the sheen of sweat on his forehead, and one hand raised palm upward on the pillow. Had it not been for the glass flagon of blood at the foot of the bed, she would have thought he was simply worn out by a long day.

"How much better he looks!" she said, standing close by Arnel.

"He was in pain," he said. "But he's better now." And unconsciously he nodded towards the bed, and Helen saw on the patient's bare upper arm a square plaster, thick and white and very clean. Then Arnel bent to pick up the leather bag he had carried, and Helen saw it contained three square paper packets labelled in green type. He swiftly zipped it, and for a moment she was conscious that he did not meet her eye; then he gave her his arm with a courteous gesture and said, "Want something to eat? Let's get burgers. He'll sleep a long while now."

They fell in love, Helen Franklin and Arnel Suarez: little sister, older brother. It was not the agonized rapture that Helen had imagined, and to which she had always doubted she was suited, nor was it the bickering and dislike that novels told her were the precursors to desire. It had instead a quality of being inevitable, or of being meant, as if each had been fitted for the other, and now served their proper purpose after years of aimless misuse. At first it had simply been a matter of liking each other, in that inexplicable way of strangers instantly at ease. They ate together; gave their personal histories (dressed up, just a little, to please); produced for each other, with a flourish and bow, the songs they liked best, the films, the food. She asked to be taught the names of the chemical compounds he memorized as he studied; she taught him German words that ran to fourteen syllables. He was, she discovered, studious, serious, sometimes seeming older than his years; he often studied late, and his eyes grew tired, so that she would say, "No books for you today, *Kuya*," and walk with him to Manila Bay with her arm in his, to eat jackfruit and ice cream on the harbor wall. One afternoon she'd looked at him, and laughed, because he'd made some joke, and he had been her friend; then she had looked away over the Pasig to the tower blocks glittering in the lowering sun, and back to the man beside her, and it was like the change of season from spring to summer heat. He was not her friend, could not be merely that: all at once he was a body, also, urgently present, his forearms bare, with fine black hair growing densely at the wrist, his neck damp because it was hot, his fringe (she saw this tenderly) needing a cut. Then (the sun on the Pasig went very quickly down) she, too, was a body—she felt it, as if it were something newly acquired: there was her forearm, longer than his, but not as broad; there was her leg, and it was very near his, very near indeed; there was her back, which ached; there was her abdomen. It rose and fell, fretful. She put her hand there. "*Kuya*!" she said, and he put his hand there, too.

In his presence she felt herself to be enough: not too small and too drab, but that other girl secretly nurtured on Christina Rossetti and bottles of jasmine scent. Standing at the square mirror bolted above the sink in her flat she did not think her hair lank and mousy, but watched instead how sleek it shone beneath the strip light. She wound a string of seed pearls round her wrist, and he rolled them aside, and kissed her there. The instant fondness with which she'd watched him remove and replace his glasses the evening they had met seemed to have been the forecast of still finer weather. She made a loving study of him, and what she learned she stored away, privately: if she had had any other friend but Arnel, she still would not have shared them. It was all hers—how suddenly he moved from serious to playful, and back again; how he pronounced certain English words in a manner that caused her to suppress a laugh; how often he was her tutor ("No, little sister—like this."). Nobody, she felt, had ever seen in him what she had seen. When they first shared a bed that, too, was easeful, as if they had done so many times many years ago, and had forgotten it until that moment. "Elder brother," she would say, putting her hands on him, on the body that had somehow, she always felt, made her also a thing of flesh: "Have we met before? Do you remember me? Do you remember this?"

Helen, who had always been assiduous, neglected her work. Instead she traveled with Arnel to places beyond Manila, where she found the undiscovered country she had longed for. Late in July, before the first rains, they drove to a volcano in Arnel's jeep, singing to a radio that hissed and spat. As they reached the crater lake fissures opened in the rock and gave out plumes of steam; everywhere mint grew in dense green thickets, and mingled with the smell of sulphur, so that it smelt as if all the inhabitants of hell were cleaning their teeth. Helen held the hand of her lover and looked down into the green lake boiling below. She tried to summon the memory of her old room in the dreary pebble-dashed house in England, and the smell of her mother's kitchen—tried also to look ahead into a future obscured by the volcano's steam. But there was nothing either before or behind her: only Arnel, and her feet beside his on the hot earth. That first sensation of having been called into being by his presence never left her: he looked at her lovingly, and in doing so made her worth loving. In September they returned to Manila, and he devoted himself more than ever to study, growing thin, seeming irritable, sleeping late; saying once, with exasperated tears, "It's for you, you are my responsibility now, you see that? What would you want with me if I had no decent work, no way of caring for you?"

"I am not your little sister really," she had said, and laughed, and kissed him: "I can make my own money, here or in any other city!" But she had felt, secretly, that it was very consoling, to have someone to lean against. If he steps away, she thought, I'll fall.

Though they visited Benjie often, he grew no fonder of Helen in that time. She recognized in him the nature of a child who has been spoiled, and because of that will always be arrested in youth. His mother would come, clucking and squabbling with the nurses, bringing plastic boxes of the food he liked best, and which he ate in huge quantities—thick slices of pork fat cooked in peanut butter, or meat stewed in pints of its own blood. She paid little attention to Helen, seeming merely to take her presence for granted. Helen discovered that the ease she felt when alone with Arnel was always compromised in the presence of others, as if they were all looking at her with censure and surprise.

In time she discovered that those small, square plasters which Arnel brought in his bag and took out with hesitant, secretive looks were a way of easing the kind of pain that would drive you mad, if you let it. "Fentanyl," said Arnel, and explained how morphine penetrated the skin, and kept Benjie from howling in torment as the crushed nerves in his spine transmitted bolts of pain from hip to foot. Without ever inquiring further, Helen understood that these were costly, and beyond the purse of either the hospital or the Suarez family; that he simply helped himself to the pharmacy store now and then, amending records as required, confident he would not be caught. Helen had seen for herself the effects of the drug, which within fifteen minutes settled the writhing patient, giving him the flushed and sated look of a sleeping toddler. "The thing is to be careful," said Arnel, putting a plaster on his brother's back, pressing it with his palm: "He wants more and more but in the end it'll kill him if he lets it. But only another month they say and he'll be in a wheelchair and after that, who knows? Walking, maybe."

Whenever she felt unwelcome—because Mrs Suarez came bustling in, or the mocking schoolgirls who, it transpired, were cousins, and children of cousins—Helen felt herself drawn to the narrow corridor beyond the little ward. It was always the same:

the feeling that here were those forgotten by staff and family—
that here the cleaners and the administrators didn't care to come.
A bloody footprint remained on the threshold of the doorless
room, and had not been cleaned off: it simply wore away with
time, until all that remained was the scant impression of a heel.
Sometimes it would be silent in there—only the sound of the
scarlet bougainvillea tossed in a breeze and rustling against the
shrouded windows—and sometimes she would hear it again:
the frantic rubbing and scrabbling, accompanied by a rhythmic
groan. One afternoon, made brave by curiosity, she went in. The
room was small and dark. A single bed was set against the far
wall, its curved white-painted frame identical to those she had
seen elsewhere. A glass of water and an empty dish were set on
a stool beside it. Someone had dropped a piece of sweet food in
the corner, and masses of ants busied themselves there. The chair
where she had seen the weary woman with the bleeding feet was
empty. The air was moist, so that Helen felt it against her skin,
as if it had substance; there was the strong scent of flowers past
their best. Through the gloom Helen made out the figure on the
bed: a woman, very thin, lying naked under a thin sheet. The
sheet was not white, as hospital bedding should be: it had once
been floral, and the pattern had faded to indistinct pale blotches.
Here and there were darker marks which (Helen stepped closer)
perhaps were blood. One arm lay above the sheet, and the fine
tubing of a saline drip entered the back of the thin dark hand. All
this Helen saw with relative calm; but as she drew closer she felt a
kind of sinking contraction in her stomach. The worn sheet was
damp with sweat and enclosed the woman closely, and the whole
impression was of a body somehow disorganized. The arm above
the sheet was, she saw, thin but whole; the one beneath it seemed
almost to have dwindled to nothing at the bicep, as if there was

nothing there but bone fine as splinters. The torso was uneven: the sheet sank deeper than it ought at the woman's breast. The left hip and thigh were worn down; the left foot truncated, as if shorn of its toes. Then the woman's head, which had been turned away, rolled against the thin pillow, and dark eyes met Helen's. They were vast, and wet; they regarded her with a steadfast appeal. Her nose was only two black slots above an upper lip half gone. As Helen watched, she raised her arm and began to rub at her stomach with a frantic motion and to grunt as she did it; the action seemed to relieve something in her, and she gave out a high sustained moan. Appalled, Helen turned and ran. It was not the grotesquerie of the woman's mutilated face and body that drove her from the room, but the feeling that to witness such degradation and humiliation was to somehow take part in it: that her eyes might wound as much as knives. Walking blindly down the corridor she jostled a nurse with an armful of linen and said: "I'm so sorry—I'm so sorry." Evidently there was something in her voice which gave the nurse pause. Smoothing the sheets with a swift practiced movement he tilted his head and looked at Helen. Then he looked beyond her, to the open door, from which the sound of rubbing and groaning came quietly out, and rolled his eyes, and smiled. "Ah, you've been in that room? It's all right: sometimes people look. One time she was in the papers and they came with cameras, you know? I sent them away. I like her. It's not good or fair, what happened. But it was months ago now, and nobody comes. They forget everything in the end."

"What did happen?" said Helen.

The nurse shrugged. "Acid," he said. "Her lover was a janitor. He had strong acid to clean with. He thought she was a cheat, threw acid on her, teach her a lesson. It happens. Some men like to keep their possessions safe and tidy for themselves."

Helen swallowed at bile rising in her throat. "Will she get better? Does she have family, that comes to see her?"

"She's poor, *di ba*? No family. There's a charity pays to keep her here but the money doesn't go far. We do what we can, but I think the acid goes on burning—every day, it goes a bit deeper, gets to her bones. How does she live, that's what I say. How does she go on living? I ask the Blessed Virgin to take her but still she goes on."

"Is she in pain?"

"Oh yes: very bad. Too much. Well, we do what we can about the pain, but the itching we can't stop. You've seen her scratch, scratch, scratch? That's the scars coming. All day sometimes, *scratch scratch scratch*. I tell her: Rosa, you stop that, you're bleeding, but on she goes."

"Why does no one help her?" Helen heard the childish, bewildered rage in her own voice, and could do nothing to quell it. The nurse shook his head. "What can we do? There's no help, no hope." He paused, and smoothed at the folded sheets in his arms. "You want to help? There's a chair in her room, always empty. Sit in it. You think you could do that?" Then he left, giving Helen a chastening look, which was not unkind.

Not always empty, thought Helen, seeing again that weary woman resting her head in her hands, and how her feet had bled against the hard tiled floor. Then she heard her name—*Helen? Little sister?*—and love made her forgetful. "Coming, *Kuya*!" she said, and went, shedding with each step the pity and horror that filled the small dark room behind her.

At night she gazed up at the turning ceiling fan. She saw the thin hand on the sheet, and the misshapen body under the worn sheets; saw, still more vividly, the seated woman with the bleeding feet, and how slowly she'd raised her head. That old sensation of being watched overcame her: never the feeling of being scrutinized by a paternal being intent on admonishing her every sin, but something more intimate, more attentive. It was almost possible to believe that the woman with the bleeding feet had been waiting for her—indeed that she had been watching and waiting for many years—that if Helen had only waited she'd have seen a gaunt face gazing at her with a horrible love. In the thick heat of the Manila night she began to shiver: what ought she to do? How might she ease that feeling of being watched, and moreover of being weighed in the balance and found wanting? She thought again of her old, small life—of the begonias in her mother's garden, of her father tapping the barometer in the hall, and saying "another fine day"—and though her lover's body was only inches away, and it seemed impossible that they could ever be parted by more than the reach of her hand, she thought: *I think I'd go home if I could.*

In the morning she woke Arnel. "I want to do something good," she said. "When you visit Benjie, I am going to sit with a patient in the hospital. Her name is Rosa, and she has no one."

"If she has you," said Arnel, "she has everything." Then he said, "When Benjie comes home there'll be a party and I think it might be soon. Yesterday he walked up the steps—he complained the whole way but then he always was lazy. He won't need the Fentanyl much longer. I'm glad. I am not clever enough to be a thief."

Two days passed, and Helen felt herself followed. In the offices of the Q.A.F. she wrote letters and filed papers and heard the frantic rub of a thin hand on a thin sheet; in the muddy heat of the afternoon, caring for a nursery class, she cradled a sleeping child on her lap and grew cold, with the alert chill of one who knows they are watched. She had failed, she had failed: this was all she knew. She had stood beside a woman in distress—a woman as she was, in distress as she supposed she might one day be—and she had run. Well: this would be remedied. That evening she took to the hospital a bunch of pink bougainvillea picked from where it poured over the wall of the Q.A.F. home, and two bottles of iced tea. Then, having watched the petulant Benjie hold out his arm for Fentanyl, she went down the dark corridor, half-hoping to meet the nurse again and have a witness to her virtue, and stood for a moment at the empty doorway. The bloody heel-print had worn away. Then, quietly, in case the woman was sleeping, Helen stood beside the bed. The dark head on the pillow turned. Above the ruined face the large and liquid eyes glowed. "Rosa?" said Helen. "Rosa?" She sat on the little stool set beside the bed.

The woman blinked. Tears were pressed out from beneath the lowered lids.

"I'm Helen." She put the sheaf of flowers on the bed. "I'm Helen Franklin," she said, and touched the arm that lay on the sheet. The woman in the bed moaned, very faintly; not with distress, but (Helen thought) with surprise, and almost with pleasure.

"I'm not American," said Helen. "Everybody thinks I am. I shouldn't mind, but I do." Again, the woman blinked, and Helen went on—in a light, inconsequential way, as if she were talking to a stranger on a station platform when all the trains are late—"I've been here three months. Sometimes I want to go home, sometimes I want to stay." The woman closed her eyes and rubbed at a place on her thigh. "I know about you," said Helen. "About what happened. I think it's the worst thing I've ever heard. Does it help, to have someone say so?"

A gardener working in the grounds outside turned on his radio, and music blew in. Rosa went on rubbing at her thigh, reaching for a place beyond the grasp of her hand. "The nurse told me you shouldn't scratch," said Helen. "You might do more harm than good." But the woman rolled her head against the pillow and opened her eyes. Helen saw in them a desperate appeal, and thought she understood. "You want me to help? All right: but no telling the nurse." Idly, as if it were quite normal, Helen put her hand on the woman's thigh, and felt heat rising up from it, as if it had been burning all the while, and would go on burning until the body was consumed. Lightly she began to scratch. The woman moved the remains of her mouth in a smile. "Is this all right?" said Helen. "Is this what you needed?" Scratching and petting as if the woman were a dog at her knee, Helen said, "Do you like the music? One thing about this country: everyone can sing. Do you know this one?" Quietly she sang to the radio, all the while scratching at the woman with a gentle rhythmic motion; this went on a long while, as Helen watched Rosa settle against the pillow, and saw a softening of all the hard pained lines of her limbs. "If I saw the man who did this to you," said Helen conversationally, "I'd kill him, and I'd enjoy doing it." Then she said, "Is that enough now? Look, there's a little bit of blood, here, just a little bit; I think we should stop." She took her hand away, and the woman sighed, and lay still. Helen said, "I brought something for you to drink. You should drink, in this heat." Then, as if Rosa had been one of the smallest children at the Q.A.F., Helen slipped her arm beneath the woman's shoulders and raised her from the pillow. The dark head rested for a moment in the crook of her neck, and Helen smelt the scent of a body failing in every function—dusky, hot, half-sweet, half-sour. She held the bottle of iced tea to Rosa's mouth and poured the liquid in, watching it dribble from the corner of the spoiled mouth, and run into the sheet. "There you go," said Helen. "There you go," and with half the bottle gone laid the woman down. Outside, the worker with the radio had moved closer to the window, and Helen made out the words of a sentimental song. "Oh, I loved this when I was young," she said, fastening the cap on the plastic bottle: "I'd listen to it in my room and sing along, wanting any life but the one I had." She set the bottle on the floor, and put her hand on the woman's. "*I dreamed I dwelt in marble halls,*" she sang, very softly, "*with vassals and serfs at my side.*" Rosa lay on her thin pillow and watched her visitor with gratitude and kinship. Helen went on singing until it seemed Rosa was sleeping; then she stood, and moved quietly towards the corridor. When she reached the empty doorframe she was arrested by a sound coming from the bed. It was very quiet, so that at first she thought it came from beyond the open window where the radio was playing; then it came again, and again, and she realized Rosa was speaking. She had raised her head from the pillow with an effort that made her body tremble; her voice was high, and hoarse; she said: "*Mamatay, mamatay. Hayaan mo akong mamatay.*" Helen thought: she is calling for her mother. "Maybe she'll come soon," she said. "Maybe she's coming soon and you should sleep until she comes." Then she moved on down the corridor until she found a toilet. Here she was very sick, then having wiped her mouth she went to find her lover.

That evening, beside him on a concrete wall, watching the polluted air above Manila Bay burn coral and gold, she said, "I sat with her for half an hour. Poor thing: you can't imagine how she suffers. I think she was calling for her parents when I left—maybe she thought it was me?—she was saying something like *mama . . . tatay,* over and over." In the bay a cruise liner left pleasure boats rocking on the Pasig river. "Oh, little sister," said Arnel Suarez. "No, she was saying: *let me die, let me die.*"

Each time Helen went to Rosa's room it was always the same. She sat on the stool beside the bed and rubbed at places Rosa could not reach, and lifted her head and helped her drink. She talked idly about her day—about the girls in the Q.A.F., about the cock fights she saw from her window—sometimes made the confidences that are possible when no reply will come. Once, when Helen had faltered, remembering how far away her mother was, Rosa's hand had moved across the sheet and found hers, and held it in a loose dry grasp. Often the gardener turned on his radio, and Helen would sing the songs she knew, and watch with pleasure as Rosa's body, rigid with unease and pain, softened and sank against the thin mattress. Sometimes there would be adverts between songs, which meant nothing at all to Helen, but to which Rosa would respond with a hoarse sound that was unmistakably a laugh. Then Helen would see, coming towards her out of the ruins, a young woman who laughed readily and sang sometimes when the beer was good; who had favorite dresses and ones she unaccountably disliked; who read in parks and preferred this film to that one, this shop to the other; who perhaps fought with her mother and made penance with the one dish she could cook; who had walked happily into a snare set by a destroyer of worlds. One day Helen encountered once again the nurse in the corridor. "She's got something for you, this time," he said, moving quickly past her behind a trolley of soiled linen. "Just a small thing, cheap. She asked me to bring it from the market. I said: 'Rosa, she won't want this,' but you can't say no to her, not now." And there had been in Rosa's eyes that day something beside the pain and the appeal: a glitter, secretive and excited, and before her visitor sat down she lifted her hand from under the sheet and put it in Helen's, and left there a square of pink fabric. It was stiff and fine and glinted in the dim light, its fibers woven in the Filipino fashion from pineapple fiber, its edges scalloped and stitched. "Oh!" said Helen, and felt her throat close with sadness. She opened it, and smilingly praised the stitching, the pale color; then for a time the woman on the bed was lifted out of her body with pleasure, and patted Helen's knee, and nodded, and smiled.

Each time Rosa spoke only once, as Helen reached the empty doorframe on her way out: "*Hayaan mo akong mamatay, mamatay, mamatay . . .*" Then in time there was another word, which Helen knew, because she had been taught it by the children at the Q.A.F.: "*Aking kaibigan,*" said Rosa, and as she said it she began to shake, not with pain or with effort, but because she had begun to cry. "*Aking kaibigan: hayaan mo akong mamatay.*" My friend, my friend. Let me die.

Later in life—in that narrow, exiled life, without friends or pleasure, the memory of Arnel concealed in a place she could not reach—it seemed to Helen those words caused a curious hardening in her that led to what followed. *My friend*, Rosa had said, and in doing so had brought Helen into a contract which she had never sought but could not break. That night she lay awake and imagined taking the thin pillow from beneath Rosa's head and pressing it against what remained of her mouth, her nose. It was impossible, of course: such violence lay beyond her hands. But would the end not justify the means? Would it not be worth a moment of her own suffering—the revulsion, the guilt—to end that of another? Helen examined the problem coolly, as if it were a matter of integers and proportions—as if she might move a number from one column to another and find she reached a solution. The question of duty struck her most forcibly: it had been her duty not to turn from Rosa's door—not to flinch at her wrecked body—to hold, to what was left of her mouth, something cool to drink. Where did her duty end—what was being asked of her? How could she tell what was good, what was right; what legal, and what just? It seemed they had little to do with each other.

The following morning—a Sunday, very bright and clear, with no sign of the promised monsoon rains—Arnel met Helen in the shade of her apartment block. She held a bunch of cheap carnations. He had bought a pair of sunglasses in green plastic frames, and coaxed his hair into a quiff; as he approached her he paused, and danced, and swung his leather bag about. Helen laughed, and danced to meet him; he kissed her and said, "We had a call from the hospital—Benjie's coming home!"

"Your poor mother," said Helen; and Arnel laughed, and kissed her again.

"Don't like him, huh? Well, that's OK. He's a pain—what are these—have you brought them for your woman?"

Helen bent to smell the flowers, but they were scentless. "Then I suppose this will be the last day I see her," she said. "I'm glad I brought her flowers."

"Poor little sister," said Arnel. "You've been kind."

"Have I? I just sit with her, and sing sometimes, and you know my voice is no good."

"That's true," said Arnel, very fondly. "You are always flat."

"Sometimes I think it upsets her more, to have someone watching. I wonder whether everything would hurt more if there was someone there to see it."

"The trouble is"—Arnel frowned, and pulled Helen back from a jeepney rattling too close to the curb—"only children think closing your eyes makes a thing go away."

"But I can't help her, can I? How can I help?" The white hospital was across the street. Two dogs roamed, thin and avid-looking;

one had recently whelped, and her teats dragged on the pavement. A girl sat under a striped awning boiling in steel pans: she
called out "*Mais! Mais!*" and the plaintive sound rose above the
traffic. Arnel drew Helen into the shade of an electronics shop
and put his hands on her shoulders. He looked very grave, as he
sometimes did when he was not quite sure what to do.

"You saw what I gave Benjie, yes? The Fentanyl."

"Of course."

"I have more." He shrugged. "It was too easy. Change a date
here, a number there. Take one for her. You put it on like a plaster: no one will see, no one will know, she'll just have peace
for the day. Isn't some peace better than none?" Helen was not
sure: it seemed to her that release from pain was a cruelty if only
brief—that the fall into despair after would be too much to be
borne. But still Rosa was behind her, walking, with a shuffling
gait—she heard, very clearly, as if the woman really had left her
white iron bed, the *scratch scratch scratch* of a thin hand on a thin
sheet; heard also that dry, pained voice: *my friend, my friend.*

In Benjie's room there was much to be done: the petulant
patient in his plaster cast soothed with corn from the market
stall; nurses praised and blamed in equal measure; papers signed,
filed, withdrawn, re-signed, filed again. "Go on," said Arnel,
giving Helen the leather bag. "Go and see your friend. Do what
you think is right, *hindi*? I trust you, little sister."

What Helen heard as she walked for the final time down the
dark and narrow corridor was not that frantic scrabbling and
scratching which had first drawn her in, but a high soft keening.
It was so high, and so soft, that for a time Helen thought it was
only that her ears had begun to ring because the storms were
coming; but as she neared the room with its empty doorframe it
became unmistakably human. *If I leave now I won't hear,* thought

Helen, *but it will still go on and on. Only a child would think otherwise.* The chair beside the door was empty; a shadow lay across it. Helen went in.

Rosa was not as she remembered. Her liquid eyes had acquired somehow the same fine layer of dust and neglect that lay on the tiled floor. She huddled against the far side of the bed, as if forced to share the mattress with an unwelcome stranger. In her distress she rocked back and forth; in doing so she tugged at the sheet and Helen saw for a brief shocked moment the body beneath it and the damage done. It took a great effort of will merely to stand beside the bed, beside the stool, and say, "Rosa. Rosa, I am here—do you remember me? Do you know me?"

She waited. A window was half-open; scarlet bougainvillea seeped across the windowsill and dripped petals on the floor. "Rosa?" said Helen. Someone moved past the window, and stopped; there was the sound of tools striking hard surfaces outside. A man laughed, was silent, laughed again, and clicked on a radio.

"Rosa?" said Helen, and music came in. Helplessly, Helen sang, not knowing the words, stumbling along to a half-heard melody. It stilled Rosa, as music sometimes did: the rocking and keening slowed. The woman fixed her eyes on Helen and it was possible to see the pupils settle, focus, grow clear: her character—which Helen had begun to know: courageous, frank, humorous, kind—returned. "It's OK," said Helen, wiping away the sweat and tears on her own cheek. "It's OK. I brought you flowers, look—I'll put them where you can see them. I can't come back: I'm sorry."

Rosa gazed and gazed at her and began her silent weeping. "I'm sorry," said Helen. "I'm sorry, but I can't come any more . . ."

Then the woman spoke, stiffening her body with the effort of it, and Helen met the words before they reached her, knowing what was coming: "*Aking kaibigan: hayaan mo akong mamatay . . .*" My friend: let me die.

"How can I?" said Helen, and her voice was indecisive, querulous, unsure, and very like her mother's. It was this that caused her to feel again a hardening of resolve: how could she? How could she not? She was not a thing made of clay, molded by circumstance for one sole purpose, likely to break if misused. She was an independent being, and her will was free: there was no restraining hand on her now but her own; no purpose other than to do what seemed—in that small hot room, if not elsewhere—most compassionate and just. She sat on the stool beside the bed, and Arnel's bag was heavy on her lap.

"Rosa," said Helen—steadily, slowly, as if questioning a child—"Rosa, do you really want to die?" The face turned towards her softened. "I never called you *Ate*," she said. "I should have called you *Ate Rosa*, my older sister. I haven't got anything right, have I?" The hand beneath hers twisted, and moved palm upward; the thin fingers threaded through hers, and very faintly Helen felt the movement of a stroking thumb. "Thank you," said Rosa: "Thank you."

"But I've done nothing," said Helen. Her hand was wet with sweat. "I've done nothing."

"Thank you," said Rosa: and for a long moment her eyes looked lovingly at Helen—more lovingly, she thought, than any eyes had ever done. Then something struck at her nerves, her bones, and she arched back against the bed and began to wail. It was angrily done: the howling of a woman who knows herself beyond the remedies of justice. Then there was a final calculation in Helen: one last assessment of her own soul set against another's—of the likely cost of doing what must be done. She opened the bag. Arnel had not stinted in his theft: seven white packets were concealed within a small square pocket. Steadily Helen removed one. It was thick, and soft; in the heat of the day it had the warm and pliant quality of flesh. Rosa had turned to the wall and the sheet had fallen from her shoulder. Softly Helen placed the plaster there and pressed it with her palm. "There, there," she said. "*Shh—*" Outside the workmen downed their tools and took away their radio. Helen stroked the thin hard flank beneath the blotted sheet: "*I dreamed I dwelt in marble halls,*" she sang, and went on singing. An hour passed of feeling the taut racked body under her hand—*how soon will it work— how much more can I stand?*—and still no respite: reaching for the bag she took out another patch and fixed it beside the first. Her hands did not shake. "*I also dreamed which pleased me most,*" she sang, and suddenly Rosa settled and stilled as if she'd been a small vessel riding out a storm. She turned towards Helen again. "There, *ate,*" said Helen: "There, older sister—be quiet now." Then Rosa smiled, and sighed, and her head swayed on the pillow; the pupils of her eyes dwindled to a pinpoint as if she were gazing into light.

"*Mamamatay ba ako ngayon?*" said Rosa, whispering.

"*Mamatay?*" said Helen. She stroked the woman's forehead where her hair lay wet against the waxy skin. "You think you're dying now? Maybe, *Ate.* Maybe." Rosa closed her eyes and her mouth moved wider in a smile. The room filled with the scent of flowers—very heady, very sweet; there was a rustle at the window and a head of bougainvillea dropped from its stem and splashed on the floor. At the back of Helen's neck cool air passed, as if at last fans had been brought in to alleviate the heat; slowly she turned, imagining that someone sat silently watching beside the door—but there was only an empty chair and a soft black shadow on the seat. There was a long quiet moment, and later Helen thought of it as a single indrawn breath: no men working beyond the window, no footfall in the corridor, no sound from the bed. Then she took out another of the white paper packets. "You're my sister and I won't leave you like this," she said. She pressed another plaster beside the other. "There," she said, and lay beside Rosa on the bed. Heat rose from her, and with it a smell like meat already gone over, mingled with the scent of flowers. Helen let the ruined body roll towards her: it seemed very soft, very pliant, like a body resting after love. Helen kissed Rosa's forehead. "There, there," she said. "It's nearly over now." The damp air caused the sheets to fasten against their skin. Rosa's breath was easeful and shallow. Sometimes Helen sang. Shortly before dusk, when the room's dark air began to cool, Rosa breathed out, and went on breathing out, until there was no air left in her. Slowly her pupils bloomed large and black and Helen saw herself in them. "There," she said. "There." She did not weep; her hands did not shake. She had simply done what was required of her. Swiftly she took the three white patches from Rosa's shoulder and put them in the leather bag. She stood beside the bed, and looked steadfastly at what it contained, because that, too, was her duty. She touched the hand that rested on the sheet—but what use was it to say goodbye? She might as well say goodbye to the stool, the dying bougainvillea, the white iron frame of the bed. Silently and quickly, she left.

At ten minutes past eight in the evening, three days later and the rains not yet come, Arnel Suarez was arrested in his mother's home. It was the promised party, with Benjie at the head of the dining table, flushed with the pleasure of being spoiled. Cousins and second cousins ate long-life noodles and bowls of beef braised in vinegar and anise; they drank beer from the bottle and teased Benjie without once causing him to scowl; Helen laughed as the others laughed at how ineptly she sucked at the noodles in her dish.

The men when they came did so politely, with the politeness conferred by a weapon at the belt. What need was there of harsh words, when there were metal alloys and jacketed lead so readily to hand? They were implacable. Their uniforms and their badged caps were blue. At the sight of them Mrs Suarez began stormily to cry in a curious passive fashion as if she could think, off-hand, of any number of felonies for which her sons might be indicted. Benjie meanwhile began to rail and rant: it was not necessary for Helen to understand the words to discern his rage at being no longer the sole focus of the day. Arnel, meanwhile, stood. He removed his glasses and folded them and put them on the table. He looked at Helen, and inclined his head. He patted the pocket of his shirt as if something stolen was kept there. "I told you," he said. "Didn't I say I was a very bad thief?"

But it was not, the policemen said, merely a matter of stealing from a pharmacy. They were concerned, more properly, with the murder of a woman known as Rosa, done away with one afternoon by an overdose of opioids while she lay sleeping in her hospital room. Of all this, Helen understood only *Rosa, Rosa, Rosa*: saw, as she heard the name, the dark head cradled on her shoulder, heard the frantic rub of a thin hand on the sheet. There was a sensation as if all that she contained—her blood, her viscera, her bones—lurched and settled and lurched again. She gripped the table. She looked at Arnel. The skin drew white and taut across his cheekbones; she saw in him the old man biding his time. Quietly, shaking his head, he spoke. Helen heard his deference, his placating disbelief; watched the movement of his hands; understood him to say: certainly not, certainly not—what use would I have for killing a woman I've never seen? Then (very politely, very placidly) he was cuffed, his arms drawn behind his back, and Helen called out, "Be careful! Be careful!" and felt in the joints of her own shoulders a matching tug and pull.

All around her there was noise: Mrs Suarez, on the floor, on her knees, pleading; Benjie blubbering, incoherent in bewildered fury, still unable to stand. In other rooms oblivious children were singing. Arnel shook until the cuffs rattled on his wrists. The men drew him politely and placidly towards the door. Helen opened her mouth. There were words on her tongue that had the weight and taste of copper coins. Her mouth was open, and she said nothing. Arnel turned and looked at her again. In that look she saw query and comprehension: saw his image of her alter, break, and be remade. She waited for the raised hand, the accusing finger; stood, with the notion that she ought to meet justice on her feet. But Arnel Suarez shook his head. "Sit down, little sister," he said. "Sit down."

Was there someone watching then—was it the gaze of the Witness that passed coldly across the nape of Helen Franklin's neck? Standing, she felt it—felt many eyes upon her: not merely of Arnel, his mother, his cousins' cousins; not merely of the police officers registering with very mild surprise the Western woman at the table. There was something else: the demands of justice made incarnate, peering at her as if from behind a magnifying lens. "Little sister," said Arnel, and his voice was not steady. "Little sister, sit down." Obediently, and with a shameful elated relief, Helen sat down, and the coins on her tongue went unspent. Then there was a hard indifferent jerk on the cuffs at Arnel's wrists, and with an infuriated cry of pain, he had gone.

They are very quiet, very close, Helen Franklin's listeners. The table has been cleared, wiped, filled again: there are sweet yellow squares of the cake they call "little coffins," interred within mounds of cream; there are pieces of *sachertorte* so thickly glazed the chandeliers sparkle on the plate. (Freddie Bayer eyes the cake.) Helen clings to the table and her fingers are sore.

"I went home after that," she says. "My mother said: we knew you'd be back before long."

Is it disgust that silences the women? Is it contempt? She cannot lift her head. "They took him to prison," she said. "I suppose there was a trial. I couldn't bear to ask." The marble on the table is cold. Then a hand—white, capable, its nails pared short—reaches hesitantly towards her. "What a very wicked thing you did," says Adaya, but the inflection is gentle, kind. Helen looks up at the thick glasses, the short fair hair, and is astonished to encounter the same shy smile that attended her in the chapel of mirrors. "I know," she says. She is conscious of a feeling of lightness.

Albína snorts. She is attending to a piece of *sachertorte*. There is very little about her ensemble now that is white, pristine. "Fool of a boy if you ask me," she says. "Nobody asked him, did they? Nobody said: take the blame, take the punishment. Did you? No. Well, then. What was all this for?" She gestures with her fork—up, down, up: it is both contemptuous and triumphant. "Miserable little English *myš*. He gave you a life and what did you do but build your own prison. Idiot!"

"I deserve it. I deserve it." (Josef Hoffman, solemn boy, nods.)

"You know," says Adaya, cool hand on Helen's, "it is not always necessary to suffer, even when it's well deserved." Her thumb moves, once, in a caress.

Thea has not yet spoken. She frowns. It is a look Helen knows well: judicious, inquiring, examining the facts. Her eyes rove about—take in the piano, the waiters adroitly tending to their patrons, the National Theatre sailing by. She unfastens, refastens, unfastens the splint on her left wrist: experimentally opens and closes her fists. Her hands these days are puffy and weak. The bee on her finger goes about its business in the eye of the silver skull. Then she says, "It is hardly unprecedented. Remember the law of Leviticus: think of the goat who took the sins of the people on his back and went out into the desert to die. Well: if Arnel Suarez made himself the scapegoat, justice has been served. And served twice over, what with all this denial, this self-punishment." Confidingly she leans forward. "We always tried to guess what it was, Karel and I. In the end we concluded you'd been brought up by Jesuits and whipped yourself on Tuesday afternoons."

It is preposterous, this lightness, this acceptance of her: Helen rebels against it. "You are not taking me seriously," she says. "If you did, you would leave."

"Well." Albína shrugs. "That woman. Rosa. You did what you were asked. I would have done it and without singing." Helen believes this: imagines, for a moment, waking one morning to find Albína approaching with a pillow.

Thea, pondering, says: "Were I his lawyer I should have a case, I suppose. But I am not. It is time to set a statute of limitation on your crime, little Helen."

Adaya pours seed pearls from hand to hand. She says, gently, apologetically: "It may be, of course, that she cannot; that her sentence is a full life term."

"It is!" Helen is grateful that Adaya, at least, is not fooled— does not attempt to bring mitigating circumstances before the court, to extend the hand of mercy.

Thea says: "Adaya, put those down, and get my bag." It is withdrawn from beneath the table: a satchel on which is painted a Renaissance army going elegantly into battle. Thea fumbles with the buckles—resists Adaya's offered help—takes out a folded sheaf of paper. It is placed on the table, its edges straightened, a breadcrumb brushed from the title page (*The Cairo Journals of Anna Marney*); it is all done slowly, reverentially, as if it were a document retrieved from the ashes of Lindisfarne, and not fifteen sheets of A4 run through Karel Pražan's printer. Meanwhile there is dancing now beside the piano: a woman of fifty in the arms of a boy who wears a velvet scarf. Thea says, "I'll give you this. You'll wish I hadn't—but in the light of it you'll think yourself a saint. Take it—go on, put it in your bag: it's heavy, and I don't want it."

"Melmotka again, I daresay," says Albína. "You girls and your fairy tales. How do you know she's not here already, huh? Might be me! I've had my eye on you for years now, did you think of that?"

Helen, folding the document into the pocket of her coat, says lightly: "I shouldn't put it past you," but finds herself looking swiftly up at the shining window, the open door. There is a piece of cake on a plate in front of her. It is dense, moist, almost black; it is spiked with liqueur, and wet with apricot preserve. There is the scent of almonds, a silver fork on a brocade napkin, a strawberry cut and splayed into almost a flower. It no longer seems to Helen impossible that she might take a bite: that she could permit herself the taste of sugar. She looks up—looks for Franz Bayer, with the open sores beside his mouth; looks for Alice Benet tending to her burn—looks, with a yearning guilt, for Rosa shuffling over wrapped in her worn-out sheet. They are gone. Albína is looking at her over a raised wine glass: seems to say, *Go on, go on, no need for all that now*. She takes the fork, and presses it through the glossy chocolate, the apricot, the cyanide-scented crumb; Thea says, "We should probably go soon."

"I'm hungry," says Helen. It is a surprise. She puts the fork in her mouth. The cake's sweetness, its softness, is a delectable shock. She tastes apricot orchards in August, almonds cracked open in a silver dish. The fork is cold and smooth on her lip. She awaits the sensation of revulsion which is her just reward, but feels only the simple pleasure, the child's joy, of sugar in the blood.

"Eat up, eat up," says Albína Horáková. She is putting on her velvet coat, tying its grosgrain ribbon.

"Eat up," says Thea, and she is smiling, and putting her hand on Helen's shoulder.

"Mind you don't feel sick," says Adaya, blushing, tugging at the very white cuffs of her shirt: "It can happen, if you're not used to it."

The dancers are waltzing by the piano, by the Danube. The National Theatre goes on sailing by; Helen Franklin goes on eating.

Silly Rusalka, swooning water nymph, is straightening her wig. She is none too bright, and made still more foolish by lust: within the hour she'll exchange her voice for the love of a portly tenor and be swindled by a witch. But first she'll sing to the rising moon: it waits, pale paint peeling from its disk of wood, somewhere by a pulley in the wings. Here is Ježibaba, witch and swindler, provider of potions and knives: she is fretting over a worn-out shoe and eating cheese and cucumber on a piece of brown bread. The portly tenor is at the mirror and contemplating a drink—he is not (he thinks) all that he once was, but at any rate is more than he soon will be.

It is twenty minutes past seven. Helen Franklin is in her seat. Albína Horáková has paid for a box: they are enclosed, these four women, in a velvet casket, flanked by plaster gods.

Thea—breathless, triumphant, refusing aid or praise—came slowly up the stairs, her chair stowed among furs and travelers' cases in a basement cloakroom. She says, "Helen, you really needn't stay," concerned that the sweetness of Dvořák will be worse for the penitent than even the sweetness of cake.

But: "I'm fine," says truthful Helen. She feels drunk. A woman in black is tuning her harp. "I'm fine," she says, and looks for Josef Hoffman, for Alice Benet, but they are gone.

There are three seats and a stool in here in box 7. Adaya, perching straight-backed and patient, sits on the stool beside the door. She has the look of a sentinel: nobody, thinks Helen, not even Melmoth, could pass without permission. Albína, leaning on the balcony edge, shedding a feather, shedding a tear: "This was always my best, my favorite. I could sing it all. I could go down on stage and sing it all for you now." The feather lands on an old woman's shoe: she looks down, looks up, smiles. She has garnets dripping from her ears.

"Karel hated *Rusalka*," says Thea. "Idiot of a girl, he said. Who'd give up eternal life, he said, for the sake, of all things, of *love*?" Her voice, when she remembers Karel, breaks: all the same, she is courageous. She says, "I suppose that was quite telling, in its way."

Albína is still eating. She has, wrapped in a napkin, a piece of bread and butter. *"Ekni mu, ekni mu, kdo na eká!"* she sings. She grins wickedly at Helen. "'Tell him: who is waiting for him!'" Somewhere in a rehearsal room Ježibaba is sending a message to her son: *Remind me*, she says, *to buy milk*. Rusalka is at the mirror whitening her face with paint. Her hair is red and many yards long: scraps of green nylon are stitched across her breast with silver thread. *How lovely I am!* she thinks. A man in an apron is cleaning the moon. The minor gods sleep on the balconies;

the chandelier has been put out. To Helen Franklin it is as rich
as the cake which is still on her tongue, and even more forbidden. A baton is raised in the pit and it is the signal for silence
above and music below: Helen sees, in each face turned towards
the stage, the pure sweet pleasure of anticipation. She is not
immune. There is a lightness in her which she cannot trust. Is
it wine? Is it the striking of the opening timpani, felt as much
as heard? Is it the sight of Thea, dimly lit, glowing, seeming her
old self; as if the past year—sickness, frailty, loss, pernicious old
Melmoth with her bleeding feet—has been erased? Is it (here are
the timpani again; here, a flute, very serene!) merely that Helen
has made her confession—that like Bunyan's pilgrim sinner she
has set her burden down? Albína, leaning forward, lets loose
another feather; it rocks and drifts on the air. Helen finds she
is smiling: that she can barely recall the faces of Hoffman, of
Alice Benet; would be hard pressed, if you asked her, to recall the
sound of footsteps behind her in the streets. It seems she is on
parole. She permits herself to indulge in the thrill of the rising
curtain, which stirs also Thea in her seat, causes Albína to lean
still more towards the stage: here is Rusalka with her red-gold
hair, her alabaster skin with its greenish cast; here is mist rising
from the lake; here also is the moon, freshly polished: an opal on
a bit of velvet.

So: she goes about her business, the swooning water nymph.
She stands under the opal moon and lets down her hair and sings
clear as a blackbird in the morning. Poor Helen lacks the necessary
armor to withstand the beauty of it, which is no less intoxicating
for being false. She experiences it as if she'd been kept in a dark
room and let loose without warning on a fine spring day—it is
too sweet, too sad, too much: the sound of the harp, the thousand lights, the white smoke pouring from stage to pit. Rusalka is

singing the end of her song. She kneels. Her small hands cannot reach the moon. Her red hair hangs to her heels. Black birds descend from high in the wings and all their eyes are blue. They come down to the water nymph, who is singing now one single note which rings up to the gods. It is impossibly high, impossibly sustained: in wonder Helen looks and sees Thea motionless, sees Albína Horáková leaning forward while a seed pearl falls from a string of beads. On come the birds, very black, very real: Helen cannot see the wires that hold them. Still Rusalka sings that one high note and does not breathe or pause—not when the birds are by her side, not when there comes onstage a witch.

"Ježibaba!" whispers Helen, delighted as a child, for she has read the program: and indeed here is all she'd hoped from that wicked enchantress. Beside kneeling Rusalka the old witch is tall and wears a coarse black wig. It is long, this wig, and by some trickery moves of its own accord, so that coils of it lift and fall about her, languidly, as if she were underwater. Her robes also move, stirred by onstage breezes—they are of the finest silk worn very thin; they pool at her feet like spilled ink. "Ježibaba!" says Helen, turning to Thea, who remains motionless, fixed with wonder perhaps; turning to Albína, whose seed pearls are still falling. But—how can that single note go on—how can Rusalka still be singing? What soprano's trick is this, that defies the need for breath? And Albína is pouring pearls out over the balcony, and Thea does not move—Helen begins slowly to rise from her seat and there is the sensation in her throat of something very sharp lodged there. Down on the stage the witch hangs her head as if in weariness and shame—her black hair falls forward—her hands are by her side. And Albína is pouring pearls out over the balcony, and Thea does not move, and Rusalka goes on singing. Then—Helen cannot move; cannot draw a breath—the witch raises her hand. It comes slowly up as if movement causes pain in every muscle and bone, and there is a gaunt white hand among the deep folds of her sleeve and it is pointing, and (Helen reaches for Thea and Thea cannot move) pointing at her—unmistakably, it is pointing at her, at Helen Franklin, who was taught to pass without notice—at the frail black net of her dress, the skin on her breast, the ribs beneath it, the heart beating there—pointing at what is kept concealed, what can never be set down. That weary head, hanging forward, begins to lift, and Helen dreads and longs for what's beneath the moving coils of hair—there is a sensation in her which is part terror and part desire. Her courage fails—she looks away, down to the auditorium below where the patient audience waits out Rusalka's song. Are they patient? Do they wait? The elderly woman twenty feet down with garnet dripping from her ears turns in her seat and looks up at Helen and does not blink. The man beside her, holding her hand, slowly moves his head: he looks up also and his eyes are black behind their glasses and they are fixed on her. One by one, then in their dozens, and in their several hundreds, every face is turned to Helen—children in buckled shoes and dresses of tulle, lovers pressed together, diligent students taking notes; from the cheap seats, the gods, the circle, the stalls; from the velvet boxes and from down in the pit each musician, each visitor, each usher waiting in the aisle, is looking placidly and with bright unblinking eyes at Helen Franklin where she stands. Then in an instant, as if each were whispered a secret all at once, those impassive faces change: register contempt, disgust, surprise. The air is full of the smell of lilies, of jasmine, as if flowers have been hurled in tribute on the stage. And here at last—out of the pages of the Hoffman document, out of the pen of Sir David Ellerby alone in his room, out of a farmer's field in a cold village by the Eger—is the face of Melmoth the Witness. Her skin is dappled as though many shadows cross it and her unblinking eyes are spheres of smoky glass. It is as strange as a nightmare and as familiar as home. There is a look on it of the most profound unswerving devotion: it is possible to believe that she has waited out millennia for this one moment of witnessing Helen Franklin in box 7 of the National Theatre. On her knees Rusalka goes on singing and a pearl falls from Albína Horáková's neck. Helen reaches out her hand—over the balcony, towards the stage—imagines the touch of Melmoth's palm, very hot perhaps, very soft against hers, coaxing her up, drawing her down. So after all her parole has been revoked: she hears the slamming of the iron gates. But she hears, also, very close by, a grunt and choke. It is Albína Horáková, in a deep sleep brought on by wine, by good rich food, by the warm air rising from the velvet walls, the deep plush seats. She snores once more, and it is loud. Her head tilts back; there are feathers in her lap. The sound silences Rusalka, down there on her knees—at last that single ringing note stops. Thea picks her program up and fans her face, which glows with pleasure: she whispers, "Poor little Rusalka! Would you trust that witch? Would you trust her an inch? Look at her!"

Helen Franklin—sick, bewildered—looks. And what is there but a mezzo-soprano in dyed green rags that hang from waist and wrist, and green tights worn thin at the foot? What is there but a cardboard moon on a pulley, and painted birds on silver wires? There is a seed pearl on the balcony and it hasn't fallen yet. She picks it up. The faces of the crowd below, of the musicians in the pit, are turned away—to the scores on the music stands, to portly Ježibaba under her papier-mâché tree; they have no interest at all in Helen Franklin. "*Melmoth*," says Helen, whispering, as if she might very well summon her up; but no, it is all stage sets, contrivances, illusions—all conjured out of tales for children, and the fertile ground of her guilt. Still, it is not so easy to shake the illusion off—there is again the slam of the prison gates; there, she is certain, is Josef Hoffman up in the gods, and Rosa is sleeping on his shoulder.

"I must go," says Helen—but Adaya is cool and calm on her stool beside the door, hands folded in her lap, a blushing sentinel. She catches Helen's eye. She smiles, and puts a finger to her lips. Helen, whom confusion and fear has made biddable, returns to her seat. The stage is busy with water nymphs imploring Rusalka to come to her senses, but she is thinking only of the portly tenor, pays no mind to his slipping wig, and cannot be dissuaded. Then—"*Shh!*" says Thea, laughing: Albína is snoring, still more loudly; surely there is a look of censure from the first violin? "*Shh!*" says Thea, but the old woman shudders, and the many layers of white in which she slumbers rise up around her, shed fragments of satin and pieces of net, and settle against the chair. She is a white bird on the riverbank shaking itself out, tucking its head beneath its wing. There is another choking, gasping snore, which is very long, and very loud—the first violin suppresses a smile and turns a page of his score. "Albína Horáková, really!" says Thea, in an admonishing whisper, turning in her seat: "So much for your favorite opera; so much for singing it by heart."

But something is not right: the old woman's head has tipped too far, her mouth hangs unevenly open. Helen takes Albína Horáková's wrist. The skin slips over the bones as loosely as a length of silk. There is no flutter there, no blood beating at the pulse. Albína's eyes are open and they are fixed on the stage, and they're as wide as those of an enchanted child. Her lap is full of pearls.

"Oh," says Thea. "*Oh*—" She puts out her hand, clumsily; rests it on Albína's knee.

"It's nearly finished," says Adaya. She is standing. It is not possible to see her eyes behind their lenses.

"But we *hated* each other," says Helen, and cradles the cool thin hand between hers. She feels a fissure open. She glides apart. She falls in the cavity, and all the griefs she has denied herself—for Rosa, for Arnel, for Thea, for Karel, for her own life, interred within a cardboard box—are waiting down there: in the unlit cul-de-sacs, the dark unentered places, she had no idea she contained.

The water nymphs have deserted the stage, and the witch is returned to the wings. Rusalka is drinking a glass of water and the audience drifts to the aisles. Slowly the chandelier blooms with light. Act Two has finished.

Part 3

From *The Cairo Journals of Anna Marney*, 1931

Tuesday 19th May

I saw the beggar again today. There's a place under the awning of the Heliopolis where they let him sit. How can they leave him there? You'd think they'd sweep him into the gutter with the rest of the rubbish. I took his photo. I don't think he saw me.

Sissy just came home. She thinks she's bought saffron at the market, but it's only sawdust and ink. I said nothing. Let her find out.

Wednesday 20th May

Mother and Pa have gone to Karnak. Sissy refused to go with them. She'll do nothing but lie in her room eating dates and rubbing oil into her shoulders.

I'm sick most days and my head hurts. I want to be back home with Lou and David, with turpentine on my clothes, drinking at our old place on Floral Street. Lou wrote and told me she's sold three gouache sketches and will spend the money on a canvas two yards long. She says she's bored of representational art. I wish she were here!

Tonight I saw the beggar walking to his usual place. He sidles along like he's ashamed. I took his photo again, then he sat down and rattled a tin spoon in a tin bowl. A man ran out from the Heliopolis and put bread and olives in the bowl and went back in without saying a word. I can see him there now, down in the shade, eating olives, spitting the stones into the street.

Thursday 21st May

I spoke to him today. I was standing at the window and he beckoned me down. He must have seen the sun on the camera lens. His arm looked as if it got broken long ago and nobody bothered to set it straight. He was looking directly at me and waving and I thought: why shouldn't I go? There's nothing else to do.

He's even worse close up, squatting against the wall, smelling: if he were a dog, you'd shoot him. His right arm is wasted and his left has got some kind of disease—it's covered with black lesions like fungus. Something is wrong with his eyes: they've gone pale, but he doesn't seem blind. I thought he'd ask me for money. I said, "What do you want? Why did you call me down?"

His English is good. He said, "I've got something to tell you," and then he started to cry. He blubbered and sobbed and nuzzled into his arm and it made one of the lesions lift off, and underneath it was raw and red. He said, "I've got something to tell you, please don't go."

I thought he had mistaken me for someone else. Sometimes
here they think I'm a boy, because my hair is short and I won't
wear frocks. "You don't know me," I said. "I'm only Anna
Marney from London. I'm not important. We've never met."
Then he told me his name was Isimsiz and he'd waited fifteen
years for me to come. He said, "Allah is merciful, and has sent
you to me!"

There is no god of course, and if there were, why would he
send me? I said, "Is this because I took your photo? It doesn't
mean anything. I take photos of everything here. I've got nothing else to do."

He started to say something but then he stopped and his
awful eyes went very wide and he started to scream. I realized
I'd never heard anyone scream before. Sissy loses her temper
when she doesn't get what she wants, but this was different.
Then he scrabbled against the wall as if he wanted it to open
up and swallow him down and said, "Look, look, look, look,
look!" So I did look and realized he was pointing straight at the
window of my room. He said, "Do you see her?" First there was
nothing, but then I suppose the sun got in my eyes because I
saw the strangest thing. It wasn't a person. It wasn't a shadow.
It was like a swarm of flies—like one thing made of many
other things and all of them black and moving very fast. Then
I blinked and it was gone, and the beggar was at my feet in a
pile of dirty white cloth. He patted about trying to find me but
I backed away because for some reason I felt sick and afraid.
There was nothing there, I knew that—it was my head and
the heat and the man screaming—but I kept thinking of Sissy
alone in her room and I wanted to see her and be sure she was
all right, so I ran across the road.

Of course as soon as I got inside our apartment block I

heard Sissy singing along to the gramophone and Salma in the kitchen taking bread out of the oven, and I knew what an idiot I'd been. Salma saw me and called me in and told me off. She said, "Don't go talking to that old fool. And don't touch him. God knows what disease he carries."

I said, "Where is he from? Is he Egyptian? He says his name is Isimsiz."

"It's not a name," she said. "It's Turkish. It means 'nameless.' Maybe one time he had a name but he doesn't know it now." I sat on the wicker chair in the corner and watched her kneading dough and I said, "Tell me more about him."

She said, "He was a prisoner of war—of the English, you know. Kept here in camps with men from the Turkish army. I remember them. Bored and unhappy, wearing the fez, asking for something to read. The English know nothing about food and gave them this bad diet. They all got pellagra—you've seen it on his arm?"

I said it was like fungus and she said, "Yes, like tree bark, like he's not human. The only doctor in the camp was Armenian and Isimsiz wouldn't let him touch him, so." She shrugged. She took her apron off and put her hands on my face and said, "Don't go giving your pity there, Anna. Other people deserve it. See his eyes, all burned out? Maybe it was just too long in the desert. Maybe it was something else." She shrugged again. Nobody shrugs like her.

I could hear Sissy upstairs singing. I said, "Did anyone come to the house today? Was anyone in my room?" She looked at me as if I were mad and said, "Nobody came, only Fatima to bring the flour, and she had nothing to say for herself, because does she ever?"

Saturday 23rd May

I am sitting at my desk. It's dark outside as if all Cairo has turned out its lights. I want to turn round but I can't because if I do I'll see someone sitting on the end of my bed waiting patiently for me. I can hear something moving and I think maybe it's only my pen as I write or maybe it's long black clothes dragging on the floor . . .

Yesterday I woke up feeling guilty. This Isimsiz was just a mad old man, not even wanting money, and I had run away. All those years I thought I was different—not a simpering English girl good for nothing but men and babies, but willing to look the world dead in the eye, then the world came to me and I ran. So when I had my coffee I asked Salma to give me a dish of *ful medames* and some of the bread she made and I went over the road to give it to the beggar. He was in the same place as always. When he saw me he held out his tin bowl, and ate it all without speaking to me.

"What do you want to tell me?" I said. He said, "I knew you'd come, for is Allah not most merciful to those who most need mercy?" Then he took my hand and kissed it and his mouth was wet with tears and the juice of black olives but I didn't flinch. He stood up, and it was like watching an animal stand that had only just been born, and I wondered if underneath his robes his legs were as scarred and broken as his arms. "Come with me," he said. I thought for a moment of Sissy and Mother and Pa. I thought of their faces, which are like my face, and of the way they live, which is not how I want to live. Then I said, "I'll go with you."

He led me down Emad El-Din Street and I could hear trams and I thought of London. I could see buildings with white balconies and Arabic slogans painted on the plaster and posters pasted up full of bright colors, and men selling newspapers in kiosks. There was a cart with its donkey gone and its load empty, and yards away a Ford with its motor running and a woman putting on lipstick in the back. There were basket-sellers and awnings and at the end of the road a gold-and-white minaret. I looked into a café with a green tiled floor and men in gray suits were reading pieces of paper with the government insignia on them, and two girls walked past smoking cigarettes that smelled like the cigarettes Lou smokes sometimes. I felt happy—I thought I'd forgotten how—here was everything I thought I had left behind: just ordinary life, badly lived and well lived, going on all around me! Then Isimsiz turned into an alley where there was only one shop. It was a café that was empty except for a young man standing by a silver urn. He didn't look surprised to see a beggar and an English girl come in, but brought us coffee on a copper tray. I drank mine right down to the grounds at the end then Isimsiz said, "Everything I tell you now you will write down, and you will call it 'The Testimony of Nameless and Hassan,' and since Allah is most merciful to those who most need mercy, it may be that I who am nameless will then be lifeless also, for what other hope do I have?"

Then he began to speak. But it's as if I was drugged because I can't remember anything that passed between then and now. I don't remember his words, or whether I spoke or whether anybody else came in. I remember nothing until I woke in my bed an hour ago and when I woke I was full. I knew that I had been an empty vessel that would ring hollow if you struck it and that now I was full and that the fullness would be heavy and painful in me for the rest of my life. I lay there in the dark until I saw on my desk a pile of empty paper and my father's pen and knew that I could do nothing now but write down everything Isimsiz had put in me—

The Testimony of Nameless and Hassan

He was born in 1890 to a modest family in Constantinople. Altan
Sakir his father was a tailor, and made suits of broadcloth and
linen in a room of their home on a sewing machine which he ped-
alled all day without rest. His brother Hassan was a government
official. The brothers were friends. Each enjoyed the company of
the other, and would have sought it out even if they had not been
born in the same house eighteen months apart. They were alike
in appearance, in diligence, in a fondness for any activity that
was governed by rules, and their inability to appreciate, or even
tolerate, music in any form. All three men were dark-haired and
dark-eyed, with mouths that would have been girlish and pink if
they had not grown beards very young. Aysel Sakir, their mother,
had died too early to inhabit his memories; they admired and respected their father, who taught them to play chess, and told them
the stories that all children are told: of the wolf who bore ten sons,
of Timur's iron sword, and of Melmat, the woman who watches.
Neither Nameless nor Hassan were married, out of shyness, and a
feeling that their lives, for the moment at least, required nothing
more than what was already their lot.

When he was eighteen Nameless joined a minor bureau in a
minor department not far from the bureau where Hassan was
employed. Here he developed a skill with drafting letters and

documents which passed from one desk to another, and kept the infinitely small wheels of government infinitely turning. The brothers traveled together in the morning by tram, and home again the same way, and met sometimes during the course of the working day. Hassan taught his younger brother all the skills of the petty bureaucrat: the correct etiquette relating to the titles of government officials, the best method for laying out a set of minutes, the nearest café serving good strong coffee.

Nameless and Hassan had been born under a dying star. They knew, as all good Turkish boys knew, what was their due as heirs of the Ottoman empire. Theirs was the race that had calculated precisely the motion of the earth around the sun, built the watch which could measure time to the ticking minute, depicted for the amazement of unborn historians the skills of surgeons who were also women. But the last of the Sultans, fearfully watching his borders, thought it wise to put in place means to indicate the inferiority of other races. So it was that Armenians were forbidden to annoy their neighbors with the ringing of church bells on a Sunday morning, or build houses so much as an inch higher than those of their Turkish neighbors, who after all had truer claim to the land. These same Armenians wore red shoes and hats. Greeks meanwhile wore black; Jews, turquoise. None were permitted to wear collared kaftans, or silk, or cuffs made from the pelt of the Astrakhan lamb. (Meanwhile, in villages hidden behind hills, Sultan Abdul Hamid II earned the nickname Abdul the Damned, for more direct and efficacious enterprises; but of these, Hassan and Nameless knew nothing.)

Late one evening, as Nameless and Hassan and their father ate a dinner of lamb, they heard the howling of an animal. "Do you hear that?" said Nameless.

"Don't be afraid," said Hassan. "Perhaps a dog has been hit by a tram. It will be over soon." But the howling went on and after a time they heard in the howling the words of a boy crying for his mother. Hassan put down the knife he held, and said, "Stay here. Let me see what has happened." When he came back, he had become pale with rage.

"It's Asil next door," he said. "Come back injured from the war. You can see his jawbone, like an animal that died in the desert. Pray to Allah he dies soon."

"It is a tragedy," said their father Altan. "Every day I pray you will be kept at your desks in your departments." Nameless watched as his father, who was mild and even-tempered—who, so far as they knew, had led a life of quiet civility—spat upon the floor. "I have seen it," he said. "The mess a gunshot makes. I have heard the weeping of the women. I pray you will be spared it."

Nameless and Hassan grew anxious and mistrustful. When, for the Easter festival, Anoush Agopian, who lived five doors down, brought plaited Armenian *chorek* bread and painted eggs as a neighborly gift, Nameless turned her away at the door. "Better that way, I think," he said to his father, who was stitching buttons on a white linen shirt. "If you lie down with the blind, you get up cross-eyed." When Loys Gregorian stumbled and broke his ankle against a kerbstone, Nameless and Hassan—who really had never by either mischance or misdeed caused a moment's pain to anyone—laughed and jostled the fallen man and went on their way.

Soon it seemed this anxiety and this mistrust had entered the waters of the Bosphorus and was drunk by the gallon. On the tram in the mornings Hassan said to Nameless, "It is important you see that to be a Turk is to inherit the kingdom. And there can be no false heirs, or the kingdom will be divided." Young men gathered in city cafés and beneath the trees in small town squares and formed societies dedicated to the promotion of the Ottoman ideal. Hassan joined

Turkish Hearth. Nameless joined Turkish Strength. In the evenings they laughed and played chess and fought over which was the superior society. Each walked a little more briskly in the evenings, when it was warm, and they strolled on Galata Bridge over Golden Horn, greeting their neighbors and friends, eating pastry soaked in honey. "Do not neglect your studies," said their father, presenting them with a volume of *The Divan of Nejati*, "*For though every leaf of every tree is verily a book, for those who understanding lack doth earth no leaf contain.* The battle of the mind is the war which can never be won."

Those young men with their ardor and their societies and their pamphlets became in time the nation's ruling party. Sultan Abdul Hamid II, who was called Sultan the Damned, was dislodged from his throne, and took up residence in the Palace of the Lord of Lords on the Bosphorus, where he turned his hand to carpentry. "Union and Progress!" said Hassan to Nameless, standing straighter than he'd ever done before. "It cannot be achieved without a degree of unpleasantness I suppose, but think of the end and not the means!" Then: "Keep it from our father. He is old. There are things he need not know."

The time came when neither Nameless nor Hassan walked so often on Galata Bridge over Golden Horn. It seemed the skills of the humble civil servant were no less essential to the pursuit of unity and progress than those of the secret militias said to roam the villages out in the east ("I heard there's a revolt among the Armenians," said Nameless to Hassan. "I heard they are making weapons that could destroy whole masses of Turkish women and children! So we need these militias, to keep our borders safe!") In the spring of 1915, Nameless—in a fresh suit his father had made: double-breasted, gray flannel, with a white silk handkerchief in the left breast pocket—was instructed to compile, in the precise and unambiguous language for which he was so admired, a memorandum relating to the movement of certain elements of the population from one place to another. This he drafted five times, mindful as never before that with every syllable he contributed personally to the dawning of a new age: of Turkish men and women living in unity beneath the sickle moon on the scarlet flag. Never did he allow himself to grow grandiose. Nobody could have been more humble than Nameless, none more modest. "I am just a cog turning in a big machine," he said. And after all what had changed? Flowers still bloomed in their beds in Taksim Square. Everything he did seemed both momentous and inconsequential.

The memorandum was drafted, and approved, and signed in triplicate; it was signed by his superiors, and by his superiors' superiors. By morning it awaited attention on desks further afield than Nameless himself had ever traveled; within the week those black marks on that white paper became deeds, not words, and 235 Armenian intellectuals were deported from Constantinople to Ankara.

"It is only a precautionary measure," said Nameless to Hassan at breakfast. They ate *lavash* bread with sour cherry jam and sheep's milk cheese. "It is only the troublesome sort. Intellectuals, you know? The writers of pamphlets and papers. If you had an infection in your toe, would you not rather lose your foot than your whole leg?" On the windowsill three tomato plants were coming into flower.

"I suppose," said Hassan, warming his hands on the silver coffee pot which his mother had been given by her mother on the morning of her wedding, "further orders might be made, to preserve the peace of the population. But after all it is not their land, is it? It is yours, and mine, and our father's, and our father's father's."

Altan Sakir, who always woke early to work, stopped the movement of his foot on the pedal of the sewing machine and said, "My sons, beware the pride of nations. There were those whose land this was before your ancestors were born, and there will be those who claim it when your name has passed from memory. A bird may as well make its nest in a tree and say: no other bird shall nest here, for these branches are mine alone."

Later that same year Nameless and Hassan Sakir—whose diligence, humility, good nature and rather frail appearance endeared them to all their colleagues—were posted together to the coastal town of Trebizond. They were twenty-five and twenty-six years old.

(MUST I GO ON?)

They were neither pleased nor displeased with their new positions. There was no advancement in wage or status, and it meant leaving behind their home—the treadle of the sewing machine which had attended them all their lives, the tomatoes on the windowsill they'd never eat now, the perfectly matched games of chess with their father—but it was a change of air, and Trebizond offered a view of the Black Sea, and of a monastery set high up within the cliff. What was more, Trebizond was a little nearer to what each had come to think of as the heat of battle: sometimes at night it was possible to hear gunshot and the screams of men. These troubled Nameless, who was peaceable by nature and breeding, but allowed him to feel that at his life's end he would feel that at least he had counted for something: that his diligence and exactitude, if dull, had been part of a glittering whole.

Nameless found his work in Trebizond arduous. It was necessary to devise a practical means of moving ten thousand Armenians into the interior, where they could do no mischief. "The trouble is," said Nameless to his brother in the small apartment they shared not far from the Black Sea shore, "that a strong laboring man can do more than a mother who has just given birth. Besides, mothers fuss, don't they? They fuss about the children and so on, and grow emotional, when really it is only a question of moving house. Didn't we move house, without complaint? Sometimes life is not as easy as one might like, but the noble thing is to keep going."

In the end, it was decided (Nameless, at a table with seven other men, in the suit his father had made, dipped his pen in ink and continued taking minutes) that the men should be despatched first, to be put to some useful purpose. The women and the children, meanwhile, would be sent to Mosul Vilayet: a long walk, certainly, but no harm would befall them there. ("Mosul," said a senior official to Nameless, knowing he was not well traveled, "is not unpleasant, and they can swim in the Tigris.")

"And what of the children too young to walk?" said Nameless, and put down his pen. He'd often thought he might one day have a son of his own, and the longing made him tender. "Might we give them to good Muslim families?"

The senior official surveyed Nameless for a time. Then he smiled, and said, "You have a tender heart, Sakir! It is a good solution. The infants will be kept here in Trebizond."

Emboldened by praise, Nameless said, "I understand the American consulate has been poking about. Let them take children, too. Let them bear the burden. Why should it be carried by the Turks alone?" Then he returned to his desk (it was spring, and the scent of wildflowers under the open window was like that of a perfume bottle broken on the path) and with all his usual diligence set out the required minutes and memoranda.

That night, four hours before dawn, he was woken by an undulating cry. The air was still, but the sound seemed carried on a wind which rose and receded and rose again; now it was so loud it dwelt there in the room, on the carpet—now it faded, and could not be heard no matter how hard he strained into the dark. It was voices, he supposed, and many of them, though whether of men or of women he couldn't say; then on a single report from a firearm it stopped and the silence that came after was absolute. He could not sleep again. In the morning, eating eggs and bread, his brother told him that a column of Armenian men bound for Gumush-Karna had been set upon by a band of militia, who'd cut their throats and left their bodies for the wild dogs. "It's highly regrettable," said Hassan. He put salt on the yolk. "It's really very regrettable indeed. But what can we do, brother? Are you and I responsible for villains and fanatics coming down from the mountains with knives in their belts?"

Nonetheless in the weeks that followed both Nameless and Hassan were altered. They were made of that material most essential to government machinery: soft enough to be pliable, hard enough not to break. But there in Trebizond it became necessary to grow harder, and harder still. How else could they continue to sign and countersign, to prepare agendas and correspondence, when in the midday heat there came into the room the scent of a butcher's floor which has not been properly washed?

When they spoke it was only to recall, as if from the distance of many years, not many months, how they'd played chess with their father Altan Sakir, and how it had been Nameless the younger and not Hassan the elder who'd first beaten him. Of the work which each undertook, they never spoke at all.

One evening towards the end of July Nameless prepared the final document of his career. It was brief. It related to the movement of Armenian children from the care of the American Consulate to an institution some distance from Trebizond, where they would join many other children of their heritage. *It's better for them this way,* he thought. *Better to be with their own kind. Who knows what they eat, or what stories they tell, or which God they worship?* This document he signed, and folded, as he had been taught, very neatly, matching corner to corner, and placed in a tray to be sent to its recipient. Returning to his rooms, he slept well, as men do when their work is done.

Then he fell ill with a sickness that had come to the town. Three days passed and he did nothing but vomit green froth into a bowl his brother held. In the night he dreamed a woman watched him. In the dream he saw first nothing but a column of black smoke rising as if from a great distance away. Then each time there would come a sudden sharp shift in perspective, and he would see that it was not far but near—very near—and coming closer; and not smoke, but many layers of fine black fabric moving as if in the wind. Dreaming, he knew that inside the garments was a woman's body, which he could not see, but which he somehow desired; and above it a face, which he could not see, but which he somehow feared. When he woke he would find he had risen as if to greet her, and would always fall back whining against the wall. "It is her!" he said to his brother, who brought him water on a tray. "It is Melmat, the woman who watches! All along she has been at my shoulder—behind me—watching me then, and watching me now! Hassan, if you love me do not leave me here alone!" So Hassan brought a chair into the room and watched his sleeping brother, marvelling at what vivid and material dreams shook his body, then in the heat of the night, and the weight of his own weariness, he too fell asleep, but dreamlessly.

Hassan Sakir and his brother who is now Nameless—young men of modest gift and modest ambition; who admired and respected their father Altan Sakir, and had been the pride of their mother Aysel Sakir; who all their lives had undertaken their work with diligence and skill, and would have shrunk at harming even a mad dog—were woken at the same moment by the ringing of bells. It echoed from the Black Mountains above the Black Sea and shook the glass in the window frames. First Nameless and then Hassan woke, and stood amid the sound which entered the room like water and washed up against the walls. "It is the monastery!" said Hassan.

"How can it be?" said Nameless. "They said it was abandoned, and all the Christian monks gone home to Greece!"

Drearily they stood in that small room halfway between sleeping and waking. "It will wake the whole town," said Nameless; but when he stood at the open door he saw not one lighted window, and heard not one raised voice.

"We should go," said Hassan.

"Does it ring for us?" said Nameless.

"I think so," said Hassan. "We should go." But they did not go yet, only stood hand in hand as they had when they were very young, before their mother died, when they'd followed her through the market with their eyes fixed on the scarlet scarf that covered her hair. The bells tolled louder, enough to wake the deepest sleeper in the deepest bed, but there was no sound of men waking or women throwing open windows, or dogs and children running in the street.

"We should go," said Nameless, and they went. Overhead each star was extinguished one by one, like flames pinched out at the wick. The temperature of the air was the temperature of their blood. The bells tolled and drew them down through the town towards the Black Sea. Nameless held his brother's hand and said, "Look, do you see it! Allah be merciful—you must see her!" What Hassan saw then was this: not a woman, but the mere shadow of one, moving up ahead. It paused when they paused—moved on, as they moved on—then hurried on to a street corner, between places of business and worship, and seemed somehow to lay in wait. Sometimes it sank against the wall as if weary, and sometimes pulsed and throbbed and grew darker as if it were a cavity into which all the wickedness of the world had been poured. "It is her," said Nameless, very calmly and quietly, and on they went.

The town ended—the path went down to the shore—the black cliffs of the Black Mountains rose up from the black water and there was no moon. The monastery high up on the cliff was a coat of white paint on the rock. Then the bells stopped ringing and there was the silence of a storm that has blown itself out. "It is Melmat, I tell you!" said Nameless. "She had been watching—all along she has been watching, when we thought her just one of Father's tales—we must go down! How can I stand here knowing she is waiting for me?"

They went on. "What is this I see?" said Hassan. "Has a ship gone down and lost its cargo, and it's all washed up on the shore?" Sacks were scattered all across the bay. They lay there singly or in groups of two or three; some were large, and well-stuffed, others lay flat against the sand. Hassan bent to look and saw they were hessian, and tightly tied with rope. "A merchant ship, perhaps," he said: "And here are sacks of wheat or bolts of cloth."

"Do you hear her?" said Nameless, and Hassan heard: a deep low keening without hope of consolation that struck each man silent. Then the largest of these sacks moved, or seemed to move— it shifted against the sand, then altered its shape, very slowly; stretched upward, expanded, until they saw clearly against the low sky a woman standing there. She wore a long dress of such fine dark stuff that it lifted and fell all about her as if she were submerged in water. Her hair was dark and heavy and it covered her face. She held something soft and dark in her arms and sometimes she lifted it to her breast like a mother nursing a child. "I can hear her," said Hassan. Then, quickly as an indrawn breath, the woman crossed the twenty feet between them and stood very close by. The fine black cloth across her breast rose and fell as she breathed; she bent to the bundle in her arms and keened and crooned at it. Then with a swift hard motion she raised her head and the brothers saw her face. Nameless could not speak. It was the face he had sought and dreaded in equal measure as he dreamed in his bed: shadows shifted across the skin, which was now dark and now pallid as wax; the lips were full and drawn back from her teeth. Her eyes were like upturned bowls of glass within which coils of bluish smoke were moving. Under them the bones were visible and cast gray shadows on the skin. When she spoke, her voice was sibilant and soft.

"Brothers," she said. She lifted the bundle she held and crooned to it. "Brothers, didn't you expect to find me here? Don't you know me? Don't you know my name? I, who saw your mother's pain as she gave birth? Didn't you see my shadow on the page as you went about your work? Didn't you feel me at your shoulder as you sharpened your pens into knives?"

It had always been Hassan's way to grow angry at false accusations. He said: "What is it you say we have done? Why have you brought us here? We have nothing to do with you."

"If you have nothing to do with me," said the woman, "how do you know my name?"

The wet sacks at the water's edge lifted and moved. "We have nothing to do with you," said Hassan. The woman lifted the bundle she held. She patted it and crooned at it and pressed her lips to it and Nameless saw that her mouth was stained with red. Then she tugged at the cord that tied the sack and moved aside the fabric and the brothers saw the face of an infant. Her cheeks were soft and flushed and her hair curled against her forehead. Her eyes were open and they were the color of the cap of a mushroom. She was naked, and somebody had cut her throat. The woman held out her arms—"See what you have done?"

Nameless vomited. "See?" said the woman; and vomiting again, he fell on to the wet sand. Light bloomed behind the monastery on the cliff. Nameless saw that all the sacks scattered on the shore had come undone, and that in each sack was a child, or an infant; or several, or merely two. Then Hassan fell to his knees beside his brother, and Nameless heard that he was counting: "*Fifty-two— fifty-three—fifty-four—*" he said, as if he might well be called on in the morning to make a report, like any diligent government official.

Then the woman was kneeling there on the sand with them and her feet were bloody and bare. Lightly she touched Nameless on the cheek. Her hand was very hot. She said, "These are the children that were safe, until you signed your name. Here is Taniel, who only learned to write his mother's name three days before he died. Here is Siran, who wears her sister's scarf. See? It will never be clean again now. Here is Petros, who broke his leg playing and wanted to be an engineer. Do you see what you have done?"

"I did nothing," said Hassan. "I did nothing."

The woman came very close, and whispered. In the folds of her fabric was the scent of lilies dying in a hot room. "It was your hand that held the pen, and yours that sealed the letter. It was you that led them to the boats in the bay, and you that held the knife, and you that put the living and the dead together in the sacks piled on the deck. Did you think I wouldn't see? Did you think there was no witness?"

Hassan was bewildered and afraid. "I did nothing!" he said. "Nothing!"

"All this, and more," said the woman. Then she opened her arms and drew the brothers towards her: Nameless on her left shoulder, Hassan on her right. It was softly done, but neither could release themselves from the hands that held them. "Let me show you," she said. Her breath on their cheeks was warm. "Let me show you—" and suddenly weary, Nameless and Hassan leaned against her, half-dreaming. They saw a desert, and wild dogs hopelessly rooting in the dust, and some distance away, the torso of a fallen woman. Nothing remained of her below the hollow of her ribs, within which some animal had made its nest. Above the empty cone of bones a skull smiled and smiled up at the blue sky. Then they saw a town square and heard the murmur of a crowd which was excited but polite, and in the square were six tripods of new wood, made very fine and sturdy for the occasion. And hanging from the tripods on short ropes six men hung, their robes white and clean, and their feet not a yard from the ground. Sometimes they moved and kicked like sporting boys. Then again they saw a child on a stool, and this child wore a white shirt, and a hat of white Astrakhan fur, and a pair of good dark trousers mended at the knee. He held up his hands and stretched out his bare feet, and on each hand and each foot was the mark of crucifixion. On his face was a look of bewilderment, as if all the world spoke a language he did not know, and could never learn.

Then the brothers were roused from their dreaming by the sound of laughter. Holding them tightly, the woman laughed and laughed. Then she grinned at them with a wicked good humor and said, "Did you see what you have done, with your letters and documents? What great things you can accomplish from behind a wooden desk with three drawers, and a filing cabinet kept in good order!"

"It's not fair!" said Hassan. "I've done nothing! I've done nothing!" He put his thumbs to his eyes and pressed them very hard, as if he thought he might put them out of their sockets and with them everything he had seen. Then he stood and the sacks were all around him and the rising sun shone on the upturned hands of the children that spilled out. He walked steadily and without stumbling into the sea. The water was at his waist and something floating there pitched up against him and caused him to cry out. "I have done nothing!" he said, and went on walking, and the slow black water closed over him.

Nameless watched with an acceptance of his own guilt which was almost placid. He knew himself beyond redemption's reach: no hand of grace could come so far, no light could penetrate. Well, then: he'd seek neither light nor grace. The woman breathed beside him. He knew her name. "Melmat," he said. He heard in his own voice longing and fear in equal measure. What else was left to him now, but she who'd seen what he had done? Who else might accompany him now, but she for whom life was an eternal punishment? "Melmat," he said. "I know you, as you know me."

She petted the sack beside her on the sand. She sang to it, and her soft voice thrilled and appalled him. "What do you know of me?" she said.

"That you are damned, as I am damned."

"It's true: I am damned." The shadows that shifted across her face stilled for a while, and Nameless saw clearly the broad gaunt bones of her cheeks; the smoky eyes, and behind them the old light burning. "What else do you know of me?"

"When I was a child they told me you wander the earth watching all that's most base and most wicked in mankind—that wherever sin is greatest you are there, and you are the witness. They said you come to those in the blackest despair, and hold out your hand and offer friendship, because your loneliness is so terrible."

"It is true. I am lonely."

"Then take me!" said Nameless. "What's left for me now? My brother and my only friend is dead—I cannot take my guilt to my father—I have been the cause of such suffering my eyes will see nothing else until the day of my death!"

"You would be my companion?" said the woman. She stood. The low sun slid behind her. The black silk of her robes lifted and fell as if immersed in clear water.

"Take me with you! If you and I are damned, can we not be damned together? How can I return to the life I had, which all along was the life of a devil? I am not worthy of my home, my land, my family, my name!"

"Your name!" The woman began quietly to laugh. Her merriment among the scattered sacks was more frightening than anything he had seen before. "Your name," she said. "Tell me your name."

Nameless opened his mouth and his tongue did not move. It lay there like old meat.

"Tell me your name!" she said; and he found he had forgotten it—that it had gone, like his brother had gone.

The woman went on laughing, and put a hand within her robes. She took it out, and Nameless saw that she held a letter. It was not the kind that passed through his hand hourly, or so it seemed, in the course of his working week: it was white, and very small, and the name on it was written in blue ink blotted long ago by water.

"I have something for you," the woman said. She held it out. She grinned, and watched him, and the old light flared up and was blue. Nameless took out the sheet of paper folded inside. Morning had come now, drearily and weakly, with enough dreary light for Nameless to read. When he had read it, he began to shriek without words, without purpose, without any hope of comfort. He groveled in the sand. The grinning woman reached out with her bare foot and nudged him once or twice. The water lapped the shore. The eyes of the infant in her wet sack looked up at the sun. Nameless patted blindly about in the sand—looking for Melmoth, looking for mercy—and could not find her. An hour passed. When he raised his head there was nobody else on the shore.

Here Anna Marney's journal ends.

Editor's Notes

1. In 1940 Marney was recruited as an official war artist by the War Artists' Advisory Commission at the Ministry of Information. She produced more than 300 charcoal sketches, some of which are held in the collection of the Imperial War Museum. They are distinguished by an impressionistic style, and by the inclusion of a figure in black located towards the edge of each work, suggestive of the artist herself as witness. She died in Cairo in 1974 after a short illness.

2. Marney's journals present a puzzle to historians of the period. The change in style between the first diary entries and that of the "Testimony," together with the abrupt abandonment of the journal, indicate that Marney may have suffered a psychiatric illness involving a dissociative episode. Others suggest the journal is merely a piece of fiction of no historical value.

3. Since much official documentation relating to deportation orders and the creation of special militias during the period 1914–1918 has been destroyed, it is not possible to identify Nameless or Hassan. Nonetheless significant points of interest remain. Correspondence between an official at the American Consulate in Trebizond and the US Secretary of State in 1915 testifies to the treatment of Armenian children in the area at that time, as does an eyewitness account from a Turkish lieutenant circulated to the British War Cabinet in 1916. Red Cross reportage on the condition of Turkish prisoners of war interned in British camps in Egypt bears striking resemblance to details recounted in Marney's journals. These documents, now published online, would not have been available to a British woman in Cairo in 1931. In addition there are notable inconsistencies: for example, there is no bell tower in the Sumela Monastery outside Trebizond.

4. Perhaps the most striking aspect of the Marney journals is a letter discovered within the pages, which is reproduced here:

Trebizond
1889

My brother, I kiss your hands. I will not see you again. Our papers are secured, and tomorrow we depart. In Constantinople we will live beneath the crescent and the star, and not the cross; we will be good Turks, and not despised Armenians. You will think me foolish. You say the Great Massacres, which we saw with our own eyes, are the past, and not the future. But I have learned to trust hope less than knowledge and I still hear drums in the night.

Yet I have hope, brother, and it is this which sustains me: that the suffering of our people does not go unwatched—that there are those not yet born who will know my name, and that of my wife and of my children, when all our bones are dust.

So it is that I, Hrant Hachikian, now called Altan Sakir, willingly forgo my name, home, faith, customs and inheritance, that I may preserve the lives of my wife Zabel Hachikian, now Aysel Sakir; my son Emmanuel Hachikian, now Hassan Sakir; and my child who is yet to be born, and is nameless.

Forgive me, and hold me always before the eyes of God.

ALTAN SAKIR

Look, if you can, at Helen Franklin now. It is morning. She is curled on the bed with her face to the wall. She's grown thinner in the days that have slowly passed since Rusalka sang to the painted moon: the bones of her back show plainly through her nightshirt like the ribs of a trilobite. Winter has turned unkind. She shivers. Albína Horáková is present in the spiders dawdling in the dried flowers, the doilies, the ugly useless objects on the mantelpiece— she is present in the scent of old incense, old drink, old food. At night Helen hears her shuffle and drag on the carpet, and wakes expecting to see the old woman at the door, but there is only her walking frame toppling like a drunk in the hall. The memory of Helen's last sight of her—face turned up among her bridal finery; conveyed like a duchess on a palanquin through Prague's opera-going classes, who twitched their good clothes in distaste—cannot dispel the notion that she might at any minute appear at the door with a plate. A phone is on the floor beside the bed. Sometimes it lights up, rings, falls silent; it is ignored.

The testimony of Nameless and his brother Hassan is scattered across the carpet. Helen has read it three times. She sees in her sleep the wet sacks scattered on the Black Sea shore. She cannot turn and face the room, because she is by no means alone. Here is Hassan shivering and wet. Here is Nameless, here is Josef Hoffman: they have much to say to each other. Here is Freddie Bayer: she is choking, and nobody pays her any mind, because nobody can help. Here is Rosa, behind Helen, actually on the bed: she is laughing, in her husky wordless way, at something Helen cannot hear. There is a shadow on the wall. Helen averts her eyes.

It is dense, deep—it pulses, sometimes, so that she draws up her knees, her feet, makes herself small, insignificant.

She is broken, then, as I suppose you thought she would be. Is it the manuscripts, the stumbling stone, the reckless consumption of sweetness, of pleasures she does not deserve? Is it her watcher, who even now—this minute, while she shivers on the bed!— stands on the pavement, in the hard cold light of the morning, looking steadfastly up at her window? Is it poor Rosa: did she fight against the fatal dose—was it, in the end, not mercy but malice? Is it Melmoth? Has it always been Melmoth, in fact: were those glassy calculating eyes, that longing look, not mere tales told to children, but fixed on her all along? Is it (and perhaps you think this more likely) Arnel Suarez, older brother, unlocked from the chamber where she kept him hidden, let loose in her memory? Many hands have made light work of dismantling the barricades behind which Helen Franklin has made herself safe. She is exposed to pleasure and fear alike. Her constrained life, her genteel suffering, her penitence, have all amounted to nothing. She has fewer defenses than at the hour of her birth, because there is nobody now to give comfort.

There it is again, the insistent phone. Its blue light flickers on the wall. Hunger rouses Helen. She lifts her head from the pillow, and slowly—very slowly, like an animal which expects nothing but harm—turns on the bed (Rosa covers her face with her hands and slowly rolls aside). Standing, Helen reels, lightheaded and sick. She puts her hand to the wall to steady herself and the shadow there thickens, reaches out, recedes. The phone rings. Dumbly Helen looks down at the screen: it is Thea, who has called many times, who has left messages. *It is today*, she reads. Helen picks up the phone, crosses the carpet (Josef Hoffman offers her his arm), takes her dressing gown from the door. She does this slowly, flinching, expecting to find that there beneath the thick pink folds is Melmoth the Witness, patient as she always is—watching, as she has always been.

There is a little food in the fridge. There is a plate of small iced cakes in which Albína has left a clumsy thumbprint. There is meat which has gone over. The smell of it mingles with the smell of Albína's greenhouse lilies dying in their vase. Helen eats, with small unwilling bites: stale bread, cheese which has acquired a bloom of mold, a tomato which has gone sour (Franz Bayer sits at the table and eats potato peelings). *It is today*, reads the message. She drinks water from the tap in a cup which has not been cleaned. Somebody is singing on the pavement outside. Helen looks at her phone. She recalls, with the effort of moving aching muscles, Thea in her wheelchair at a table in a café not far from Charles Bridge, in black cashmere and black linen, her russet hair neatly parted and combed. "I don't mean a wake, exactly," she had said, frowning, judicious: "That's not it. But I hate to think of anyone passing out of the world without notice. Helen, you're not sleeping."

Adaya had been there, too: Helen recalls her serene presence, her clumsy shoes, her look of a postulant nun. She had said, gently: "I suppose it is guilt, still. It is a heavy thing. Does it make you tired, Helen?" Lightly, she had touched the gold cross resting on her blouse. "You look sick. I don't think you should eat, but perhaps some tea."

"Let her be!" Helen recalls Thea's scowl. "Leave her alone. Her friend has died. She is mourning."

Helen said: "I hated her." She missed that hatred, the warmth of it, more than she missed Karel's teasing or her father's anxious affection.

"All the same." Clumsily, Thea had passed her coffee. "Not a wake, but we should meet after she is cremated: next week, say, and toast her in *sekt* . . . oh, she was dreadful, I know, but wasn't it a good way to go? All that wine, the pearls on the floor. In her sleep, at the opera, on her birthday—"

Hesitantly, Helen had said, "Did it all seem ordinary to you—the birds on the stage, the witch?"

"Were they puppets, do you think, those birds?" The café door opened: Helen averted her eyes. "And that fat old witch with ladders in her tights! What I always love about the theatre," said Thea, "is looking for the artifice—for who it is that pulls the strings."

Helen takes a bite of stale bread. The kitchen floor stiffens her feet with cold. Helen supposes she agreed to it—to raising a glass to Albína Horáková, who alone is missing from the zealous faces that cluster about her now. And why not? She does not fear the city streets, the lanes and alleys—what is there to trouble her in the sound of footsteps following hers, when she already knows herself haunted? She sets down the dirty cup, the bread. It is very quiet on the street outside: the air is sharp, the snowfall slick and frozen over. No children play. Somebody outside is singing (. . . *marble halls, with vassals and serfs at my side* . . .) but Helen does not flinch, or seek to distinguish between what is present, and what is remembered. She is acquiescent now. She accepts her punishment. The phone on the table rings. Thea is growing impatient. Helen replies: *I am coming.*

The city has wearied of winter. The place where the Christmas tree in the Old Town Square played Strauss just four weeks back is empty and slick with ice: last night someone slipped there and broke two bones in their foot. Master Jan Hus huddles deeper in his overcoat, and might well prefer the flames of the martyr's fire to the cut of the winter wind. In the Jewish cemetery folded notes of pity and contrition left on the jostling graves freeze hard to the headstones and will never be read. Nobody sits outside the cafés, the restaurants: chairs are stacked against the wall. The air is spiteful. The soft lips of children split with the cold and old men are in bed with pneumonia. The Vltava is freezing at the edges and each morning a swan must be broken free. It is one minute to noon. Helen is down by the river. The sky is pale with a frozen haze and behind it the white sun is a paper disk. She wears no gloves: her hands are scarlet and they ache. A minute passes and an eerie sound rises from the east of the river, then from the west; from behind the National Theatre with its golden crown, from the ticket booths and pizza stalls, from the Black Light theatres and the library at the Klementinum, where a student at desk 209 turns the pages of a textbook. It is a low note, melancholy, ringing up from the pavements and down from the eaves of apartment blocks—startled jackdaws are tossed from their ledges and bicker in the stripped black branches of the linden trees. The low note rises and nobody pays it any mind. One or two tourists, braving the wind's bite, pause, lift a finger, exclaim: but it is generally ignored. Helen reaches the Bridge of the Legions. It is empty. The siren tires of its own voice and slowly dwindles to a low note, which is cut off by a man indistinctly speaking Czech from a speaker ten feet above Helen on an iron pole. The silence it leaves is uneasy—you might imagine the city to pause a moment to recall the rattle of tanks coming over the bridge before going about its day (though listen carefully and you'll hear, quiet in that uneasy silence, somebody is singing). Helen stops on the kerb and awaits the passing of a tram, empty save for an elderly woman too doughty to be dissuaded from her tasks by mere weather. It passes, and reveals a man standing on the pavement opposite. He wears black trousers and a padded coat within which he is shivering. The black hood has fallen back. There is little hair left on his head: what remains has receded from above the cheap glasses cracked across one lens, and grows sparse and black above his ears. His skin has a sickly pallor and hangs loose at the jowl. When he opens his mouth to speak there are black places where teeth have come out. He raises his right hand; he is carrying something in his left. "Arnel," says Helen. It is no surprise to see him there, because he is not alone: Josef Hoffman, boy of fifteen, is just behind his shoulder; Sir David Ellerby, wringing his hands, stands poised on the kerb. "Older brother," says Helen, but does not respond to the raised arm, the sound of her name. She walks in a daze past Legion Bridge, down Smetana Embankment, along the freezing banks of the Vltava. The man with the broken glasses follows her. So do his companions.

Thea waits in the appointed café and has been there since the appointed hour. The place is dimly lit from behind green glass shades; the light is like that of a forest at dusk. Green velvet curtains hang from the windows and against the door; there are green glass ashtrays on the tables. Dimly, Helen recalls—as if from a distance of many years—having once sat here, at this table, under these green lights, as Karel Pražan said, "Do you see her? *Has she come?*" Thea gestures in comic admonition to the clock ticking on the panelled wall. As if nourished by loss, by shock, by her encounters with Melmoth the Witness, she looks very well indeed. Her hair springs from her forehead; her cheeks glow with good health, and with the application of a powder that glistens with gold. She wears black, in deference to the occasion, but her trousers, her blouse, the patent shoes on her feet, have nothing melancholy about them, nothing remotely sombre. Her lipstick is scarlet and neatly applied. There is something almost malignant in her vitality when set against Helen's depletion. She has come not in her chair at the hands of a helper, but on two crutches that lean on the table. If this has proved arduous there is little sign of it. The café is otherwise empty, and the staff lean bored on the counters. Thea has prepared two chairs beside her.

"You are late! Never did I think I'd see the day. But Helen, darling, have you been ill—did you catch a cold? God knows it's easily done in this weather. Sit down, won't you? What is it—what's happened—what have you seen?"

Helen turns her back on Arnel Suarez and Alice Benet, who wait patiently outside. Obediently she sits. She places a hand on the empty chair. Might it be possible to confess to Thea that the veil which hangs between what is real and what is not has been torn—that she wanders about in a daze, and cannot tell which side she walks?

"Is it Melmoth?" says Thea, teasingly, with none of the concealed malice with which she used to say the name, and Helen realizes that Thea is done with it now: that having passed on the Melmoth manuscripts she has washed her hands of the affair. Her yoke is easy; her burden is light.

Helen says: "It is all of them." A girl in a white shirt brings three glasses and a bottle wet from the ice. "Melmoth," she says. "Nameless, Hassan, Josef Hoffman. They have been with me for days." Her hands in the warm air throb with the sudden rushing of her blood.

"Won't you pour?" says Thea. It is evident she has concluded that Helen is indulging in the absurd. "I'll only make a mess of it. Adaya said she would come. Odd how a stranger becomes an acquaintance, isn't it? Very quickly, and as if they hardly mean to."

"Last night," says Helen, "I had Rosa in my bed."

"All right then: I'll do it, but it's your fault if it gets spilled. Then you've had a temperature, to be seeing things like that? Poor lamb, poor thing. Perhaps they'll make you a toddy, if I ask, like in an English pub—"

"And there's this place on the wall where the shadow looks dark and deep and I thought: if I touch it my hand will go all the way in—"

"What I think we need is plenty of lemon, for the vitamins, and at least two fingers of whisky."

"—I think she has been watching me all along. I think, even, that I might not have done it, if I hadn't felt her watching me—"

"And take off your coat. You won't feel the benefit, as my mother would say."

"In all those stories nobody said that. Nobody said: I know she was watching, I knew it marked me out, and that's why I did what I did." Helen pauses. She says, with a mouthful of spite which tastes delicious: "I'm surprised you either remember or care what your poor mother would have said."

"Look, Helen, they've made you a whisky and lemon. Sit quietly for a bit and drink it. You're not being very nice."

"Nobody said, it was her fault—*it was her fault*—I would never even have done it without her—"

"How odd. There is somebody on the pavement, just standing there in the cold." Thea has spilled the wine.

"Oh yes!" Helen smiles. "I told you. Hoffman, Alice, Arnel—Sir David Ellerby, not dressed for the weather." She does not say: Melmoth, because it is both too much to hope for and too much to dread (and do you wonder what she might say, were Melmoth the Witness to come now, and offer Helen her hand? Oh, so do I—so do I!)

"Drink up, before it gets cold. It's a man in a black coat with the hood up. He looks absolutely wretched. His glasses are broken. He looks sick."

Helen's blood surges in her like a tide dragged by the moon. She cannot speak.

"Poor man ought to come in out of the cold. He is shaking."

"Do *you* see him, then?" It is a whisper, this: of hope, fear, disbelief.

"Of course I see him. I may be a wrecked ship, Helen, but my eyes are all they ever were. He is looking at you, actually." Thea frowns. She has the look of a lawyer surveying dubious evidence. Is it possible it occurs to her that here is Arnel Suarez, having crossed the years and continents, and pitched up in a café in Prague, where the beer mats on the table show Charles Bridge at midnight? Perhaps: certainly she loses a little of her good cheer.

Helen says: "Is he alone?"

"Yes. Strange how quiet it is today."

Helen turns in her seat. Her body rebels against the command and it is a great effort to move. The café has three windows, long and deep, which face the cobbled street. Through them she sees the black pole of a street light with a bike tethered to it, the façade of a shop selling Moser glass, a board on which are papered flyers for concerts in deconsecrated chapels. There are no passersby, no children in winter coats, no tourists holding paper cups of honey wine. In the middle window—precisely in the centre of it, placed as if by an artist on a canvas—stands the man in the hooded coat. His face is up against the glass. His breath blurs it. Light strikes the cracked lens of his glasses and gives him a blind bewildered look. His mouth is moving: he might be speaking or singing but the glass is thick and Helen cannot hear. He raises his hand and presses his palm to the window.

Helen Franklin stands. She shudders; her hip knocks the table and Thea's glass breaks on the floor.

Thea says: "Do you know him? Helen, what is it: you're frightening me." She fumbles with the crutches propped against the table.

"He's here," says Helen. "He really is here." The words are a whisper because there is a cold hand at her throat. Frantically she looks for her old companions—for Hoffman, for Alice, for Nameless and his brother: if they are there, Arnel is not. But—no: it is only that solitary figure, patiently waiting.

"Who is it? You look so afraid."

"I am afraid! I am afraid!" Helen is hot now, with the old wet heat of a summer in Manila before the rains have come. Sweat has broken out on her face, on her body: her eyes sting with it. She looks down and sees the hard green tiles of a hospital floor and the print of a bleeding heel. Twenty years slip from her like the sloughed skin of a snake: she is twenty-one, ardent, believing herself marked out, believing herself merciful and just; she is twenty-two, appalled, shaking in the bed where she slept as a child, knowing herself condemned.

"So it was *him*." Thea is trying to stand, grasping the table's edge: "Who has followed you, all this time?"

"What does he want?" Helen's voice—she hears it; she despises it—is high, querulous, plaintive. "Has he come to punish me? How he must *hate* me—what can I do? What can I say?" With a very great effort she lifts her head. The window is empty and he's gone. There is a single moment of elation and reprieve before she sees him at the door. His hood has fallen back, and she can almost make out, behind the gaunt loose skin gone sallow from confinement, behind the high forehead which has lost its thick dark fringe, Arnel Suarez, who once held her aching arm very gently and turned it this way and that, who stood with her at the mouth of a volcano, who danced towards her in the street and kissed her, who had sat with his brother and been very tender and worried all night that he wouldn't bear the pain. "I did that," she says. "I did it." Because it is not merely time that has decayed Arnel, that has sucked the flesh from his bones, that has knocked the teeth from his head. He is on the threshold now and he is carrying a plastic bag. The handles are torn and it slips from his fingers and is clumsily pulled up. The atmosphere in the room is thick, oppressive, its particles charged—two waiters leaning on the counter seem indolent, weighed down by the heavy air. Thea, leaning on the table, shaking with the effort of standing on wasted legs, says, "You will have to face him, Helen—there is no way out, I'm afraid." She has lost her vital, happy look. She says: "I think Melmoth would be better than this."

"How has he done this? How did he find me? How did he come all this way—"

"Anyone can find anyone, these days—there are no hiding places, not any more!" The door closes. The velvet curtains hanging over it stir and are still. Helen hears herself breathing rapidly and each breath is a whimper. The curtains part and here he is, the man who has pursued her from the Pasig to the Vltava, who sang to her in the streets, whom she sentenced to a kind of death with her pride and cowardice. He puts down the bag he carries and takes off his glasses. The lenses are white with steam. He lifts the hem of his shirt, and wipes them carefully, and carefully puts them back on. Then he stoops to pick up the bag and clutches it to his chest. All his movements are slow, considered, and his hands are shaking. The greenish light gives his face a still more sickly look. He comes forward. Helen finds her mind and body are wholly immobile: she cannot move—she can scarcely think— she is suspended between dread and anticipation, between pity and fear, and it leaves her stupid, insensible. He is hardly ten feet away. He stops. He says: "Helen? Little sister?" and his voice has a break in it. "Little sister?" he says; and then there is a violent bang. The women are startled out of their stupor and the man flinches and drops what he carries on the table. They all turn. High up on the centre window there is now the imprint, very plain to see in the thin cold light, of a bird. The uplifted wings, the smooth full breast, glint on the glass. The shock of it rouses Helen from her disbelief. She studies the man who stands closer now, wringing his hands. There is nothing there to frighten her, nothing to justify those days, just passed, of lying shivering on her bed. He has the humble, shy look of someone who expects nothing but contempt and refusal and accepts it as his due. He is shorter than she remembered—much shorter, as if something has dwindled down his bones. He says, "I have come a very long way and I'm very tired. Can I sit down?" What color remains on his cheek fades. He sways where he stands. Thea—regaining her customary control by degrees—says, "Of course you must sit. Here. You ought to eat. You ought to have something hot to drink." There is a pause, in which you might, if you looked closely, see Thea's anxiety do battle with good manners, which in the end win out. She holds out her hand. "I am Thea," she says. "I am a friend of Helen's." The man looks at the outstretched hand (there again is the diligent bee in the eye of the silver skull), bewildered, then grasps it with both his. He clings to her. "Ma'am, thank you," he says. "Thank you. My name is Arnel Suarez."

"So I infer. Helen, sit down. Mr Suarez, give me back my hand."

But Helen cannot sit. How can she take part in this pantomime of good manners, of introductions, of a glass of wine and something to eat? She rubs absently at the scar on her forearm—rubs harshly, as if that small wound was the cause; as if all of it—Rosa sharing her bed at night, Karel's desertion, the shadows deepening on her bedroom wall, Melmoth herself with her implacable eyes—was caused by nothing more than a cockroach nymph getting hungry in the night.

"Is it you?" she says. Still, she doubts it, and well she might: what is there in this small, cringing, gaunt old man, with his broken glasses and torn plastic bag, to make her think of her lover? He cannot meet her eye: has not, yet, looked directly at her. "How did you find me?" Anxiety makes her imperious. "How dare you?" she says. "How dare you follow me here?"

He fumbles with the bag and takes out a child's exercise book. It is stained; the corners roll and fold. "I didn't know where you were," he says. "I didn't know where you went. I couldn't write or call. So all that time, all those years: I made this. Look." He opens it with care. "I made it for you," he says. "I'm sorry I didn't make it better. I wanted to show you what it was like. I wanted you to know what I did for you."

"But what do you *want?*" says Helen. "What can I do? What can I say?"

"I went to the Q.A.F. the day I came out. My mother, she'd died by then; my brother is a lawyer, you remember. I am no good for him. So I went to the Q.A.F. and then I wrote to your family at the old address, asked where you were. I am sorry. I just wanted you to see." Humbly, he pushes the book across the table. Helen will not touch it. But after all there is something familiar in the way his hair grows at the nape of the neck, in how he straightens his glasses: Helen hears, as if it is an echo delayed by many years, her own voice, half-laughing, half-tender, saying, "Older brother, I'm thirsty, get me something to drink." Deep in her stomach, where the flames have so long been damped down: an ember. There are moles where his neck is bare above the worn collar of his coat. She knows them. They have thickened, coarsened by sun and age. They revolt her and she'd like to touch them.

"Let me look." Thea cannot conceal her curiosity. She draws the book towards her, and with awkward movements flicks through the pages. It has the look of a sketchbook kept by a student: drawings in ink and black pencil, annotated, erased, drawn over. Or rather: it is like a book in which many students have sketched. Here, bushes of bougainvillea so finely drawn the petals curl from the page; here, a man, squatting against a wall, looking up, very haphazardly done. Across a double page, what seems at first to be many insects going about their business, but (Thea peers a little closer; Helen cannot help but look) is men, dozens of them, seen from above, lying beside and upon each other, confined within a cage.

"Nineteen years," says Arnel Suarez. "I said I was innocent. But then, it was a long time before the trial. A year. I lost heart. I didn't care."

"Here," says Thea. It is not that she doesn't pity him: her attention is merely elsewhere. She points at a page—turns it, points at another: at a barely sketched figure in black outside a barred window, or standing watchful at the corner of a yard. "This woman, here, at the edge of the page—and here, at the foot of the bed . . ."

"Yes, ma'am." Arnel removes his glasses and puts them in the pocket of his shirt. The movement causes Helen a new pain so sharp she presses a hand to her side. "We saw her sometimes. Not all the men, but some. When things were bad. There were too many of us, you see: not enough food, and what we had wasn't good. Every day in the summer it smelt, worse and worse. Our skin went bad, we got sick. And then sometimes we saw her. Just watching. We said: won't you help, won't you tell someone how it is for us in here? But she just watched. Some of the men called her Saksi and thought she'd come back. Saksi," he said, "means witness."

"What do you want?" says Helen again. His hands are folded on the table. A black cross is tattooed on the left, beside the thumb; the right is scarred at the knuckles with thick padding as if he has repeatedly struck something hard. He says, humbly, "You don't have to give me anything. I don't want money. I want to know it was right, what I did. I want to know it counted. That was how I stood it, all that time, knowing you were free." He looks at her then. His eyes are bloodshot, and the remains of an infection is reddening the lids. "*Kuya*," says Helen. "Older brother—"

Listen! There is the sound of something striking the window— then another, and another. It is jackdaws—gentlemanly, blue-eyed, watchful jackdaws—coming down from the eaves and ledges of the buildings opposite, coming up from the Vltava and down from the shoulders of St. James and St. John; from the library bell tower and from deep in the folds of the coat of Master Jan Hus. They come so thickly down the street the light of the winter sun is obscured: the café darkens, the lights glow more ardently behind their green glass domes. There is another strike, and the indolent waiters, exclaiming, come forward, and stand beside Helen, beside Thea: the windows now are marked all over with the greasy imprints of broken wings. The glass cracks. Thea says: "There she is," without surprise or horror. "She's coming."

"Oh—" Helen, shaken, finds herself coming closer to the man who has risen from his seat—against whom she instinctively presses, in her anxiety and surprise. "Adaya," says Thea, who is on her feet. And, look: it is Adaya, coming in view—to your left, to the first of the windows, among the jackdaws' hurl and eddy. Her thick fair hair curls up at the collar and a gold cross sits on the cheap gray wool of her winter coat. She is smiling, in her hesitant way, and her young face is flushed with the cold. Then she passes from view and appears again, in that window where Arnel stood and pressed his palm against the glass; Adaya is tall now, and her smile is gleeful and merry and red, and her hair is dark and long and it lifts with the wind. Look: again she is gone, slipped out of sight; again she appears, in the third window, the last, which is beside the door: Adaya, but by no means Adaya, in black clothes of a fine thin fabric, many layers of it, that trail behind her like a shadow, that snare the panicked jackdaws, that drip like spilled ink in the gutters. She is monstrously tall, she must surely stoop to cross the threshold; her gaunt face flickers with passing shadows; she grins.

Helen Franklin feels neither fear nor surprise. She recalls Adaya's soft hesitant looks and her way of saying: "Have you been punished? Do you despair?"; thinks of her at the cold marble table overlooking the National Theatre and of how she held a seed pearl and said, "What a very wicked thing you did!"

And here she is, on the threshold, between the parted curtains: Melmoth the Witness, the wanderer, she who is cursed, who is lonely beyond endurance; she who cunningly concealed herself; made herself useful, attended to Albína, to Thea, to Helen—to their small wounds, their confessions—with gestures of caution and care. She is smiling. Her feet are bare and bleeding.

"I have come," she says. "Helen, my friend: did you know it was me? I wanted you to know—I hoped you would know: I even told you my true name, which I have not heard spoken since the days of my transgression!"

"Adaya," says Helen, and all the lamps grow dim.

"My own mother named me witness: did she see my curse at the hour of my birth? Oh Helen, my loved one, to whom I gave my name—you have waited for me long enough!"

Helen turns, and finds that everything about her is arrested. The waiters are at the window, exclaiming at a jackdaw, which is breaking itself against the glass. Thea has fallen into her seat: she is aghast, amazed; her right hand is pressed to her mouth. Arnel stands, and has put out his hand, as if to fend off something he does not want to see. But all the while the jackdaw struggles, and the waiters exclaim; all the while Thea breathes heavily against her palm; all the while Arnel sways, and his raised hand trembles.

"Oh, I have no need of them," says Melmoth. Contemptuously she dismisses Thea, Arnel, the waiters at the window. She comes nearer. The bones of her feet are breaking. "It is only you that brings me!"

"I knew." Helen cannot take her eyes from those of the Witness: they hold hers with an unblinking implacable gaze. "It has been a long while. I felt you—at night, when I couldn't sleep, in my bedroom, when I was young—"

"Yes! Yes!"

"Was it you, in Rosa's room—beside the door—on the chair—"

"The chair was left for me."

"Did you see me? Did you watch me when we lay on the bed—"

"I saw you. I heard you sing."

"Then you know what I am! You know what I have done!"

She is very close now, very attentive: her eyes in her gaunt dark face are like oil spilled on water. Lightly she puts out a hand, touches Helen on her shoulder; her palm is warm, and very soft, and Helen, who has denied herself so much, responds with something like desire. "My love"—the hand moves in a caress—"I know what you are. I have always known. How could you fool me, whose eyes have never left you?"

"These past few days I have been mad—I have seen them all— they were in my bed, they were at my table—" Helen is faint. She sways where she stands—she covers her face: "I don't believe it, I don't believe you are here. I am sick—my head hurts: I don't know what I'm seeing . . ." How is it possible? It is fantastic, bizarre. It is simply that she has read too much, slept too little, carried her shame for too long; it is all just a shadow moving on the wall. The scent of lilies is all around her; it is strong, sickly, and there is something else there which is like the sweetness of things left to decay.

"Don't you believe that I am here? Oh Helen, my friend, my dear! You are tired—won't you rest your head on my shoulder?" And Helen is drawn down in arms that wrap her like a winding sheet. She cannot move—she does not want to move; she hears the beating of Melmoth's old heart, rapid and strong; she hears her murmur: "Let me show you what you did." Helen, half-dreaming, sees a jail cell. It is scarcely larger than the room where she sleeps and it contains twenty men. They lie on a concrete floor which is wet with monsoon rains that pour from gutters overhead. The men are listless and thin; all have lesions and rashes that make their skin tender and raw. There is a yellow slop-bucket full to the brim. There is Arnel, young, squatting, his face buried in his hands. Beside him a boy of sixteen is clutching his stomach and asking for his mother, and Arnel pats his hand, his hair, and says he would help him if only he could. Then again here is Arnel, older, in a frenzy of despair, punching a wall until the skin splits across each knuckle, and not feeling it, and Helen knows beyond doubt he is thinking of her. And again: Arnel, on a high bunk, eating a kind of broth, reserving the few noodles, the few pieces of meat, for later, because he is afraid there'll be no more. And there is nothing left of him now—no fury, no kindness, no despair— there is nothing: he has been emptied of himself, left hollow.

"You see?" Melmoth is murmuring now—her voice is very soft, very sweet: it is the voice of a lover. "You see what you did? It would have been better for him, for his mother, for everyone who loved him, if you had never been born. Who would want you now? Who could bear to look at you? If they knew what I knew—if they'd seen what I have seen!"

"I know. I know." Helen is humble. The jackdaw is breaking its beak on the glass.

"Then come away with me! What remains for you here but shame and disgrace? Come away with me, little Helen: be my friend, be my companion! Won't you take pity on me? Won't you take my hand? I've been so lonely!"

The old heart is beating beneath Helen's cheek and the scent of flowers is heady and rich. She is tired. It would be so easy and so sweet to submit.

Helen says: "Is there no hope?"

"None—how could there be?—but a loving companion in your despair."

No hope, then, thinks Helen—but she cannot believe it. There is something there—something in her, fluttering, weak, making itself felt. She thinks of the box beneath her bed, and its remnants of the time when she had lived. Then she thinks also of another box, another girl—a lid lifted, and all the world's wickedness let loose. But something had remained then—hope, very small, very frail, like a white moth looking for a flame. She puts a hand to her stomach and imagines that she feels it—nothing urgent, nothing grand: only a faint lifting that draws her up towards the light. She thinks then of Karel Pražan, and of the choice he made—of how it was Melmoth, in the end, who roused in him the belief that justice demanded he stand witness; who made him not cowed and despairing, but something more large and more free.

She looks down, and there on the table is Arnel's notebook. It has fallen open at a place where he has drawn a garden. This garden is in a valley and above it there is a mountain and the peak is obscured by cloud. Flowers in the foreground bloom on the page—there is honeysuckle and bougainvillea, and there are leaves of mint. Deep in the valley, scarcely more than a scribble of a worn-out pencil, are two figures standing close. Lightly she touches the page. It offers, in its little sketch, something she thought beyond her grasp—the prospect of redemption by meeting hope with hope.

She says: "No."

"No?" The jackdaw's beak is breaking.

"I won't go with you."

Helen is thrust from Melmoth's arms and the eyes that hang in that gaunt face are burning blue. "You reject me? You—a murderer, a coward? You would leave me here to my sorrow, to my solitude?"

"I am sorry for it"—and it is true, because what Helen feels now is pity, as she looks down at the bare feet bleeding on the carpet—"but I do have hope, I feel it in here like a pain! I must try, I must!"

There is a change in Melmoth. She who was all softness, all coaxing warmth, who retained something of the hesitant appealing look of the young woman she had briefly been, hardens, grows rigid as a stone grotesque high on the castle wall. She stoops beneath the low dark ceiling and her hair is all around her in greasy coils that lift and fall. She is grinning now and her mouth is wide and red. She says, "Idiot!" and begins to laugh, a laugh which has in it as much misery as wickedness. "Idiot!" she says: "Then I will leave you here, to wallow in your shame. Do you think you can be redeemed? Do you think you have anything to set against all these years? There is no redemption—there is no hope—there is nothing you can do, to make the balance even!" (Do you think it's only malice, that makes her speak like this to Helen? Do you think it only spite? It is not—it is her loneliness, her grief!) The shadows on the wall deepen, pulse, acquire substance: Helen sees in them Josef Hoffman, and he is kneeling, and Franz and Freddie Bayer stand over him, and torment him with blows and with kicks; she sees Nameless and Hassan among the sacks on the Black Sea shore; sees Rosa, hears the rub of hand on sheet, the grunt of pain and relief. All the lights in their green shades go out one by one, and there is movement now at the window: jackdaws, in their hundreds, in a frenzy, pouring down the lane, hurling themselves in stupid rage against the glass. Melmoth is shrieking, but Helen cannot make out the words above the sound of it, of small bodies striking the window, of beaks sheared off, of broken wings: then the window shatters, and they are all around her—on the carpet, struggling, beating helplessly against the carpet, opening their beaks—*why? why? how? why?*

Then—it is light again, with that greenish forest light, as if the low sun comes in through a canopy of trees; it is light, and Thea is saying, "She is coming," and is half-rising from her seat; and at the window the staff in their white shirts are exclaiming at the glass, and the glass in the window is cracked, and there is the imprint of a bird.

"Oh." Thea frowns. She returns to her seat. "I thought I saw Adaya—I thought I saw her coming down the road." She shrugs; does not see how white Helen is, how she leans against Arnel.

"Strange," says Thea, "how quiet it is today."

"She was here," says Helen. The green lamps are glowing on the walls. "She was here, and now she's gone."

"Helen," says Arnel. He is humble, quiet. "Little sister," he says. "Won't you sit? Won't you sit with me for a time? I don't want anything. Can't you sit here with me?"

"Do sit," says Thea: "For goodness sake." She has always had a certain impatience, a certain briskness, where the frailty of others is concerned. "Is it the birds? The glass was polished too well, that's all: they thought they could fly clean through." The staff shrug, lightly press the window where the pane is cracked, and draw the curtains. The soft green light is still more soft, more green; they bring candles, and set them on the table in green glass bowls.

Helen's legs are shaking. Her heart beats as hard as Melmoth's heart was beating. Arnel puts his hand on the chair beside him and looks at her with a shy and frank appeal. She sits down. She says: "I've got so little to tell you."

"There." Thea surveys them both with a placid contented air, as if their presence together—their improbable, their astonishing presence, in the same room, at the same table—has all been her doing. "There. Now, Arnel: will you forgive us if we make a toast? We came to raise a glass to a friend, who died. She was old and dreadful, but we miss her."

"I do!" Helen begins to laugh, and Arnel's face, which has been so melancholy and so gaunt, lightens in a smile. "I hated her, you see," says Helen, confidingly, watching Thea, clasping the bottle with both hands, pour glasses of Bohemia *sekt*. "I can't really remember why."

"If I may, ma'am: what did she die of?"

"She died of life, as I suppose we all do, in the end." Thea is regal: her hair is a gilded crown. "A toast, then." She lifts her glass. "To Albína Horáková," she says, "who will never really die, so long as Rusalka goes on singing."

"To Albína Horáková," says Helen Franklin. The glass in her hand is cold. Now there is music. Beside her Arnel is cleaning his glasses on his sleeve and she knows the movement well. He looks up at her, shyly; looks away. "To Albína Horáková," she says. The lamps glow against the green curtains and on the green walls: it is all verdant, warm, a forest in summer at dusk, and Helen closes her eyes. She finds herself on a path with a dark wood enclosing her. It is dense and deep and there is no light. The road narrows and turns and then there is a house among the branches and something shining in the dark. It is a candle on a windowsill. It has burned so long the flame is small on its charred black wick—but it does burn, it does shine. It shines on David Ellerby holding Alice Benet's hand and commending her to God; it shines on Josef Hoffman, melancholy boy, and his sole act of virtue. It shines also on Arnel Suarez on his narrow bunk, refusing despair; it shines on Hrant Hachikian as he bends over his letter and hopes only that his name is remembered; it shines on Rosa, with a pink fabric scrap in her hand, waiting for her friend.

Helen opens her eyes. Thea is turned towards Arnel with solicitous care, because now she is not the most wounded at the table. Arnel is saying, "The snow is not as hard as I thought it would be," and a candle is burning in its green glass dish. Helen raises her glass again and again, silently, with tears. Here's to Alice Benet with the sacred wound on her hand and here's to Freddie Bayer and her brother dancing in their white buckled shoes. Here's to Rosa, burning in her bed. Here's to Karel Pražan, gone for a time; to Sir David Ellerby and Josef Hoffman; even to Nameless, even to Hassan: because isn't it always those who have been forgiven most, who find themselves most able to forgive?

The bottle is empty. Helen puts down her glass. Somebody opens the door, and beyond it the afternoon has lost its cold severity: the wind coming off the river does not sharpen itself against the eaves, only billows in the awnings of the cafés and the market stalls. "Shall we go?" says Helen. She stands. Thea drains her glass, puts money on the table; Arnel closes his notebook and tucks it in his winter coat.

The streets are busy, and nobody pays Helen any mind: the jackdaws on their ledges have other matters at hand, and Master

Jan Hus, who feels a change of season, is shaking out his coat. Arnel stumbles on the cobblestones and Thea on her crutches is slow. "Come on," says Helen. She offers each a hand. A pleasure boat is moving on the current of the river, down in the gleaming shadow of the bridge. There is music playing on the deck, and it comes blowing up the alley like a scent. She says, "Come on."

Look! It is midnight on the Vltava. The banks are white with sleeping swans and ice that creeps from east to west. St. John of Nepomuk on Charles Bridge has little to entertain him: the street lights blooming on their iron stems show no passersby, no lovers, no children let out late. But it is not empty, not quite: look at this solitary figure leaning on the high stone balcony, gazing down into the river, with an eternal, an absolute solitude! Think of a black ship adrift in a windless calm—think of the last star burning in an empty sky! Doesn't pity light an ember in your heart—don't you long to reach out your hand?

My reader, my dear—you know her, you have been waiting for her: it is the witness, the wandering woman—the punished one, who is lonely beyond endurance, before whose eyes the world's wickedness unfolds! Oh beloved one, my companion—it is I, Melmoth, whose voice you have heard all these hours, these days—who first put Hoffman's letter in your hands! It was I who told you to read, and to bear witness—it was I who showed you how degraded we are, how far we have fallen from all that we ought to have been! Didn't you know? Didn't you guess?

Dear heart, I've watched you so long. I was there when you were a child and wondered how much you were loved; I was there when you lay awake in the dark and wondered who stood at the foot of your bed! There is no tear you've shed that didn't wet my cheek, and no joy you've had that didn't lift my heart!

Oh, and I saw what you did when you shouldn't have done it—I know what thoughts plague you most, when you cannot keep hold of your mind—I know what you cannot confess—not even alone, when all the doors are bolted against your family and friends! I know what a fraud you are, what an imposter—you never had me fooled: I know how vain you've been—how weak and capricious and cruel! What might they all say, if they knew?

And don't you know you were born to sadness, as surely as sparks fly up from the fire? I have already seen it! I've seen how sorrow will break your bones! But my love, I won't leave you here to bear it on your own—I have walked to you on bleeding feet: who else could want you like this?

Oh my friend, my darling—won't you take my hand? I've been so lonely!

About the author

About the book

Read on . . .

Insights,
Interviews
& More . . .

Meet Sarah Perry

Jamie Drew

SARAH PERRY is the internationally bestselling author of *The Essex Serpent* and *After Me Comes the Flood*. She lives in England. ∽

Reading Group Guide

1. At one point, Helen and Thea have a discussion about Melmoth's victims, and whether they are damned from the start or not. Do you think Melmoth chooses her victims, or is she summoned by them?

2. Does Helen's guilt cloud her view or make her more perceptive? How does her interpretation of the world and the people she knows change over time?

3. Do you think every act of wrongdoing is worthy of Melmoth's attention? If not, what might the distinction be?

4. What is the appeal in the way in which Melmoth's offer is expressed?

5. Did you suspect that Melmoth was the narrator all along?

6. Is it accurate to say that Melmoth watches those who have learned not to watch?

7. In the sections of the book that deal with genocide, the characters haunted by Melmoth are but a tiny subset of those who participated ▶

About the book

in the savagery. Do you think everyone in the larger group is similarly pursued? If not, why might that be?

8. What is the "best defense" against Melmoth's notice and pursuit—and do you think you live your life accordingly? ∽

An Excerpt from *After Me Comes the Flood*

WEDNESDAY

I

I'm writing this in a stranger's room on
a broken chair at an old school desk.
The chair creaks if I move, and so I
must keep very still. The lid of the desk
is scored with symbols that might have
been made by children or men, and at
the bottom of the inkwell a beetle is lying
on its back. Just now I thought I saw it
move, but it's dry as a husk and must've
died long before I came.

There's a lamp on the floor by my feet
with painted moths on the paper shade.
The bulb has a covering of dust thick as
felt, and I daren't turn it on in case they
see and come and find me again. There
are two windows at my side, and a bright
light at the end of the garden throws
a pair of slanted panels on the wall.
It makes this paper yellow, and the skin
of my hands: they don't look as if they
have anything to do with me, and it
makes me wonder where mine are,
and what they're doing. I've been
listening for footsteps on the stairs
or voices in the garden, but there's only
the sound of a household keeping quiet.
They gave me too much drink—there's ▶

An Excerpt from *After Me Comes the Flood* (*continued*)

a kind of buzzing in my ears and if I close my eyes they sting . . .

I've never kept a diary before—nothing ever happens to me worth the trouble of writing it down. But I hardly believe what happened today, or what I've done—I'm afraid that in a month's time I'll think it was all some foolish novel I read years ago when I was young and knew no better. I brought nothing with me, and found this notebook pushed to the back of the drawer in the desk where I sit now, hidden by newspapers buckled with damp. The paper smells dank and all the pages are empty except the last, where someone's written the same name on every line as if they were practising a signature. It's a strange name and I know it though I can't remember why: EADWACER, EADWACER, EADWACER.

Underneath it I've written my own name down, because if I ever find this notebook again I'd like to be certain that it's my handwriting recording these events, that I did what I have done, that it was nobody's fault but mine. And I'll do it again, in braver capitals than my name deserves: JOHN COLE, underlined three times.

I wish I could use some other voice to write this story down. I wish I could take all the books that I've loved best and borrow better words than these, but I've got to make do with an empty notebook

and a man who never had a tale to tell
and doesn't know how to begin except
with the beginning . . .

Last night I slept deeply and too long,
and when I woke the sheets were tight
as ropes around my legs. My throat felt
parched and sore as if I'd been running,
and when I put on the grey suit and grey
tie I'd laid out the night before they fit
me poorly like another man's clothes.

Outside the streets were eerily quiet,
and it was the thirtieth day without
rain. People had begun to leave town in
search,of places to hide from the sun,
and sometimes I wondered if I'd go out
one morning and find I was the last man
left. As I hurried to work there were
no neighbours to greet me, and all the
other shops had lowered their blinds.
I'd imagined customers on the steps of
the bookshop peering in at the window,
wondering what had kept me, knowing
I am never late—but of course no-one
was waiting. No-one ever is.

When I let myself in I found that in
the dim cool air of the shop I felt sick
and faint. There's an armchair I keep
beside the till (it was my father's, and
whenever I sit there I expect to hear
him say 'Be off with you boy!'), and as
I reached it my legs buckled and I fell
onto the seat. Sweat soaked my shirt
and ran into my eyes, and my head hurt,
and though I've never understood how
anyone could sleep during the day I
leant against the wing of the chair
and fell into a doze. ▶

An Excerpt from *After Me Comes the Flood*
(*continued*)

My brother says the shop fits me like a snail's shell, and though I feign indignation to please him he's right— I've never sat in that armchair, or stood behind the till, and not felt fixed in my proper place. But when I woke again just past noon everything had shifted while I slept and nothing was as I'd left it the day before. The clock in the corner sounded ill-tempered and slow, and the carpet was full of unfamiliar birds opening their beaks at me. All the same my headache had receded a little, so I stood and did a few futile little tasks, waiting for someone to come, though I think I knew no-one would. I've never much wanted the company of others and I'm sure they don't want mine, but as I fumbled at the books on the shelves I was hoping for the bell above the door to ring, and for someone to stand on the threshold and hear me say 'How can I help you?'

I crossed the empty floor to the window and looked out on the street. I heard someone calling their dog home and after that it was quieter than ever. For all that I've never believed it possible I felt my heart sink. It was a physical sensation as real as hunger or pain, and just as if it had been pain I felt myself grow chill with sweat. Looking for something to wipe my forehead I put my hand in my pocket, and pulled out a postcard I'd folded and shoved in there a week ago or more.

It showed a boat stranded on a marsh,

and a sunrise so bleak and damp
you'd think the artist intended to keep
visitors away. On it someone had drawn
a stick figure walking in the shallows and
beckoning me in. I turned it over and saw
a question mark written in green crayon,
and under it the name CHRISTOPHER
in letters an inch high. My brother
keeps a room for me in his house on
the Norfolk coast, with a narrow bed
and a bookshelf where he puts the sort
of novels he thinks might interest a man
like me. He often says 'Come any time:
any time, mind you,' but I never do,
other than at Christmas when it seems
the proper thing to do.

I turned the postcard over and over
in my hands, and lifted it up as if I could
smell salt rising from the marsh. If I went
to see my brother, there'd be a houseful
of good-natured boys, and my sister-in-
law who seems always to be laughing,
and my brother who'd sit up into the
small hours talking over whisky. But I
could put up with all of that, I thought,
for clean air and a cool wind in the
afternoon. So I took a sheet of cardboard
from the desk, wrote CLOSED UNTIL
FURTHER NOTICE on it in as tidy a
set of capitals as I could manage, and
propped it in the window. Then I turned
off the lights and made my way home.

I'd hoped the weather might be breaking
at last, but the sky was blank and bright
and my head immediately began to ache.
I let myself into my flat and packed a ▶

small bag, then left with the haste of a
schoolboy playing truant. Twice I walked
up and down the road before I found my
car, feeling the heat beat like a hammer
on the pavement, hardly knowing one
end of the street from the other. When
at last I saw it, the bonnet was covered
in a fine reddish dust and someone had
drawn a five-pointed star on the
windscreen.

Should I have turned back then?
A wiser man might have seen the journey
was cursed—on a balcony above me
a child was singing (we all fall down!)
and in the gutter a pigeon had died on
its back—but when I looked up at the
windows of the flat they seemed as empty
as if no-one had lived there for years.

It wasn't until London was an hour
behind me that I realised I hadn't
brought a map, or even the scrap of
paper where once my brother wrote the
simplest route to take. I thought I knew
the way but my memory's always playing
tricks, and in less than two hours I was
lost. Black boards by the roadside warned
SLOW DOWN and the sun began to
scorch my right arm through the glass;
I opened the window, but the air that
came in was foul with traffic fumes,
and I began a convulsive coughing that
shook my whole body at the wheel.

I began to panic. My stomach clenched
like a fist, and there was a sour taste in
my mouth as if I'd already been sick.
My heart beat with a kind of fury that
repeated itself with a new pain in my

head, and I couldn't move my hands on the wheel—nothing about me was doing what it ought and I felt as though I were coming apart in pieces. Then I thought I was losing my sight and when I realised it was nothing but steam coming from under the bonnet I shouted something—I don't remember what, or why—and gritted my teeth, drifting on to a byroad where the traffic was sparse and slow. When the dark fringes of a familiar forest appeared I was so relieved I could almost have wept.

I drove on a little while, then finding shade pulled over and stood shaking on the bracken verge. The pines stooped over me while I vomited up a few mouthfuls of tea, then I sat on the verge with my head in my hands. When I stood again, feeling ashamed though nobody saw my disgrace, the pain behind my eyes receded and I heard nothing but the engine ticking as it cooled. I was afraid to drive again so soon—I needed to sit a while and rest, and though I know little enough about the workings of my car or any other, I thought the radiator needed water, and that I couldn't be too far from help.

I found I'd driven almost to the road's end, and saw ahead of me a well-trodden path so densely wooded it formed a tunnel of dim green shade. It seemed to suck at me, drawing me deeper in, so that I walked on in a kind of trance. All around I could hear little furtive movements and crickets ▶

An Excerpt from *After Me Comes the Flood*
(continued)

frantically singing, and there was a lot of white bindweed growing on the verge. After a time—I don't know how long— the path became little more than a dusty track and I found myself at the edge of a dying lawn sloping slightly upward to a distant house.

How can I explain the impression it had on me, to see it high up on the incline, the sun blazing from its windows and pricking the arrow of its weathervane? Everything about it was bright and hard-edged—the slate tiles vivid blue, the chimneys black against the sky, the green door flanked by high white columns from which a flight of steps led down towards the lawn, and to the path where I stood waiting on the boundary.

It seemed to me the most real and solid thing I'd ever seen, and at the same time only a trick of my sight in the heat. As it grew nearer it became less like a dream or invention—there were stains where ivy had been pulled from the walls, and unmatched curtains hanging in the windows. Someone had broken the spine of a book and left it open on the lawn, and near the windows rose-bushes had withered back to stumps. A ginger cat with weeping eyes was stretched out in the shade between them, panting in the sun. The painted door had peeled and blistered in the heat, and as I stood at the foot of the stairs I could see a doorknocker shaped like a man's hand raised to rap an iron stone against an iron plate.

I was standing irresolute at the foot of the steps when someone pulled open the door and I heard a child's voice calling. I thought they wanted someone else, who maybe stood behind me and had followed me unnoticed all the way, but when I looked over my shoulder the path was empty and I was all alone. The child laughed and called again, and I heard a name I knew from long ago, though I couldn't think whose face it should call to mind. Then suddenly I realised it was my own name, called over and over, and the shock made me stop suddenly with my foot on the lower step. I thought: it's only the heat, and the ringing in your ears, no-one knows you're here.

The child's voice came nearer and nearer, and through the blinding light I made out the figure of a girl, older than I'd first taken her for, running down the steps towards me with her arms outstretched: 'John Cole! Is that you? It is you, isn't it—it must be, I'm so glad. I've been waiting for you all day!' I tried to find ways to explain her mistake but in my confusion fumbled with my words, and by then the girl had reached the bottom step and put her arm through mine. She said, 'Do you know where to go? Let me show you the way', and drew me up towards the open door. The girl went on talking—about how they'd been looking forward to meeting me, and how late I was, and how glad she was to see me at last—all the while leading me into a stone-flagged hall so ▶

An Excerpt from *After Me Comes the Flood*
(*continued*)

dark and cold I began to shiver as the door swung shut behind me.

She must have seen my pallor and my shaking hands, because she began talking to me as if I were an old man, which I suppose I am to her. She said, 'It's all right, we're nearly there', as if these were things she'd heard were said to elderly people, and thought they'd do all right for me; and all the time I was saying 'Please don't trouble yourself, there's nothing wrong—I'm all right', and neither of us listened to the other.

At the end of the dark hall we went down a stone step dipped in the centre and into a large kitchen with a vaulted ceiling. I just had time to register a dozen meat hooks hanging from their chains when she dragged out a stool for me and I nearly fell on to it. The beating behind my eyes stopped like a clock wound down leaving in its place emptiness and release, as if my head had detached itself and was drifting away. It must have been a little while later that I opened my eyes to see the girl sitting opposite me, her palms resting on the table between us. She was frowning, and examining me with unworried interest. Then she asked if I wanted water, and without waiting for a reply went over to a stone sink. I saw then how mistaken I'd been—she wasn't a child after all, although she talked like one, rattling on in a light high voice without pausing to breathe or think. . . . ❧